# KEEPER OF PLEAS

## KEEPER OF PLEAS BOOK 1

## ANNELIE WENDEBERG

*The office of the coroner originated in the 12<sup>th</sup> century England and was referred to as "custos placitorum coronae" - keeper of the pleas of the Crown.*

# CONTENTS

ALSO BY THIS AUTHOR:

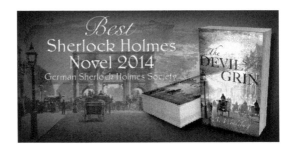

www.anneliewendeberg.com

**Bonus material at the end of this book:**

Preview of book 2: *Spider Silk*

# PRELUDE

## IN WHICH NINE BODIES ARE FOUND AND ONE GOES MISSING

*Why not become the one*
*Who lives with a full moon in each eye*
*That is always saying,*

*With that sweet moon*
*Language*

*What every other eye in this world*
*Is dying to*
*Hear?*

Khwāja Shamsu ud-Dīn Muhammad Hāfez-e Shīrāzī

## APPLE TREES

*I*f you ignore the faint smell of death that clings to *Alexander Easy no matter how well he washes or how fresh his clothes are, you will arrive at the conclusion that there is nothing special about the man. Perhaps you might think his waist is a little too thick, his breath a little too short, and his upper lip a tad too hairy. To you, he might even look and sound like a walrus, the more so when he chases the omnibus, which happens rather often.*

*But dare raise a mocking eyebrow and turn away now, and you'll miss a drama of great proportions. Mr Easy's last moments on Earth are approaching swiftly. The prelude of his death will be announced in a heartbeat by none other than a young man with a flowerpot.*

ALEXANDER EASY ENTERED the mortuary of St George-in-the-East sharply at nine o'clock in the morning of Friday,

December 10, 1880. One embalmment and two hours, sixteen minutes later, a policeman rumbled through the door, sputtering 'Bollocks!' under his breath as a handful of soil spilt from the large clay pot in his arms.

The young man placed the pot on the floor, brushed the dirt off his lapel, and lifted his hat in greeting. 'Mr Easy, sir. Peter Culler's my name. I'm constable of the Metropolitan Police, Division H, and I have a... ah...delivery.'

Constable Culler wearily regarded the three bodies on the tables before him. He gulped in an attempt to keep his meagre breakfast down, and waved a hand through the stench of decomposition and Thames muck. The cold air stirred lazily, refusing to cease the assault on Culler's nose.

'A delivery?' Mr Easy straightened, gently patting the knee of the distended corpse he was working on.

Constable Culler's gaze slid from the mortician's hands to the corpse's grotesquely swollen testicles. Pale fluid dribbled from the blackened penis.

Culler's face grew hot and prickly. The nape of his neck felt as though a hundred spiders were building a nest beneath his skin. He told himself to stop looking. However, the repugnant harboured a sickening fascination for many a man, no matter how much the stomach protested.

Mr Easy wiped his hands on a handkerchief and, for modesty's sake, deftly placed it over the dead man's privates. Then he ran a finger up along the body's middle line, stopped at where the balloon-like abdomen met the ribcage and the skin's colour spectrum of black, green, and purple had turned a little paler. With a click of his tongue, Alexander Easy pushed the sharp end of a long, hollow lancet through the dead flesh. A hiss issued from the lancet's upper end, which Mr Easy swiftly lit with a match. *Woompf,* it said.

The stink, if at all possible, grew stronger. Constable Culler felt his stomach heave. He blinked. Everything below his chin seemed strangely disconnected from his brain.

Mr Easy, hearing his visitor's faint gurgle, looked up. Rather puzzled by the constable's chalky face and wide-open eyes, he arrived at the conclusion that an explanation might be called for.

'That's only gas. It's surprising, given the low temperatures, isn't it? As if the guts had a wee furnace inside that keeps them warm enough to produce gas. Now, there's no need to sway like a pendulum, young man. You've seen a floater before, haven't you?'

At that, Peter Culler's legs did what needed doing: they propelled him backward through the antechamber and, finally, the doorway. He doubled over and the porridge he'd had a few hours earlier neatly hit the frozen ground. The roar of nausea in Culler's ears rendered him deaf to the mortician's cry: 'But my dear man, this is a trifle! You should see them in the summer heat. Sometimes, they burst before we can prick them.'

With his hands pressed to his lower back, Culler gulped the comparatively fresh air, and, after having had enough of it, lit a cigarette and leant back against the mortuary's icy brick wall.

The December wind combed his hair in dank smells

from the docks. He recalled his hat then, which still sat on the one unoccupied table inside the mortuary. He sucked at his smoke with abandon, and chased away any theories as to what might have been on that table before his hat had touched it. Or which smell and consistency it might have had. The door behind him opened without the faintest creak; it was as new as the mortuary it hinged to.

Alexander Easy stepped out onto the walkway. The oak above him sprinkled flecks of molten snow onto his shoulders.

'So?' Easy demanded.

Constable Culler flicked his cigarette toward the mule cart that stood nearby, and cleared his throat. 'Inspector Walken and Coroner Sévère sent me. They need these ex...examined.'

The mule snorted, shook its head, and aimed a kick at the shafts but missed by an inch. The cart wheels creaked on the cobblestones and crows in the oak tree cocked their heads, perhaps expecting bits of food or, at the very least, entertainment.

'Coroner Sévère. Hum.' Easy scratched the folds of his chin.

'Sounds French, doesn't it? Thought so myself before the inspector told me all about the man. British gentleman through and through. Well-bred, he said. His name is a bit unfortunate, though. "Gavriel", his mother named him. Jewish, I think she was. His father, I heard the inspector say the other day, was a—'

Easy interrupted. 'Will there be an inquest? Here?'

Culler nodded and spat on the ground.

Easy wondered how a jury could possibly fit into his

small viewing room, whether he should call for the char-woman to sweep the floors and polish the windows, and if the gentlemen would require a brazier.

The two men approached the cart, the one in uniform with some hesitation, and the one in death-stink with some puzzlement. Six large clay pots stood on the vehicle, a scrawny sapling sticking out of each of them.

'Flowerpots?' Mr Easy asked, and twirled his mighty moustache.

'Erhm…' Peter Culler missed his hat — specifically, the well-fingered rim. Without it, his hands felt out of place. 'The coroner says it's sus…susspishuss. Suspicus. Somewhat.'

'Suspicious flowerpots?'

The constable tried to hide his reddened cheeks in the upturned collar of his coat, and Mr Easy tried to hide his impatience by squeezing his eyes shut for a moment.

When the policeman pointed at a pot that was in obvious disarray — a crack running up its side, the sapling lopsided, soil spilt — Mr Easy noticed a pale something sticking out of it.

'Could that be…a bone?'

'Yes, from a baby. The housekeeper found a skull as she dug in the…' he flapped his hand at the cracked pot. 'Then she called for us. Inspector Walken and the coroner questioned her. She said all these were purchased at Covent Garden. The coroner is sending a surgeon to ex…examine the…uh…pots. Today.'

'Where is the skull?'

'What skull?'

'The skull you just mentioned! The one the house-keeper found. Whichever housekeeper that is.'

'Oh,' said Culler, and eyed the inside of the cart. 'Must have lost it on the way.' He shrugged and sucked air through his teeth. His fingers plucked at the seam of his second-hand coat. He wanted to be done with this already. Dirty business, that's what it was.

'Well, my dear man, get on with it and bring in the pots, will you.' Mr Easy huffed and gave the constable a hearty clap between the shoulder blades.

---

CORONER GAVRIEL SÉVÈRE stood on the small balcony, tapping his cane against his left boot. He barely registered the street below him, the bustle of pedestrians, shop-keepers and shoplifters, of cabs and omnibuses. In his mind, he arranged observations, evidence, and witness statements like bits of shattered porcelain. The little information he'd gained today and the empty spaces — all the missing pieces — drew his attention and shut off the world around him.

His olfactory sense alone tied him to reality, reminding him that he was not in his office, but out in the open. Whitechapel Road was peculiar in its spectrum of odours, for it lacked the suffocating pungency of fermenting mule manure, of human excrement and refuse. Instead, Sévère smelled coal fires, burnt butter, sizzling mutton and pork, fresh bread, and perfume. An occasional scent of warm horse droppings before they were whisked away. And there! A whiff of Belgian pastries.

His mouth began to water and his expression changed ever so lightly. An observant stranger may, or may not, have noticed that the man's face had brightened a fraction. A friend would have been able to corroborate this observation, but Sévère had no friends. He felt no need for company.

With a small nod, the coroner set the tip of his cane onto the balcony tiles, and drew a line through the black marks: one semi-circle of potting soil freshly sprinkled onto the floor, and seven dark rings from the water that had seeped through seven flowerpots during the previous months. A chaos of footprints trailed muck into the apartment, much to the chagrin of the housekeeper and her maid. Sévère looked up and breathed a cloud into the chill air. The evidence slowly dissolved with the slush.

The housekeeper saw him to the door, her hands clasped below the mass of her sagging bosom, the potting soil still blackening her fingernails.

'The inquest will be held at Vestry Hall at eleven o'clock tomorrow,' he said when he took his leave.

'Cable Street?' the housekeeper asked, her voice warbling.

'The very one.' He tipped his hat and strolled out of the house, turned right and melted into nonexistence.

Coroner Sévère was a man of average height and average looks. He was neither noticeably handsome nor particularly ugly. His face bore no marks — no scars that told of disease or battle, no moustache that indicated his social standing. Most people forgot his appearance the moment he walked away from them. Except, of course, when he wanted them to remember. His jury, and his suspects in particular, never forgot the man, no matter how much they wanted to. Strangely, what they recalled most clearly was not his slight limp — the one feature that could have made him stand out had he allowed it. It was his eyes they remembered. The majority of the murderers he'd sent to gaol would have sworn his irises were yellow, like the Devil's, had one ever bothered to ask them.

It was all nonsense, of course.

Sévère considered these silly sentiments useful. Emotions in general aided his work, as long as they happened inside other people. To him, witnesses and perpetrators were an open book. Turning other people's pages brought him amusement; he might have even called it happiness, if he'd ever had the need to attain this particular state.

Whenever necessary, he let his suspects know what he thought of their mental capacities. He revealed the tricks they tried to play, tore apart the weave and weft of their fabricated alibis. Sévère was a master lie detector. He stood above the world and he liked it up there. His position as Coroner of Eastern Middlesex allowed him to lead a comfortable life. He kept an appropriate number of servants, owned a modern, well-appointed house, purchased only newly-tailored clothing of quality silk and wool, and visited London's best bawdy houses at least once a week.

Sévère considered himself a made man with very few problems. However, the few problems he *did* have frequently drove him close to crossing the line between legal and illegal. He wondered, briefly, if that would happen this time — the crossing of the line, that is. After a mere three hours of investigation, this case certainly showed potential.

Sévère shook off the thought, entered the pastry shop, and left it a moment later with a small paper bag in his right hand. He walked along Whitechapel Road and turned into Leman Street. Without sparing Division H Headquarters a single glance, he extracted a pastry from the bag, finished it in three bites, and pulled out pastry number two.

He turned left onto Cable Street, stretched his shoulders, and tossed away the bag. He slipped his right hand into his coat pocket, and modulated his limp so that the weakness of his left leg was barely noticeable. To the uninitiated, he appeared like any other gentleman on a walk. Easy to overlook.

His eyes scanned the street, the murky corners and doorways. Slum dwellers who didn't know his face or couldn't remember it, believed him to be a plainclothes detective with a pistol in his coat pocket. Surely, he was looking for someone.

Sévère moved through the worst section of Cable Street without anyone bothering him. Not even the greenest of pickpockets dared approach. Half of the men who littered the pavement melted away the moment they set eyes on him, only to reappear once he'd reached the corner of Denmark Street. Better safe than sorry.

A moment later, Sévère turned into the churchyard of St George-in-the-East. The thin layer of melting snow told him that both flowerpots and surgeon had arrived in time: tracks and hoof prints of the police's mule cart and those of a hansom cab showed in the dirty-white mush. Sévère followed the crumbs of black potting soil from Cable Street to the red brick building of the mortuary.

'Hello, Mr Easy,' he called from the antechamber, kicking the slush off his boots. 'Thank you for coming, Dr Baxter.'

The coroner kept his coat, scarf, and gloves on, for the brick walls seemed to suck all the warmth from his body. It was worse than the breeze outside.

'Coroner.' The doctor held out his hand, noticed the dirt covering it, and dropped it. 'Ahem,' he said and turned back to the evidence. 'Nine bodies. All carried to term, I should think.'

Eight miniature skulls were lined up on the table. Some were gaping at their crowns like petals of a wilting tulip, others looked more like an eggshell smashed into symmetrical pieces. The tiny jaws were toothless. Below each skull, small bones were arranged in patterns resembling flat, incomplete skeletons. The ninth skeleton was headless.

'The constable lost a skull on the way. He tried to retrieve it, but someone must have taken it,' the doctor said rather cheerfully.

Deep in his throat, Sévère produced a soft growl. Almost inaudible. Division H was a thorn in his side; it had been since he'd opened his solicitor's practice. Most of the constables were sloppy, and Division H seemed to follow neither etiquette, logic, nor work ethics. Per regulations, witnesses and evidence belonged to the man who was first to arrive at the scene. In this particular case it was the coroner. Yet, the 2nd class inspector who'd arrived more than thirty minutes later had determined that the head of the household, a Mr Bunting, was to be taken into police custody at once. Division H inspectors chronically turned a blind eye in their own favour, and it was of no use informing the magistrates of this serious slip in protocol. Sévère would have to pay a visit to the Home Office and turn in an official complaint.

Whenever he found the time.

The usual case-solving-circus seemed to be that coroner, Division H, and the bunch of plainclothes detectives the magistrates called their own, were supposed to race each other. Whoever was the first to apprehend a suspect — whichever suspect — won.

When Sévère was a young man, he'd clung to the naïve view that police work was truly about finding a culprit and keeping London safe (or comparatively safe), and not about gaining influence and power over the inner workings of the city.

'Can you say anything about the cause of death?' he asked the doctor.

'Well…' was the reply. 'There might be signs of violence.' Dr Baxter picked up a few vertebrae, arranged the individual pieces on his palm, and pointed at what appeared to be scratch marks.

'And?'

'It is impossible to tell if these injuries were inflicted ante-, peri-, or postmortem. The skeletons are all clean. There's no soft tissue to work with. Not one bit of flesh or skin left. I'm guessing the infants died five to ten years ago.'

Sévère took a step forward, leant his cane against the table and gingerly turned over the fragile bones. 'How likely is it that someone collected nine stillbirths and buried them in flowerpots?'

'The world is the strangest of places. However...' The doctor held up a pencil, bent over the vertebrae in Sévère's hand and pointed at a tiny discolouration. 'Here we might have an indication for internal bleeding. Before the heart stopped beating, that is. Or it might be dirt. It's impossible to tell. But this does smell of violence, doesn't it? If I'm not entirely mistaken, these are all illegitimate children farmed out by their mothers soon after birth.' The doctor shrugged. 'An everyday occurrence. Ask the Thames Police Office. They are sick of infants floating in the river or lying on the banks.

Sévère felt an itch at the back of his head. Baby farmers wrapped their dead charges in paper or rags, or sometimes they placed them into cardboard boxes. They threw these packages into dust yards, back alleys, the Thames. Baby farmers cared little about how they rid themselves of their charges as long as the "getting-rid-of" couldn't be connected to them.

His gaze touched on each small, planted grave, and each laid-out skeleton. There was accuracy, care. Baxter's interpretation was simple and straightforward. But it did not fit.

'I need a second opinion,' Sévère said. 'Mr Easy, would you be so kind as to send a message to the house surgeon of Guy's Hospital?'

At four thirty in the afternoon, Dr Johnston of Guy's Hospital alighted from the cab in front of the mortuary. Per the note he'd received at noon he was to wait for Coroner Sévère before he began his examination. This irritated him a little. Coroners were solicitors, their specialty was the law. Hence, they should keep their noses out of postmortems. But then, Dr Johnson respected every man who strove to increase his knowledge. Rumour had it that the newly-appointed coroner showed an unusual interest in all medical matters related to deaths caused by violence and neglect. If the police were only half as curious as that man…

Dr Johnston was torn from his thoughts by the noise of shuffling feet. That, too, irritated him. The mortician had been fidgeting a lot these past minutes, his eyes firmly stuck to the infants' laid-out remains.

'Are you quite all right, Mr Easy?' Dr Johnston asked without looking up.

'Yes, thank you. I'm all right. Might have caught a cold, though. Or something.'

'Hum,' said Johnston. He tapped his fingers on the table, extracted his watch from his waistcoat pocket and grumbled, 'I can't wait forever.'

He rolled up his sleeves and began to methodically examine the flowerpots.

---

Rubbing his left elbow, Alexander Easy watched Johnston work. Easy's arm had been aching for days. For how long precisely? he wondered, but couldn't recall when it had begun. Perhaps I should see my physician. Yes, I just might. After Christmas, perhaps? Better yet, after New Year's Eve. Less clients to attend to, once the annual wave of holiday suicides was over.

His attention meandered back to the remains of nine tiny human beings. He couldn't seem to pull his eyes away from them. And slowly, creepily, he felt something inside him begin to unfurl. There was a heaviness in his stomach and a clenching of his ribcage he couldn't quite explain. Neither could he explain why these nine corpses disturbed him so. He was a mortician. He laid his hands on dead bodies every day.

---

'MY APOLOGIES, I'M LATE.' Sévère stepped through the antechamber and into the viewing room. 'Dr Johnston, thank you for coming. I know you are a busy man.'

'Hum,' said Johnston, sorting through potting soil with nimble fingers. He didn't spare the coroner a glance or even a nod.

Sévère positioned himself at the mortician's side, and both men watched Dr Johnston examine every crumb, every square inch of clay pot surface, every fibre of root, every twig, and every bone.

When, finally, Johnston pressed his hands onto the table and huffed, Easy and Sévère leant forward.

'Well,' Johnston said. 'Complicated.' He brushed the soil off his palms. 'Let me begin with the facts: We have, as you've written in your message to me, nine small bodies in seven flowerpots that have been found on the only balcony of all of Whitechapel Road. One skeleton has recently been disturbed, allegedly by the housekeeper of the household with the balcony in question. The skull of that same skeleton went missing owing to the carelessness of a constable of Division H. This means we have eight bodies that have not been disturbed for one growth season. What might have happened to them before spring of this year is mostly based on conjecture.'

Sévère cleared his throat. 'You believe they have been relocated?'

'Most definitely. You see, here.' Dr Johnston grabbed a sapling and ran his fingers along its roots. 'The saplings were grafted three, perhaps four years ago. Judging from the development of the roots, they were replanted in spring this year. You may wish to have an expert confirm this. You can see that some of the roots have retained the shape of a smaller pot, while the newly-formed roots are stretching out through the entire space of the new, larger pot. A few of the roots are touching the neonates. Er…the newborns. Hence my conclusion that the saplings were repotted in spring this year. You will notice that the original pots must have been too small to contain any of these bodies. Whoever repotted the trees, moved the bodies from somewhere to here.' He waved at the pots.

'Now, I can't tell you much about the original burial ground of the neonates, but I can tell you where they have *not* been buried.'

'Go on,' Sévère said.

'Let me breathe, lad, and I will pour out all that I am able to glean from the little you've given me.' Johnston tut-tutted, one eyebrow raised at Sévère.

He took his time to indicate the surface of each skull and each eye socket while explaining, 'Only a few of the fresh root filaments have grown into the cavities or cracks, which tells me something about how much time the bodies have spent in these particular pots. However...' Johnston exhaled, sending a cloud of condensation into the cold air. 'Next time, do me a favour and summon me *before* Baxter-the-Axter gets his hands on the evidence.'

'I will. And I greatly appreciate your offer.'

'But I must warn you, Sévère. Should you ever call me in for a trifle, I will establish a routine of first attending to *all* of my patients before I attend to your enquiries. Which might take me several days.'

'Understood.'

'Very well then.' Johnston turned back to the table. 'All the neonates are skeletonised...meaning all bones are pretty clean. Only here and there are small bits of ligament. Especially on these two.' He indicated a pair of skeletons on the far left of the table.

'You will notice that each skeleton appears a little darker than its left-hand neighbour. The bodies on the left are the freshest, the ones on the right have been buried the longest: not only does the dark brown colour of the bones indicate that they have spent an extended period of time underground, the bones also show a higher degree of degradation.' He pointed to hands and feet that lacked fingers and toes.

'In my opinion, the soil dissolved the small bones of the hands and feet. Look, here.' Johnston picked up part of a pelvis and brushed his index finger over its brownish surface. 'It's rough. Slightly acidic soil is found in most of

England and Scotland. Bones, especially those of neonates, will dissolve — slowly, but surely. However, you'd find the pelvises disarticulated either way, as the ossification centres haven't fused yet. Er...the parts of the... Never mind. It simply means you'd find three separate bones for each innominate and five separate elements for the sacrum. If there is ligament remaining, it may hold the five separate centres that form the sacrum together — as you can see in two of the nine neonates, but the pelvises would still be found as three separate bones for each innominate.'

Sévère scribbled furiously in his notepad. 'Don't you think rats might have carried away the small limbs?'

'Rodents will take what they can gnaw off, but there are very few scratch and bite marks on these bones. And here comes my first gift to you, Sévère: these neonates were not buried in London. They spent considerable time in a less populated area before they were taken on a journey together with the apple trees. The ones on the right, the darkest ones, must have been buried for a period of about ten years. Perhaps more. If they'd spent ten years in London soil, there would be nothing left for me to examine. The rat population is rather high in the city.'

Sévère huffed. 'My list of suspects has just increased dramatically: most of England and Scotland, excluding large cities.'

The doctor tut-tutted. 'Sévère, you must learn to be patient. Let the old surgeon give you one bit of information at a time, else your brain might explode. Now, here comes my second gift to you: Someone has taken great care to protect the bodies. Someone might have loved these children.'

'What makes you think that?' Sévère found himself surprisingly undisturbed by the fact that Guy's house surgeon had thrown aside etiquette and taken to calling him "lad" and "Sévère." He wasn't sure if this was an indication of disrespect, but decided to ponder the question later.

'Mr Easy, are you quite all right?' Johnston asked.

Sévère turned to the mortician who'd been quite invisible to him these past minutes. The man looked pasty.

Mr Easy blinked. 'Uh. Yes. Thank you. I'm just…a little tired. It has been a long day.'

'Indeed it has. Is. Anyway.' Johnston turned his attention back to Sévère. 'I wouldn't be surprised if these were all siblings. They were buried soon after their death and exhumed a few years later to be carefully buried again. Not a single one of the larger bones has gone missing. Except, of course, for the skull the good constable lost. The two pairs buried together might be twins: they show almost identical signs of ageing. But this is a tad too wild of a guess for my taste. These infants were cherished; I'm absolutely certain of it. There is, however, the unfortunate evidence of their violent deaths.'

He picked up a row of vertebrae from one of the freshest skeletons and pointed to three fine lines carved into the bone. 'These are cuts. Their appearance indicates that the cutting was done around the time of death. Adjacent to these cuts, the discolouration differs from the darkening of the entire skeleton, the latter resulting from the soil it was buried in. By the way, I've found three different types of soil — you might want to consult an expert on these. But this discolouration, here, where the cuts are, is different. It's blood.'

'But…' Sévère pinched the bridge of his nose, trying to summon his limited medical knowledge. 'A surgeon once told me that when a body lies on its back, that's where the blood pools. Couldn't the same thing have happened with these children? That they were born dead, the cuts were inflicted after birth for whatever reason, and that they were placed on their backs allowing blood to stain the bones of the neck?'

'How long does a birth typically take?' Johnston asked with a patient smile, the same he applied to his students.

'Several hours?'

'How quickly does blood congeal?'

'Ah, I see.'

'Precisely. If what you have theorised were true, then all of these must have died in the birth canal only minutes before their throats were cut. Now, who cuts the throat of stillborns? Really, Sévère!'

'Who in his right mind would do this to nine children?' Mr Easy whispered, his voice a hoarse croak.

# BROTHEL

*A*lexander Easy locked the door to the mortuary. His hand paused on the iron handle. He did not notice the icy cold creeping into his palm. His gaze travelled up to the patterned tiles that ran all around the small building, the same patterns that could be found on the gateposts of St George's Gardens. Again, he tried to identify their meaning. Again, without success. He stretched his shoulders, rubbed his elbow, exhaled a cloud into the cold evening, and turned his back to his working place one final time.

On Cable Street, he climbed aboard an omnibus and sat down next to a gentleman with thick glasses and a red necktie. He smelled of fish and wet dog.

At Commercial and Brushfield he alighted. His knees were aching. He walked thirty-nine paces and opened the door to his home. He climbed twelve steps to the first floor, the keys in his hands clinking, the stairs creaking a protest under his weight. His breath shortened the farther he ascended. When he unlocked the door to his rooms, the housekeeper — who'd kept an eye on the street for the past half hour — stepped out into the hallway to greet him.

'Mr Easy, sir, nice to see you back. I expect you wish to take your supper now?'

'Yes, thank you, Mrs Dobbins. But…'

'The water. Certainly. Certainly.'

This exchange had been identical for nearly six years.

Mr Easy washed and dressed in fresh clothes, then sat down to roast of mutton with Brussel sprouts and potatoes. It smelled delicious. He gazed at the meat and couldn't muster the energy to stick a fork into it.

Sighing, he leant back and shut his tired eyes. Before he knew it, his head fell into his hands, and he wept until his shoulders trembled and his cuffs were soggy.

For nearly six years now, Mr Easy's evenings had been quiet and uneventful. Tonight, though, he felt as if his chest might explode should he stare at Agnes' empty armchair for a moment longer. So he did something entirely unexpected: Alexander Easy dashed the tears off his cheeks and left the house.

Mrs Dobbins couldn't believe her ears when she heard Mr Easy's boots descending the stairs, the door to the house opening and snapping shut, and boots clacking down the stone steps and onto the street.

For perhaps the hundredth time that day, she pushed aside the lace curtains. Just the smallest crack. Believing herself unseen, she and her cracked curtain were yet wonderfully conspicuous to all in her neighbourhood.

Her eyes followed Mr Easy, and she wondered if he'd

finally gotten over his wife's passing. Yes, that must be it. Surely, he's courting a young woman.

'Thank the Lord,' she whispered, and in her mind's eye, chubby children were already tramping up and down the stairwell. She frowned, told herself to be less nosey and more patient, and poured herself a gin.

---

HE WASN'T QUITE sure where he was going. Outside, away, was all he could think. Those nine bodies... Someone had cherished them, the doctor had said. And yet, killed them. What man or woman could have done such a thing? Alexander's belief in mankind had been rattled deeply. For ten, twelve years he and Agnes had tried to have children of their own. Five times she'd given birth to a dead girl, once to a dead boy. Then she had perished, slowly, steadily, unstoppably from under his loving hands like a cut-off lily.

A tear skidded down Alexander's cheek as he stumbled blindly through the streets. Where was he, anyway? He looked up and found that he was drifting toward the mortuary. He dug through his mind and found that there was only one proper thing to do: bury the children in sacred soil. Lay them to rest. Yes, someone had to do it and he was just the right man. But something niggled at the back of his mind, telling him that he had to wait, they had to wait. The inquest was to take place the following day. The bodies were to be viewed by the coroner, both doctors, all witnesses, and the jury.

Alexander came to a sudden halt in an unlit street.

With a shudder he realised that this was not a place to cross, or, God forbid, to dawdle. He set off again, at a faster pace. His view swam as he thought of Agnes and her children, his children, theirs. And the nine he'd seen today. He stumbled and was close to stepping into something that looked suspiciously like a very flat rat.

He stopped again, knowing all too well that middle-aged, middle-class men — who couldn't run when it came to it — had no business whatsoever in the slums of Whitechapel, and that he would likely get mugged if he didn't leave at once. Or worse.

But he was tired. Tired of running and, he had to admit shamefully, tired of life.

He pressed his knuckles into his aching sides, looked up, and found a goddess gazing down upon him. There, right before him, printed on the tattered remains of a billboard was a woman of such beauty that Alexander believed it could only be the Holy Mother of Jesus herself.

"FIND BLISS IN MARY'S ARMS!" the bleached headline screamed.

Alexander sighed. Hope began to creep into his poor heart. Swiftly followed by panic. The address as to where this goddess could be found had been torn off.

---

THE PANE CRACKLED as she turned the handle. She pulled open the window and the joints produced a squeak. The vibration dislodged ice from the pane. The crystals dropped onto the rug, melted and disappeared into the coarse wool. The winter wind sneaked through the gap in the heavy curtains, hardening her nipples and pulling her skin tight. Blood rushed to her cheeks.

She waited for the knock. It couldn't be long now.

She didn't push aside the curtains, didn't lean out to search the street below. There was no need for it and it wasn't how this game was played.

When the knock finally came, she closed her eyes and placed her hands softly on the wall on either side of the window.

The door opened and closed. Four steps. The rustle of a coat being shed and draped over a chair. The clink of a belt being unbuckled, and another clink — that of a gold coin being placed on the table.

Two more steps. Hands found her hips and pulled her back against a crotch. Large and soft hands. The hands of a man who'd never had to work hard in his life.

'Oh, no!' she breathed, making her voice a little higher, younger. 'What are you doing to me, sir?'

The anticipated result arrived at once: an erection stirred, hardened, and pressed against her thigh. He bent forward. The bristly tips of a moustache tickled her skin. Hot breath crept over her neck.

'I will show you the pleasures of the bedroom,' he hummed, excitement trembling in his voice.

'But, sir, I am a maiden.' This was far from the truth and they both knew it.

'Tell me your age, dear.'

She produced another lie. In fact, most of the words Mary uttered were far from the truth. 'I am but twelve years old. I beg you, sir, do not ruin me. What if my father finds out?'

This part of the game used to make her sick, but it had been awhile.

His hands groped her behind. The head of his penis pressed against her anus. He spat on it. 'I am certain your father would not approve,' he growled and pushed himself in. Once there, he stopped for a moment and reached toward the window. Satisfied that the window was wide open behind the drawn curtains, he began to thrust, whispering, 'You may...call me... Mr Brazen...tonight.'

And so she did. 'Oh, Mr Brazen! Have mercy! You are too big for me.'

That, too, was far-fetched.

The church bells struck ten, and every *bang* was accompanied by an, 'Ah!' from Mr Brazen's mouth and a squeaked 'Oh!' from Mary's.

He finished along with the bells, wiped himself off and said, 'Now, look at me.'

She turned and gifted him a sweet smile, then reached out to tuck his flaccid cock back into his trousers. She stopped in her movement and breathed, 'Allow me to clean this for you.'

She sank to her knees, and, tenderly caressing his bollocks, slipped him into her mouth. Mr Brazen wasn't the youngest of men, and his time of virility was coming to a close. It took Mary considerable effort to make him stiff once more. Eventually, he was all clean and provided a wad of his seed so she might wash the taste of her own faeces down her throat.

'Thank you, Mr Brazen,' she said, licked her lips, and graced him with the smile he loved most on her face: that of a little and naïve girl who had been given the most delicious candy.

Then she frowned and sucked in her lower lip. 'I will not be able to sit for days, Mr Brazen.' But at once, her face lit up. 'But I am glad I was seduced by such an experienced and talented man.'

Mr Brazen's moustache twitched. He tried to control his expression, but the blush that rose up his throat and past his perfectly starched and pressed collar betrayed just how much he believed her.

Without speaking, he buckled his belt, shrugged into his coat, and nodded toward the guinea on the coffee table.

'Wednesday,' he said as he took his leave.

'Wednesday,' she whispered, and bit her tongue hard so that her eyes would begin to water and her face would appeared as if she could barely survive the long days without him.

After Mr Brazen had left, Mary rolled her burning tongue around in her mouth, swallowed foul taste, and shut the window. She squatted over the chamber pot and watched the swirl of piss, semen, and traces of diarrhoea cover the kinked enamel.

A soft knock announced Rose, a scrawny girl of eight, delivering a jug filled with steaming hot water. Unfazed by the woman's nakedness — a frequent sight in this establishment — Rose waited until Mary had finished squeezing out the residues of her client, then she picked up the pot and said, 'It's meat pies tonight.'

'Could you bring it up?'

'Yes, *ma'am*.' With a wicked grin, Rose curtsied and left.

A moment later, she delivered Mary's supper. The girl was quick and serviceable. She would make a good whore in a few years.

Mary poured the hot water into her washbowl, brushed her teeth, and wiped her face, armpits, and crotch. She put on her nightgown and a robe, and climbed into her armchair to eat and read the papers. Her client was entirely forgotten until she stumbled over his name on page eleven: an article reporting on a new decree, ordered and signed by Chief Magistrate Linton Frost.

She tut-tutted and whispered. 'Mr *Brazen*, you are such a bad boy.'

Mary knew that Mr Frost was a connoisseur of maidenheads. He paid five to twenty pounds sterling per maiden delivered to him. Sometimes, they needed to be held down. Other times, the seductress would put snuff into a girl's beer to make her drowsy and pliable. When the girl awoke, she was in pain, ruined, and richer in experience as well as money. Although half of the latter was taken by the woman who had abducted her.

Mary assumed that she was the only experienced, if not to say, older, whore Mr Frost was visiting. But she couldn't be sure. For a woman, she was not old, not by any measure. A man who didn't know what she did for a living might well have asked permission to court her. She was sixteen now, a good, ripe age for being courted and married off. In a few years, she would be considered too old to find a good suitor.

Whatever others considered her to be, Mary thought of herself as an experienced businesswoman. Nothing more, nothing less. She'd been introduced to the trade at the tender age of nine. *That* was indeed a little illegal, although not by much. Seven years a whore. A long time to survive in this business.

Mary, though, did not merely survive. She thrived, owing much of her success to her wits — a truly unusual condition, for the main requirement in this profession was the ability to bounce a lot and moan a lot, not to think a lot.

Now, there was nothing special about cheerful up-and-down movements. Most women managed those. After all, only very few men fancied doing it with a corpse, let alone would admit to it.

It wasn't only what Mary did with her attractive orifices that allowed her to ask for a high fee. It was what she said, how she timed her sighs, the parting of her lips, the trembling of her thighs, and the words she whispered in feigned ecstasy. Men believed her. Absolutely.

She knew how to convince them how very big they were, or — if that would have been quite obviously wrong — how very *right* that nub of a prick was to stroke the most sensitive spot of her privates in *just* the right fashion. With a flick of her tongue and a flutter of her eyelids, she convinced them that she was their willing slave, not because of the money they paid, but because they were absolutely wonderful and the best thing that had ever happened to her. *Oh, will you ravage me, please?* her body asked them in the sweetest tones. And oh, they did. They did.

Only hours after she'd lost her virginity during a painful transaction with a middle-aged gentleman, she realised that no one would help her.

And then she'd calculated the amount of money she would need to set herself free.

It might appear laughable to dream about freedom when women, in general, were seen as property. Mary knew this. Hence the high fee. Rich women were free, all others had to prostitute themselves, one way or another. That's how Mary saw the world: whores were paid, wives were kept. She had no wish at all to be a monogamous, child-bearing, house-keeping version of herself.

What she wanted was freedom. Freedom as wild and as independent as it was outrageous.

To Mary, being outrageous was an ideal.

A KNOCK WOKE HER. She groaned. Pale yellow light seeped through the window. It made her think of John, the lamp lighter. The bawdy jokes he told her when he climbed up the ladder to light the lantern a mere three yards from her window.

'You have a client,' a deep male voice sounded from the other side of the door.

'I'm not taking anyone else tonight.'

'He asked for you and won't be sent away. Make an exception, won't you?'

'One of those, eh?' she called.

'One of those.'

She pushed herself up. 'Give me a few moments, Bobbie. And send Rose up with tea.'

'Good girl. He's in the parlour. The madam is filling him with wine.'

WHEN ALEXANDER WAS FINALLY ALLOWED to ascend the stairs, he stuffed his hands into his pockets so as not to wring them. He also didn't want to touch the banister. His palms felt like slugs, wet and slimy, and he pressed them against the inside of his pockets in an attempt to keep them comparatively dry until he had shaken her hand. Was he even supposed to shake her hand?

He had to let go of his right pocket for a moment to rap his knuckles against the door. When he heard soft footfalls he almost tumbled back down the stairwell. His heart was hammering so hard, he could barely think. The ache in his left elbow distracted him, but it was forgotten when the door opened.

She was slender and long-limbed. Alexander wondered if he could encompass her waist with both his hands. The thought was lost when he noticed her proud, graceful stance, her long lashes, the dark brown irises that seemed to swallow all light and, with it, himself. He felt his face flush. He felt too fat, too old, too...widowed.

Before he could shrink back into the dark stairwell, the dark corridor, the entrance hall, the streets and anonymity, she held out her hand. In a gentlemanly reflex so deeply ingrained in Alexander's nature, he softly took the offered hand into his own and blew a kiss onto her knuckles. 'My lady,' he whispered. 'I am... I...'

'Did the madam tell you about my fee?' she asked politely.

'Oh yes, here.' His fist shot out clumsily, his fingers

unfurled, revealing a small, sweaty gold coin glued to his palm.

'Would you like a cup of tea?' she enquired gently.

Tea? Confused, Alexander stumbled through the doorframe. 'Oh, yes. Please. If you'd be so kind. I'm most…'

Her smile tied his tongue. She led him to a coffee table and offered him the larger of the two armchairs. He sat, placed the guinea on the polished surface, folded his hands in his lap, and stared at his fingernails. They do need a trim, he thought, and gnawed on his cheek.

Silently he watched her fill his cup, nodded when she asked, 'Milk and sugar?' and found himself unable to tear his eyes off her beautiful, long fingers, her unblemished skin, how she held the spoon, how she stirred his tea.

'Am I so unbecoming?' she whispered.

Alexander's head snapped up. 'Oh, no… I… Why would you think that? Um…my apologies.' He pulled a hanky from his waistcoat pocket and dabbed at his brow. 'It's that I never before visited a lady of your…profession. I don't know the customs. And I…I know I'm old and fat and you are the most beautiful woman I have ever met.'

The last sentence involuntarily burst from his lips together with a fleck of spittle, which landed unceremoniously on Alexander's side of the table. He bent forward, wiped it off, and took a deep breath.

'Isn't kindness, and not a pretty face or body, the most beautiful to behold?' She gifted him a smile of such sweetness that Alexander believed his heart might stop.

'May I ask why you came to me, sir?'

He opened his mouth to reply, but was cut off as her

hand settled on his knee. 'Let me rephrase,' she said. 'Tell me what I can do for you.'

He swallowed, but his throat was too dry. He took a sip of his tea, and said, 'I am a widower of six years. I know it sounds…out of sorts, but I still miss my wife so much. My heart hurts. I used to hold her, caress her when we fell asleep together. But now…my arms are empty. My house is empty.' He looked at his hands as if, only moments ago, his wife had vanished from his embrace.

'May I know your name?' Mary asked.

'Alexander Easy.'

She rose. Her dress seemed to whisper secrets to him. She took a step forward, knelt and wrapped her hands around his. 'Alexander, my dear, shall we go to bed?'

He shut his eyes and sighed, 'Thank you.'

She unpinned her hair and turned her back to him so he might help her undress. He asked her to keep her chemise on. For now.

When she lifted the blanket for him, he sat down on the mattress and thought of his wife. He shut his eyes, reached for her, and held her close to him. She did not feel like Agnes, did not smell like her, but he tucked her head upon his shoulder anyway, caressed her hair anyway, and felt a little long-missed peace sneak in anyway.

---

ALEXANDER WOKE A BIT LATER, strangely refreshed despite the shortness of his slumber. His left arm ached more now and he asked the woman (what was her name?) for a glass of wine.

'I am Mary,' she said, as she poured him the wine. She sat down on the bed, her knees touching his thigh.

How could he have forgotten her name?

*Hail Mary, full of grace...*

Alexander smiled at the sentiment. He was surprised that her closeness didn't make him nervous. Tonight, I am a bold man, he told himself, emptied the glass in five hasty gulps, and reached out to Mary. His fingers touched her knee, her thigh, her hip. He didn't even tremble when he pulled off her chemise.

Oh dear God, he thought when her breasts were revealed — perfectly shaped, like peaches, with perfect pink nipples. He appraised her skin that was the shade of new milk, her hair that shone in the candlelight like a sleek, black creature of the deep sea.

'I want to touch these,' he said.

She smiled again, and lowered her gaze, then took his wrist and placed his palm onto her breast.

Alexander sucked in air, as if his head had just broken the surface after a too-long dive.

'I want to kiss them.'

She whispered, 'It would be a pleasure.'

He leant in and took her nipple between his lips and then the other. He felt tears spill down his cheeks. He pulled Mary down, and pressed his face between her lovely tits, and sucked and kissed her there and down along her midriff, her navel, her sex. She smelled of roses and lavender, tasted of honey and cream and, faintly, of Agnes. Groaning, he pushed himself up and rolled onto his back, pulling Mary along. She straddled him, her sex hovering above his as if asking for permission.

'Come to me,' Alexander groaned, and she lowered herself onto him and rocked him into oblivion.

When he spilt his seed inside her, the pain in his left arm intensified to an unbearable stabbing, spread to his heart, which contracted one final time, tittered, and fell silent.

A thin line of spittle ran from the corner of his mouth down along his cheek and onto the pillow, and Mary knew at once that this wasn't the look of a satisfied client. It was the look of a dying man.

'Help!' she cried and stumbled off her client. His still-erect cock gave her hope that he might be alive, but she couldn't find a pulse anywhere on his body, couldn't hear him breathe or see his ribcage move.

When Alexander's erection began to deflate, Mary threw her robe around herself, yanked open the door, and raced down the stairs and into the parlour.

# THE MISSING MORTICIAN

avriel Sévère set the tip of his cane hard against the floor. The knock echoed through Vestry Hall. To his right stood the jury: nineteen honest men of good social standing. His officer, Samuel Stripling, stood on Sévère's left and began to read aloud the witness statements in chronological order. First, the housekeeper's, a Mrs Erica Hopegood: how she had loosened the soil around the apple tree saplings, that she had used a small shovel in an attempt to dig in a ball or two of horse manure, and that she had then found the skull of an infant. How she had proceeded to scream, and — her wits failing her for a moment — had lifted the heavy pot but lost her grip on it and set it down too hard, so that the pot cracked, the soil spilt, and the sapling went lopsided.

A man from the jury interrupted. 'Did you intend to throw the pot from the balcony, Mrs Hopegood?'

The so-addressed blushed and straightened the bonnet

on her head. 'I cannot recall what I intended, but I'm certain it was not that.'

The man nodded, and Stripling took up the reading where he had left off. Mrs Hopegood fidgeted in her chair; the old wood creaked.

'Can you not recall the name of the vendor who sold your employer, Mr Bunting, the saplings?' another man from the jury asked.

Mrs Hopegood grunted a nervous laugh. 'Of course not. Do you ask all the shopkeepers their names and heritage? Mr Bunting purchased the pots at Covent Garden in summer, and I accompanied him, as I already said under oath. The flower seller was very forthcoming, but did not provide his name nor did we ask for it. He offered to send his boys to deliver the purchase to our address. And that is what happened. I gave descriptions of the man, the cart, and the boys to Inspector Walken and to the coroner.' She pointed her chin to the inspector, who nodded confirmation at the jury. She avoided looking at Sévère.

The jury turned their attention to the inspector. 'Could you identify the man?'

'We are the police, not an oracle,' Walken answered dryly.

Someone chuckled.

The inspector cleared his throat. 'Two constables are searching for the vendor.'

Next, Stripling read the statements of Mr Bunting, Inspector Walken, Dr Baxter and Dr Johnston, and finally that of the coroner himself. All the while, Sévère was the calm centre of the room.

When his officer shut the folder and nodded at him, Sévère raised his voice. 'We will view the bodies shortly. Dr Johnston will be available to answer questions relating to the cause of death and the means by which the bodies were concealed.'

There was a mighty scraping of chairs and shuffling of feet as the whole procession poured out of Vestry Hall and moved to the mortuary.

They were greeted by a discombobulated beadle, who stammered something about having to locate the key to the mortuary because the mortician had failed to arrive this morning. And then, with much huffing and puffing, he produced the key in question.

Sévère dismissed the beadle with an irritated flick of his hand. He asked the jury to enter the small building one by one, and arrange themselves around the table at the centre of the viewing room.

The nineteen men in black coats and top hats squeezed into the building and shuffled around the table. As they stood lined up so, with shoulder pressing against shoulder, they looked much like misshapen toad spawn on a string.

The men bent over the nine skeletons, eyebrows drawn low, lips clamped around their pipes and cigars. A cloud of smoke and breath clung to the ceiling. Sévère observed the jury: the twitching of moustaches, the distasteful curling of lips. Johnston's calm gaze.

'Why are these all...disassembled?' one man asked Johnston.

'The disarticulation of the neonates' skeletons is a result of natural decomposition followed by ex- and rehumation,' the doctor answered, his sharp gaze trapped between his half-moon spectacles and bushy white eyebrows.

The jury collectively frowned.

Johnston sighed. 'The skeletons were dug up and subsequently reburied. As most of the bones are not connected by tissue — it decomposed completely — they were a little scattered, naturally.'

'Are you saying that they were not decapitated?' said one man, gingerly picking up one of the skulls.

'Their heads are coming apart,' said another.

'All newborns have flexibly connected skull bones.' Johnston spoke slowly in an attempt to use simple words for the jurymen. 'When all soft tissue has decomposed, the skull bones will come apart. There is no evidence for perimortem injuries to the skulls.'

'Perimortem is what precisely?'

'Pardon my jargon. Perimortem injuries are those that occur at or around the time of death, when bone is fresh and flexible. Those can be distinguished from injuries that occurred days or weeks before death — which will show healing — and those inflicted days, weeks, or months after death.'

Johnston, finding the translation of his thoughts into layman's terms tedious, picked up several vertebrae which were still somewhat connected to one another, and ran his finger along their frontal line. 'The marks I found on the vertebral columns of the two freshest neonates reflect a cutting of the throat rather than decapitation. As you can see, these neonates' vertebral columns are fully articulated — they did not come apart, owing to remnants of tissue adhering to the spine — and cut marks are found only on the anterior and lateral surfaces of the vertebrae. Here and here.'

The men bent their necks to glimpse the faint marks carved into the bones.

'The cut marks did not continue in the vertebral joints or the spinous process, here, as can be expected in decapitation.'

'Who cuts a baby's throat that deep?' a man muttered.

'Someone who was overly excited,' Johnston supplied.

A few men nodded, a few shook their heads in disbelief. All lips were compressed to hard lines, smokes forgotten.

Johnston threw a glance at Sévère. The coroner clapped his hands once and announced, 'If the jury have no more questions, we shall move back to Vestry Hall.'

After a long series of questions to the inspector and the coroner, the inquest came to an end at half past four in the afternoon. The jury returned a verdict of unlawful killing, the inquest was adjourned, and Vestry Hall spilt its exhausted but cheerful human contents into the next public house.

---

REYNOLDS'S NEWSPAPER, SUNDAY, DECEMBER 12, 1880:

**The Missing Mortician**
*Mr G. Sévère, Coroner of Eastern Middlesex and Mr T. Height,*

*Chief Inspector of Division H of the Metropolitan Police, have sent to the Home Secretary a statement made by Sarah Dobbins, landlady of Mr Alexander Easy, mortician at St George-in-the-East, who has so mysteriously disappeared, of Mr Easy having last been seen by her as he exited the house on Friday, December 10, at ten o'clock in the evening, and behaving most curiously. The case being so unusual, Messrs Sévère and Height are hoping it may possibly be deemed worthy of investigation by the Home Office.*

# FIRST ACT

IN WHICH THE MASTER OF LIES MEETS
HIS MATCH

# THE ANATOMY OF THE HEART

THE TIMES OF LONDON, TUESDAY, DECEMBER 14, 1880.

## Murder Or Suicide?

*Yesterday the body of a man was found floating in the Thames. About noon attention was drawn to a dark object floating on the ebb tide near the Horseferry Stairs at Lavender Pond. A Thames Police galley rowed to the spot, and the object proved to be the body of a man, apparently about 40 years of age and fitting the description of the missing mortician Mr Alexander Easy. He was floating face upwards, and his clothes were found disheveled by the action of the tide. The body was secured by a tow rope and taken to Regent's Canal. It was subsequently moved to the St George-in-the-East mortuary to await identification and an inquest.*

*A*fter the external examination I can exclude physical violence as the cause of death. For now.' Dr Johnston stretched his aching shoulders. He felt the familiar knots of pain beneath his scapula and wished he could insert one of his tools there and pound the hard flesh to a soft dough.

Coroner Sévère looked up from his notes and Chief Inspector Height bent his neck to see what Sévère had written.

'No signs of injuries caused by a corrosive on the lips, in the mouth or rectum, and no peculiar odour emanating from the body — all of which would indicate the use of poison. The deceased has no stab wounds, bite marks, or any signs of blunt force trauma. He shows no defensive wounds, has no blood, skin or hair under his fingernails or in his mouth. All clothes were in order, no tears or cuts. Even the cravat was neatly tied. Are you able to tell me if Alexander Easy was suicidal, Sévère?'

Sévère lowered his head and narrowed his eyes, recalling his meetings with Mr Easy, which had always occurred in the mortuary and always when matters other than the mortician's emotional state were demanding his attention.

He looked up. 'Can we ever say with conviction that a man is *not* suicidal? I doubt it. To me, Mr Easy did not seem overly melancholic. He was quiet, but that means little. His landlady, Mrs Dobbins, said that he was a widower of six years and was still mourning his wife, but why would he jump into the river now, and not a year ago? Or six years ago?'

'That is the question.' The doctor frowned, and ran his sleeve across his chin. 'I can make one more conclusion which I will corroborate presently. Write this down, Sévère: No visible signs of putrefaction. The subject seems to have entered the freezing cold water around the time of death. It would be advisable to measure the temperature of the Thames. For now, I will assume it to be approximately three to five degrees centigrade. I will now commence the internal inspection.'

Johnston bent forward, pressed his index finger against the hollow of Alexander Easy's throat, aimed his scalpel, and began to cut. The frozen skin crackled. He stopped at the pubic bone.

Height turned his head away when Johnston sawed open Easy's ribcage and enlarged the resulting gap with a pull and a grunt.

'After the primary incision of the abdominal parietes, no peculiar odours can be detected,' Johnston said and threw a glance at Sévère to make sure the man was writing it all down.

Then he stuck his hands deep into the corpse, rummaged around and muttered, 'No signs of inflammation of the peritoneum…hum…the peritoneal aspect of the stomach…or the viscera. As visible thus far.'

Johnston picked up several short pieces of thread from the table. 'Placing a ligature around the lower end of the oesophagus and a double ligature at the commencement of the duodenum. If you don't know how to spell this, Sévère, write it down anyway. I'll know what it means.'

'Hm,' grumbled Sévère. Pencil rushed over paper.

Johnston nodded once and grabbed his knife. 'Dividing the oesophagus and the duodenum now.'

Huffing, he lifted out the stomach and placed it into a rectangular porcelain dish. 'Opening the stomach at the lesser curvature.'

In went the knife, and out came a mixture of red wine and acid. Johnston bent over the mess and sucked air through his nostrils. He smacked his lips. 'Tut-tut. Red wine on an empty stomach. And still no signs of putrefaction. And look at this, Sévère!'

He nodded encouragingly at the coroner, who stepped closer and gazed at the tip of the doctor's knife.

'Do you see the blood?' Johnston asked, running the blade along the cuts he'd made.

'It didn't coagulate? How is this possible? He must have been dead for days.'

'More evidence that Mr Easy's body entered the cold water around the time of his death. Except if... Was the man a bleeder?'

'I don't know. But his general practitioner should know,' Sévère answered.

'Inspector, please find Mr Easy's general practitioner and ask him if the man was a bleeder,' Johnston said without looking up.

'Now?'

'Tomorrow will suffice.'

Johnston picked up a magnifying glass and examined the contents of the stomach. After a few moments, he said, 'No plant material. No pigment particles or crystals, no notable amounts of river water.'

Johnston worked his way down along the intestines,

examined Easy's genitalia, then moved back up to extract the lungs and cut them open. Water gushed out of them.

'No signs of haemorrhaging. The smell indicates that it is Thames water that has entered the lungs.'

'So he drowned?' Height enquired.

'Not necessarily. In fact, it is difficult if not outright impossible to ascertain if a floater was dead or alive when entering the water. The lungs of a submerged body will fill with water simply due to the external pressure. Easy's larynx did not spasm, so his lungs were bound to fill up.'

Again, Johnston picked up his magnifying glass and examined the contents of the lung. After some humming and mumbling, he said, 'Small dirt and plant particles, as well as the smell, confirm that this is Thames water. Excellent. I will examine the heart now.' He wrapped the fingers of his left hand around Alexander Easy's heart, and with the knife in his right hand he sliced through blood vessels and connective tissue.

Squinting, he held up the organ, turned it in the light, and placed it into a dish.

Once again, Sévère was surprised by how small a human heart was. Romantics should be required to attend autopsies, he concluded. They would stop making such a fuss about *matters of the heart.*

The doctor began to cut sections. A large amount of blood oozed out of the organ, flooding the dish.

'Aha!' he exclaimed and pointed to a yellowish area. 'Complete occlusion of the left main coronary artery.'

'Excuse me?' Height said.

'The coronary arteries supply oxygenated blood to the heart muscle. Lack of oxygen can lead to tissue death and myocardial infarction. Mr Easy had a heart attack, inspector.'

'Did he die of it?'

'Extremely likely, but let me finish the postmortem examination before I come to my final conclusions.'

It took another hour of re-examining the cross-sections of all organs before Johnston finally announced, 'The cause of death was a heart attack. He had it coming. There is no evidence for violence or poison triggering the attack. How he got into the river is another question. However, you will remember the small card I found during my external examination. It was inside a peculiar little pocket of the subject's waistcoat. I believe the pocket was made to hide something, perhaps money. A pick-pocket would have problems finding it. Did you look at it, or were you so intent on staring at the corpse?'

Height cleared his throat.

'Well then,' said Johnston. He wiped his gory hands on a handkerchief and picked up the card. Sévère and Height stared down at it, then at each other as if to wrestle for the right to be the first to interrogate the suspect.

'We'll do it together,' Height suggested, and Sévère mentally prepared himself for yet another botched investigation.

---

MARY TAPPED her fingers against the windowsill when she spotted the four-wheeler down on the street. A police vehicle. She pressed her nose against the cold window-pane, trying to catch sight of the brothel's entrance, but without success. She opened the window, leant out and peeked down. A constable guarded the door, holding on to his rattle as though a crime could be witnessed that needed reporting at any moment.

She shut the window. Sweat itched on her palms. Her being a whore would negatively influence the police's judgement. But what if one of these men was a client? Would that make matters worse or better for her? Her fingers fidgeted and crumpled her dress. She pulled herself together and exhaled. The windowpane clouded, her breath froze and blocked her view. Just as well, she thought, and turned to face the door.

Several long moments later, a man entered her room without knocking. He was quite unremarkable. His cane supported part of his weight. His left leg was weaker than the right. Not by much, though. Dirty-blonde hair, smoothed back, and most of it hidden by a top hat. No moustache or beard. Blue-grey eyes, a straight nose. Well-groomed and fashionably dressed, but not overly so. It was as if one's gaze rolled right off him like water from a goose's plumage.

His gaze connected with Mary's. Her heart tumbled in her chest. She felt a chill. Sharp, highly intelligent eyes, fluid body, coiled muscle. He was exuding an air of authority and mercilessness. This man wasn't police. But what, then, was he?

Mary felt the annoying urge to shrink away. She broadened her shoulders and lifted her chin. Just then, a second man walked in — reddened cheeks, dark hair, dark moustache. Taller than the first, but slouching a little. A plainclothes policeman, probably an inspector. She relaxed her pose and retreated to her armchair.

———

SÉVÈRE AND HEIGHT found themselves in a room with floral wallpaper, dark green velvet curtains, red armchairs, and a large, virgin-white bed. The suspect lowered herself onto one of the two armchairs, her hands demurely folded in her lap, her face unnervingly calm. Sévère felt something creeping up his spine. It was the same feeling he got when he faced murderers in court or gaol: the feeling of one beast recognising another.

'I am Chief Inspector Height, this is Coroner Sévère. We will take your statement on the death of the mortician Alexander Easy. May I sit?'

She nodded and rose. 'Coroner Sévère might wish to rest his leg. I will sit on the bed.'

Sévère cursed himself. He'd made an effort to conceal his weakness — obviously to no avail. He nodded his thanks, not because he needed to sit, but because he wished to use the opportunity to bring himself down to the level of the inspector. To pretend camaraderie, coop-eration, sameness. Since the moment Johnston had announced Easy's death to be of natural causes, the coroner had lost jurisdiction of this case.

Sévère sat, and moved the armchair so that he faced the suspect. He extracted a notepad and a pencil stump from his waistcoat pocket.

'Your full name, please.' Height asked, also armed with notepad and pencil.

She regarded them both, a smile tugging at her lips, as if to say, "Aren't you cute," and then spoke with a soft voice, 'Miss Mary.'

'Your *real* name,' Sévère said.

Her eyes began to shimmer where the lower lid touched the iris. It made her look vulnerable. 'I can't remember my name. I was…soiled when I was very young.'

From the corner of his vision, Sévère observed the loss of colour from the inspector's face. He probably assumed the suspect had been seduced before the legal age of thirteen. How could a man of his profession be so naïve?

The coroner exhaled, leant back, crossed his arms over his chest, and smiled. 'Miss *Mary*, may we enquire your age?'

'Sixteen.' Her gaze slid down to the rug, her shoulders heaved. A moment later, she looked up at Sévère, blinking the moisture from her dark eyes.

Unfazed, Sévère said, 'I assume I don't need to ask about your date of birth, because you've probably forgot that, too?'

'Indeed I did.'

'Occupation?' Height asked.

'Prostitute.'

'Place of residence?'

'You are sitting in it.'

'Obviously,' Sévère muttered and wrote down the address, remembering to add the day's date to the top of the page.

'Would you be so kind as to inform me why a coroner

and a chief inspector are calling on me at this time of day?'

Oh dear God, what a voice! shot through Sévère's mind. The timbre seemed to reach out to him and softly caress his balls. Involuntarily, he crossed his legs. Shutting his eyes for a moment, he fought to pull his attention away from his crotch and back to the business at hand.

Before the inspector could utter a peep, Sévère asked him, 'May I?'

'Certainly,' Height answered, a little perplexed.

'Miss Mary, we know that Alexander Easy paid you a visit on the night of Friday, December 10, to Saturday, December 11. He died of a heart attack in your room, most likely in your bed. His corpse was thrown into the Thames. All I want to know before we apprehend you is why you did it.'

Slowly, the woman blinked. Her cheeks paled a little. When she parted her lips to speak, Sévère couldn't help but think of a vulva.

'Who?'

I'll be damned, Sévère thought. His instinct told him that this woman had yet to speak a single word of truth. But his analytical mind — despite being distracted by his animalistic urges (or perhaps because of them?) — told him she was sincere.

'Alexander Easy,' Sévère repeated the name calmly. 'Five feet, nine inches, aged forty-two, weighing eighteen stone and five pounds at the time of the autopsy — of course before his organs were removed. He had brown hair and a large moustache. He wore...' Sévère consulted his notes. He knew precisely what Easy had worn that night, but he needed a moment to take his eyes off the woman and collect himself. 'Black wool coat, yellow waistcoat, top hat, white shirt, striped trousers, brown patent leather shoes.'

'Mr Sévère, please correct me if I'm mistaken, but I do have the impression you believe my clients are in the habit of telling me their name, weight, and age?'

Height cleared his throat. Sévère threw him a glance, shook his head slightly, and pointed his pencil at the suspect. 'I believe you are intelligent and observant enough to be able to tell a man's age, height, and certainly, his *weight*.' He paused for effect. 'As for their names, no, I doubt they would tell you the truth.'

She held Sévère's gaze until he began to feel awkward. 'Would you please grace us with an answer, Miss Mary?'

'Oh, your question must have escaped me.'

That was when Sévère lost it. Blood rose to his cheeks as he leant forward. 'I doubt you are as dimwitted as you wish to make us believe. I will tell you how it stands for you: Several men have testified that Mr Alexander Easy entered two public houses in Whitechapel, enquiring about a Miss Mary at Madame Rousseau's. One witness stated that he gave Mr Easy a card of your establishment, the same card that was later found on his body. Mr Easy then entered this establishment, died here, and was discarded like a mangy dog. You will be contained for up to three years for fraud. Chief Inspector Height, arrest Miss *Mary* for concealing the death of Mr Alexander Easy and the unlawful disposal of his body.'

'Erhm...' said Chief Inspector Height and drew himself up to his full six feet. 'Will that be all, Coroner

Sévère?' There was an edge to the inspector's voice, enough to let the other man know he'd crossed the line once too often.

Height held out his hand to Mary. She cleared her throat and said, 'May I collect my belongings?'

'If it's not too much.'

'It is not.' She retrieved a box from under the bed, threw in what she found in the drawer of the nightstand, as well as her undergarments and a simple dress from the wardrobe. She didn't spare her expensive dresses a single glance. She was certain they would be taken away and sold, and her room rented to another woman before she returned. If she returned. She stared down at the rug in front of the window, then kicked it aside.

'I will now take a knife from beneath my mattress to move a floorboard,' she said and looked at Height, who took a step back and drew a revolver. That was when she knew the inspector wasn't as easily fooled as she'd previously believed. She smiled, because she liked that in a man.

She inserted the blade into the cracks in the floor, ran it around one of the boards and then jammed it in. The board gave and revealed a hollow space beneath. Eleven guineas, five shillings, and a few pence. The bulk of her savings was hidden elsewhere. She pocketed her money and stood.

'The knife,' Sévère said.

She flipped it in her hand and held it out to him, handle first. He took it from her and gingerly dropped it into his coat pocket.

They walked her down the stairs and through the

entrance hall. She didn't look at the madam, else she might have jumped at her and scratched her eyes from their sockets.

Silently, she exited the brothel and came to an abrupt halt. She tipped her face at the sky and shut her eyes. Small droplets of half-rain, half-snow caught in her lashes.

Sévère felt his skin come alive.

Height harrumphed, took Mary's elbow and helped her into the police carriage. He followed and sat down next to her.

Sévère held open the door and said, 'Inspector, I must apologise for my lack of respect earlier. You allowed me to interview the suspect although I have no jurisdiction in cases of fraud.'

Height nodded once. 'Apology accepted. You knew Easy. It must be unpleasant to have to stand aside.'

'Thank you. Yes, we…were friends,' Sévère answered, lowering his gaze to demonstrate a gratitude he didn't feel.

'You don't have friends,' Mary said, her voice so soft Sévère wasn't sure he'd heard her speak. Her profile revealed nothing to him; her eyes scanned the other side of the street.

'Pardon me?' He gripped the door handle tighter.

Slowly she turned and addressed him with politeness. 'Coroner Sévère, as your involvement in this case has ended, perhaps you can refer a colleague to take my case? I need an attorney. I pay well.'

He arched an eyebrow. 'For all I know, you could be a coldblooded murderess. But, as you so aptly observed, my involvement in this case has ended.' He shut the carriage door and nodded at the driver.

---

MARY FOUND herself in a holding cell of Division H Headquarters. She kept telling herself to remain calm, but the not-knowing made it hard. No one had told her when or if she would be transferred to Newgate, and how long she had to await trial.

She did not need to fret for long. An hour or two later, she was taken before the magistrate of Division H who sent her to the House of Detention with the words, 'The bill of indictment will be submitted to the Grand Jury and, if found true, you will be tried for fraud at the Old Bailey on February 28, 1881.'

---

AFTER A WEEK of living in a small cell with women in various states of ruin, feeding on gruel and dry bread, pissing and shitting into a common bucket, she was brought up again before the magistrate. He didn't bother to look up from his papers as he muttered, 'The jury has rejected the bill; you are to be discharged immediately.' He scribbled his signature at the bottom of a page.

'Why was it rejected?' she asked.

Confused, the man looked up. 'The normal reaction would be to whoop and run, not question the decision of the jury.'

'I am curious.'

'The police failed to provide sufficient evidence. The drunkards who testified to have seen Mr Easy could not even describe him when asked a second time. The pickpocket who said he'd given Mr Easy the card to your establishment was detained for pickpocketing and could not tell who or what Madame Rousseau's is, let alone remember if or when he gave the card of your establishment to a heavy-set, moustached man. The card being found on Mr Easy's body did in no way indicate that he had visited you, died in your bed, and had then been deposited in the Thames by you. And your madam testified that no such man had ever entered her establishment. Hence the jury rejected the bill.' The magistrate shrugged, flapped his hand at her and said, 'Off you fly, dove.'

---

MARY ENTERED her room and softly closed the door behind her. She leant against the wall, her eyes scanning the bed, the nightstand, coffee table, armchairs, wardrobe. It was as if she'd never left, as if her days in gaol had never happened. The bell struck three o'clock in the afternoon. Time to bathe, take a nap, and make herself presentable before her new client arrived.

# BLOOD, SWEAT, & BOLLOCKS

*H*is knock was answered by a soft, 'One moment, please!' A creak of a floorboard. The door opened.

'Good evening,' Sévère said, and tapped the rim of his hat. 'I am aware that this is most unusual. You might wish to send me away.'

'I might,' Mary said, and stepped aside.

Again, her expression revealed nothing to him. Not even the lie that he was a welcome guest at her lodgings.

'I was told to leave a guinea on your coffee table before asking you to undress. A hefty fee. Which services are included?'

Her lips curled in distaste and her gaze grew cold. 'Mr Sévère, allow me to be honest with you. I am not your usual street whore. Men come to me because I provide services they can't find elsewhere. Whenever a man attempts to bargain with me, I see him to the door and never let him back in. Are *you* planning to bargain with me, Coroner?'

'Far from it. I was merely wondering whether that which I'll ask of you is included in the price. Although I greatly doubt it. May I?' He indicated the armchair.

'Of course. Have a seat.'

He took off his top hat and placed it on the table, unbuttoned his coat and draped it over the backrest, slung a flat leather briefcase from his shoulder and dropped it onto the seat. Precise and effective movements.

He remained standing, and straightened his spine. 'Your payment.' The gold coin dropped onto the polished surface of her coffee table, spun, and fell flat on its face. 'The other...*special* service I demand is honesty. How much will that cost me?'

She laughed. 'You demand honesty? Here? Mr Sévère, I must have entirely misjudged you. I believed you to be a man used to spending a substantial part of his income on drinking, gambling, and women like me, one who would know just how much honesty can be found in an establishment like this one.'

'I do enjoy brandy, but I never gamble without knowing the outcome of the game in advance. And I do indeed spend money on willing women, although I've never met one quite like you.'

She tapped her fingers against her lips, feigning a yawn. 'Now I'm bored. Is it my unblemished skin? My long, black hair? The swell of my hips? The fullness of my lips, which, when I part them lightly, as now, makes you want to slide your cock into my mouth? My breasts, perhaps, that can provide the same service?'

'All of those, and yet, none.'

Sighing, she sat down on the armrest. 'What do you want from me, Mr Sévère?'

'As I said, I wish to bed you and I demand honesty. I'll know when you lie. Your moans will mean nothing to me.' The lies came easily. In fact, he *did* want her to moan into his mouth, around his cock, into the pillows. And, by God, he wanted her to beg him for mercy. The thought made him hard.

'Ah. I know what it is,' she said and connected her gaze with his. 'I am free. I've won. You've lost. And now you wish to know what really happened with poor Alexander. You believe I will tell you. Oh my.'

'I care little about Mr Easy's death.'

'You lie, it's written in your face. But that is nothing unusual. All men lie when they enter my room. You see, Mr Sévère, I am honest with you already. It is quite refreshing, I must say.'

Sévère found that he could barely contain himself. He was certain that there was much more to her than what met the eye, that she must have pushed Easy over the edge, cold-bloodedly sped up his death, and then dumped him. To Sévère, Mary was the most beautiful monster he'd ever laid eyes on. He wanted to dissect her, to rip her open. His animalistic side tugged hard on its leash and he was somewhat shocked by his strange reaction to her.

---

MARY CONSIDERED HIS REQUEST. She took in his expression — detached at first glance, but gazing deeper, there was a darkness coiled up and waiting to pounce.

Her gaze slid over his shoulder toward an invisible spot in the air and she wondered how he wished to torture her and if she should allow it. A man who demanded her honesty wouldn't wish to be seduced, wooed, praised. Such a man would want to force himself on a woman, and revel in her screams.

She wondered what she might charge should she grant his request.

'I will consider it,' she finally said. 'Wine?'

'Yes, please.'

She stood and poured wine into two glasses and offered him one. Neither of them sat down to drink. They appeared like two large cats trapped in a cage — he standing with poise; she fluidly pacing the room.

She had to admit to herself that she was scared. The man exuded danger. *Your moans mean nothing to me.* If she were to be honest, she would have to tell him she was scared. But such admissions turned men like him into... beasts. They loved it, the squirming and screeching, the begging, sobbing.

The more she thought about it, the more furious she grew.

This man must have loved the thought of her being locked up. What a disappointment her release must have been to him.

Very well, if he *demanded* her honesty, he should have it!

She emptied her glass. 'My decision is made. The price

for my honesty is this: Undress. Lie down.' She pointed to the bed.

He lifted an eyebrow. 'That doesn't quite sound like a price to me.'

'I expect it doesn't.'

She watched him as he unbuttoned his waistcoat and shirt, as he smoothed back his hair with one hand while the other held the cane he was leaning on. He unbuckled his belt and sat, pushed his trousers down his healthy leg and then the weaker one. Her eyes followed the line of his spine when he bent down to untangle his trousers from his left ankle. The vertebrae in his lower back seemed to have drifted sideways a little.

He dropped his socks and sock garters on the floor, pushed down his drawers and stood. He didn't seem to feel awkward in his nakedness. But then, it would have surprised her if he had. Despite the disadvantage his left leg gave him, he appeared able to pounce at a victim without difficulty. When he limped to her bed, the muscles in his back and long legs rippled.

She licked her lips in anticipation. 'Lie on your stomach.'

He stopped in his tracks, and cast a glance over his shoulder.

'Second thoughts, Mr Sévère?'

He knelt on the bed and stretched out his body. His feet twitched when he heard her move behind him. He tensed when she sat on his buttocks, knees on either side of him. Her hands brushed along his sides and up his arms. She lifted her dress and scooted farther up, spread her legs wider, and pressed her unclothed sex between his shoulder blades.

He exhaled gruffly into her pillow, and she used the moment of distraction to quickly bind his right wrist to the bedpost.

'What...'

'Ssshh...' she blew against his earlobe, licked the soft dusting of blonde hair at the back of his neck, and tied his left wrist to the other bedpost. She ran her fingers down along his spine, his buttocks, his balls. His skin answered to her touch, pulling tight, raising goose pimples.

'Beautiful trim arse,' she said, and, swift as a rat, she flipped around and tied first the ankle of his healthy leg to one bedpost and then the weaker leg to the other.

'Second thoughts, Mr Sévère?' she whispered and gave his rear a gentle smack.

'Now that you mention it... I think I might.' He tested the binds. The narrow leather bands held.

'You see, it is too late for that. You asked for the price of my honesty. I will be honest now. The price is pain and humiliation.'

'You forgot to gag me. I'll scream. The police will come.'

She laughed a deep, throaty laugh, and stretched out next to him, her fingers playing with the sensitive skin of his lower back.

'Do you want me to gag you? Ah no, my dear Sévère. I wish to hear you scream. The neighbours won't mind. They are used to it. You should hear the screeching of a maiden when she discovers what *seduction* really means. No one will bother to save you. And if you think your wounds will be evidence for a crime, I must disappoint you. Many gentlemen pay for punishment. The police will assume you asked for it. I am not an expert in flogging, so I apologise in advance should I cause any form of…lasting damage.'

With that, she picked up his leather belt and cracked it against his backside.

Sévère bit into the pillow to muffle a groan.

'Perhaps you wonder why I'm doing this to you?' she asked sweetly.

'I might,' he grunted.

She hit him three more times before she replied, 'Why do you think it is a woman's problem when your prick itches?' And she hit him again and again until he finally cried out with every lash.

'Damn…you…witch! You should be…ah!…locked up in an asylum! You are…mad…dammit! Stop it already!'

'I will stop when I am satisfied,' she said, her breath heavy from the exertion.

'If you plan to kill me, be quick about it!'

'Killing?' She laughed. 'One doesn't die so easily.'

She drew the belt across his skin again and again, marking him with broad, red stripes.

Unwilling to disgrace himself even further with cries of pain, he pressed his face deep into the pillow.

'I am teaching you the pleasures of the bedchamber, Coroner Sévère,' she hissed as he began to tremble. 'Five more lashes and I will be done with you. Count!'

He refused to speak.

When she finally dropped the belt and unstrapped his

ankles and wrists, she merely said, 'This was fun, wasn't it?' and threw his clothes onto the bed.

---

HE DIDN'T MOVE at first. He needed to get his bearings. His back and buttocks were on fire. He was certain she had drawn blood.

He stretched his limbs, rolled off the bed in one smooth move, and stood. He shook out his aching hands that he'd kept balled up for too long. He tried his left leg; a peculiar prickling ran up and down its side.

Mary refilled her glass, leant against the windowsill and sipped from her wine. 'You could be a little more animated next time. It pays better.'

He strode up to her, took her wine glass, and smashed it against the wall. His limp was worse than ever; his left knee didn't seem to follow his commands properly. This, together with his bruised skin and ego, tipped him over the edge.

He grabbed her neck and pushed her toward the bed, threw her onto it. 'Skirts up to your ears. Lie on your stomach. I don't want to see your face, whore.'

She made to turn, but he pounced, grabbed her hair and pressed her face into the mattress. He pushed her skirts up and kicked her legs apart. Her rear was beautifully shaped. He wanted to slap it. Badly.

Her sex. A nest of black curls; rosy lips. No wetness that indicated arousal. Of course not.

Why did he even care?

She didn't struggle, didn't say a peep.

He spat into his hand and rubbed the saliva between her thighs. She jerked away from his rough touch. A minute movement that was swiftly doused by work discipline or routine or both.

He stared at her passive form and felt as if he'd been sucked into a black tunnel and puked out on the other side, far back in time to when he was a boy, tied to a bed by a disease he did not understand. The helplessness. The humiliation. The pain that even the lightest touch had brought. Then, it had felt precisely as it had felt only moments ago. Precisely what he'd had in mind to do to her.

His fury and lust left him with a huff.

He pushed away from her and dressed. His left leg felt exceedingly tired; it trembled when he put his full weight on it. He would have to lean heavy on his cane tonight.

Mary rolled onto her back, crossed her arms behind her head, and gazed up at him, unspeaking.

'I paid for your honesty.' His voice was soft, tired, and yet, carried a warning tone. He pulled his coat over his shoulders and nodded at the guinea on the table. 'I paid for bedding you. Should we ever meet again and you dare lie to me, I will take you by force. And I promise I will hurt you more than you hurt me tonight.'

The door snapped shut, and Mary's gaze fell on the briefcase that lay forgotten on the floor.

She scrambled out of bed, tiptoed around the shards, pushed the curtain aside, and watched Sévère limp across the street and hail a hansom.

Mary picked up his wine glass and his briefcase, and made herself comfortable in the armchair. A few bills, two coins, and a thick folder. She counted the money. Six pounds sterling, two shillings. She extracted the folder and opened it. A smile curved her lips: case notes.

---

THE FOLLOWING MORNING, Mary took her time to neatly pin up her hair and dress in her finery. She left the house at half past eleven, and reached Division H Headquarters before lunch to enquire about the location of the coroner's practice.

The young man behind the desk squared his shoulders and straightened his lapel. 'Now, ma'am, you must know that there is no such thing as the *coroner's* practice. A county coroner only works part-time, you see. Coroner Sévère's *solicitor's* practice is at 9 Laurence Pountney Hill, Cannon Street E1. Do you have a suspicious death to report?'

'I wish to give a witness statement.'

The constable scratched his chin pimples and gave a noncommittal grunt. She thanked him with a curtsy and walked off.

---

AS SHE LIFTED her hand to pull the bell chain, the door was ripped open by Sévère himself.

'Damnation!' he huffed. 'The hag is walking around in bright daylight. What is it that you want?'

'At this precise moment I wish to kick your balls, because this is not how one addresses a lady. But I will refrain from doing so. Do you, by any chance, miss your case notes?'

His gaze dropped to the briefcase clamped under her arm. His mouth compressed to a thin line, and he held out his hand, palm up.

She took a step back. 'The case is closed, it appears.'

'I need those papers, Miss Mary. If you have no further wish to spend a few days in a holding cell, I recommend you hand them to me. Including the money the briefcase held.'

'Holds,' she corrected him. 'Mr Sévère, why, in your opinion, did I come here? Do you see a whip on me? Shall we begin anew? Hello, Mr Sévère, I brought your case notes, your money, and your nice briefcase. Why don't you offer me tea, a sandwich, and a comfortable seat and I'll tell you what you have missed.' She tapped her gloved fingers against the briefcase.

'What I've missed? *What I've missed?*' He inhaled deeply, looked up at the dreary sky, and shook his head. Then, he pushed aside all emotions, switched his mind back to professionalism, and grabbed the chance to interrogate a difficult suspect.

A dazzling smile lit up his face when he said, 'Oh, hello, Miss Mary. How very nice to see you. Allow me to invite you for lunch.' He pulled the door shut and offered his arm.

'Most gallant of you, Coroner,' Mary purred, and sneaked her hand into Sévère's elbow bend.

SHE PLACED the briefcase on the table and pushed it toward him. 'Three types of soil.'

Sévère picked it up and placed it on his lap. 'Three types of soil. Is that what I supposedly missed?'

'The inquest notes don't contain a statement by a naturalist or a geologist. You didn't listen to Dr Johnston who said, "You may wish to consult an expert on this."'

Sévère extracted his watch from his waistcoat pocket, flipped it open, read the time, and closed it. 'Please reach the essence of your speech, Miss Mary. My time is limited.'

'Identify the variety of apple tree saplings and how they were grafted. With a little bit of luck, this should tell you who made them or, at the least, where the man has learnt his trade. Identify the three types of soil and you will pinpoint the nursery with precision, even though you could not find the man who sold the trees to Mr Bunting.'

'You approach this case with too much enthusiasm. You believe logic is all that needs to be applied and the crime will be solved. You will burn yourself out.'

She regarded him with curiosity, cocked her head and said, 'A cold, analytic mind can solve crimes, a hot head cannot.'

'Can you explain mankind with logic, Miss Mary? Please do so because I can't. Give me a logical reason why someone killed these nine infants.'

'The reason will be revealed when the case is solved. You will find logic in it.'

'I will find logic in it? How amusing. Mankind is not *logic*. Mankind is sweat and blood and fear and bollocks.

Passion, love, envy, hate, terror — yes. But not logic. You, of all, should know that.'

She batted her lashes at him. 'Thank you for your honesty, it suits you. I must say that I find your opinions of mankind very interesting, especially as I get to see a lot more balls than you, Mr Sévère. I will think about what you've said. Will you think about what I said?'

'I did already.' He pulled two coins from his pocket, placed them on the table and rose. As he did so, he watched her expression from the corner of his vision. She kept her disappointment well hidden. Only the corners of her lips quirked a little; he would have to keep an eye on them.

'Are you coming?' he said.

'For which deed are you apprehending me this time, Coroner?'

'Grab my elbow, Miss Mary. We have to catch a cab, else we'll be too late.'

She narrowed her eyes.

'The statement of the expert is not in my notes, because he was travelling and arrived in London only yesterday in the late afternoon. If you wish to whip the man, it will be my pleasure to introduce him to you. But you'll have to hurry up now.'

Mary jumped from her chair, threw on her coat, and snatched her sandwich. Only a few minutes later the two climbed aboard a cab to Cable Street.

'Why was the inquest held so soon? Before you had all the evidence?'

'Because the police took Mr Bunting into custody and the old man would not have fared well in a cold cell for longer than a few nights. He could barely walk down the stairs of his own house.'

'What's wrong with him?' Mary asked.

'Rheumatism.'

'So you held the inquest to...do what precisely?'

'There's no evidence whatsoever of Mr Bunting being involved in, or responsible for, the killings. Besides, he can barely descend the stairs, let alone ascend them, so there's little danger of him disappearing should the police or I plan to question him further. I prefer to take all witness statements when their memory is still fresh. The case has not been closed, Miss Mary. The inquest is adjourned.'

'You did someone a favour. How very curious.'

'You once said to me, "You don't have any friends." Why would you say that?'

'Because it's true. Cooperation is against your nature.'

He snorted. 'My occupation requires cooperation on a daily basis.'

'A fact that does not prove me wrong. It only means that you have learnt to adapt to that which is against your nature.'

---

THEY REACHED the mortuary and alighted. When Sévère opened the door for Mary, he said, 'This is where Alexander Easy used to work. You wouldn't know him by any chance, would you?'

'Oh, I do know him. He is...was a very nice man.' She

bumped her elbow against his, and strolled through the antechamber into the viewing room.

He stared at her back, the bustle of her dress bouncing beneath her coat. The clacking of her heels on the hard floor.

'I'll be damned,' he growled and followed her inside.


'MR DENNIS POUCH.' The man held out his hand. Mary gave it a squeeze. Through her gloves, she felt the calluses and warmth of a working man. His eyes were those of a scholar: bright with curiosity and intelligence.

'Miss Mary,' she answered.

Pouch's gaze strayed to Sévère, searching for an explanation for the woman's presence.

'My apologies for being late. I misplaced my case notes,' Sévère said and nodded to the saplings. 'Shall we?'


'GRAFTING IS one of the oldest arts of plant craft,' Pouch explained, stroking the trees as if they were his children. 'These here are whip-on-tongue grafted. The stems exhibit marks of the band used to tie scion and rootstock together, and here,' he bent closer and scraped at the knot with his small knife. 'Here we have beeswax residues. Oh, and look at this: the apical bud has been snipped off. The grafting was done by an expert.'

'Can you identify the apple tree variety?' Sévère asked.

'These young ones? Hardly. I need to see the fruits to be certain.'

Mary inhaled, stopped herself, and crinkled her brow.

'Yes, Miss?' Mr Pouch asked.

'Can they produce fruits at all? I mean, in a pot of this size and on a balcony here in Whitechapel.'

'I doubt it. Actually, I would be surprised if the trees could survive for very long. Apple trees need plenty of space, good drainage, and full sun.'

'Why would someone put them on the balcony of his London apartment?'

'I don't know, Miss. Sentimentality? Certainly not to grow apples.'

Sévère's shoulders stiffened. 'Can you tell who grafted these?'

'Ah, that I can't say. I'm sorry. You can find this kind of grafting in nurseries all over England. In the message you sent me, you also asked about soil identification. I must disappoint you again, Coroner. The potting soil is a mixture of sand, clay, and compost with a dash of lime. I couldn't tell you where the components come from.'

'I hope you can identify the soil stuck to these.' Sévère indicated a table in a corner of the viewing room, where a linen cloth covered something bumpy.

He pulled aside the fabric. 'You may touch them and pick them up, but be careful, they are fragile.'

'So small,' Pouch whispered, visibly shaken by the sight.

'Newborns,' Sévère supplied. 'There is soil stuck to the insides of the skulls, soil that is different from the potting mixture.'

Pouch's thick fingers curled around a small skull and gingerly turned it over and over, tipping it this way and that. Then he chose another skull.

With the nail of his pinkie he scraped at the thin layer of soil on the inside of an eye socket, rubbed it between his fingers, sniffed at it, and stuck it into his mouth. He ground it between his teeth and said, 'Slightly acidic, loamy and clayey soil. Low permeability. Probably estuarine clay and silt. Not unusual around here.'

He repeated the procedure with every skull until he found a layer of pale, slightly greenish clay. That, too, he ground between his teeth.

'Fuller's Earth!' Mr Pouch exclaimed and licked his lips. 'How very unusual! I know of only two deposits within a hundred mile radius.'

'Where?' Sévère's body snapped to attention. Finally, there was a promising straw he could grasp.

'One in Surrey, stretching between Redhill and Limpsfield, and the other in Woburn, Bedfordshire.'


WHEN MR POUCH had been reimbursed for his time and services, and bade his farewell, Mary rubbed her fingertips over the small bones of hands and feet.

The door shut and they were alone in the viewing room. Silently, Sévère watched Mary. She bent down to sniff at the skulls, touched her pinky to the soil and slipped it into her mouth. She ground it between her teeth, her eyes shut, her brow furrowed.

'Hum,' she said and turned to Sévère. 'You look as if someone crawled over your grave.'

'You stuck *that* into your mouth. I was surprised to see Mr Pouch doing it, but I never thought a woman would dare do this.'

She snorted. 'A great variety of things considered unappetising have been in my mouth.' She brushed off her hands and placed her bonnet on her head. 'I think I figured out how he identifies soil. It's how the dirt distributes into the small ridges of one's fingertips, and how fine the grain is. One can actually determine the grain size even better when grinding it between one's teeth.' She cleared her throat, blushed, and added, 'I believe.'

Sévère held open the door for her. They stepped onto the narrow, paved walkway. The crows up in the oak tree said, 'Caw!'

At Cable Street, Mary and Sévère came to a halt. It was time to part ways. But he didn't offer his hand, didn't say farewell. Instead, he frowned at her and waited.

'Yes?' she asked softly.

'Alexander Easy.'

'Oh, Sévère, do you truly believe I wish to see the inside of that dreary cell once more? I very much prefer my own quarters, despite the company I keep.'

'Why not call the police? Why throw him into the Thames? Why treat a man with so little respect?'

'I don't waste a single moment wondering what you might be thinking of me. I truly don't. You may think me a coldblooded murderess, as little as I'm concerned. I'm generally very uninterested in the opinions of other people.'

'A bargain then, Miss Mary. Tomorrow, I'll pay a visit to Covent Garden for another attempt at finding the elusive creature who sold the trees to Mr Bunting, and after that, I'll take a train to Redhill. If you wish, you may accompany me. In exchange for joining my investigation, you'll tell me about Mr Easy.'

'What makes you think I would wish to do any of these things, let alone in your company?'

'I know that you do.'

She mirrored his smile. 'An amusement day for the whore. How very gallant of you. Give me your hand.'

He held it out to her. She took it and said, 'I will swallow your bait. Tomorrow, we will visit Covent Garden together, enquire about the nursery and the person who sold these saplings to Mr Bunting. We will board the train to Redhill and I will tell you the first half of what you wish to know. Once we've visited the nursery and boarded the train back to London, I will tell you the other half.'

She spat on the pavement.

He grinned, and spat on the other side of the pavement.

'What about the trip to Woburn?' she asked.

'Let us not presume, Miss Mary.'

# SAPLINGS

The train swayed as it exited Victoria Station. Mary staggered, and her bonnet tumbled to the floor before she could grip an armrest and steady herself. She brushed the dust off her hat, dropped it on a seat and sat down next to it. Condensation was dripping down the window.

Sévère slid the door to their first class compartment shut and sat, gingerly supporting the neck of the sapling to prevent it from tipping. To Mary, Sévère's expression seemed that of disinterest, except for the slight deepening of the lines between his eyebrows. Their excursion to Covent Garden had turned up nothing of interest. The vendor who'd allegedly sold the seven apple trees to Mr Bunting seemed to have been one of those irregular tradesmen who appeared only when it struck his fancy. The description the housekeeper had given of the man fit countless others: five foot five, broad build, swarthy features, large moustache, corduroy trousers and jacket, heavy boots, cap.

Sévère removed his hat, ruffled his hair, and folded his hands in his lap. His eyes rested on Mary. 'Now,' he said.

With an impatient movement of her hand, she wiped a wet gap onto the clouded window. She needed to gaze at something other than Sévère's inquisitive, sharp eyes. 'Men lie about their names. I get a lot of visits from Messrs Smith, for example. But Alexander Easy did not lie to me once.'

'You know this from reading the case files, of course.'

'They confirmed what I already knew, or believed to know. You see, the more lies a prostitute is able to detect, the longer she lives. I'm skilled at staying alive.'

For a short moment, his gaze drifted out of focus. He nodded. 'Can you tell me anything that's not in the files?'

'You want me to detail Mr Easy's skills in the bedchamber?'

Sévère slapped his thigh and laughed. It surprised her. She was certain she'd never seen him laugh freely.

'Honesty suits you,' she said, crossing her arms over her chest. 'As I've told you already.'

'Doesn't it suit us all? I can't imagine it helps you much, though. To know when a man lies, that is. Most are expected to produce a string of lies when they enter your room. How would it help you to know, for example, whether a man is dangerous?'

'I know that you are dangerous.'

'I can assure you that I am not.'

'Be that as it may.' She turned her attention back to the

window, the droplets of water crawling down its cold surface. 'The lies men tell me concern only the superficial. Their names, where they come from, what they do for a living. It's of no consequence. Beyond these lies, I get to see their true nature. You wouldn't believe the things they tell me. All the dirty secrets men don't dare tell their wives. In general, it's never the wife who knows her husband, it's the whore. I get to see the naked man, inside and out. You, for example.' She shot a sharp glance at him. 'You are a liar through and through. You resent your position as a coroner. I'm guessing it's because of Division H's new superintendent, who is even hastier with his warrants than his predecessors. Or is it because the bunch of imbeciles the magistrate employs as plainclothes detectives spoils the fun of your investigations? Don't look so surprised. Don't believe all *fallen* women are uneducated and stupid. Besides, certain news spreads quickly among…shady individuals.'

'Well…' Sévère produced a quick smile. 'For people who *can* and *do* read the papers, it must be common knowledge that coroners don't mix well with the police force.'

'You want me to tell you something about you that's not common knowledge?' She bent forward and lowered her voice. 'Something only a woman can know?'

'Try me.'

She let herself sink against the backrest. 'The question is, what you are willing to pay for an answer.'

'Oh dear God, not *this* again!' He threw up his hands in mock terror. 'You promised not to bring your whip.'

'I don't require a whip. However, I'm afraid I might

lose my chance to investigate this most intriguing case with you, because what I'll say might disturb you.'

'I promise I will hold up my end of our bargain. Besides, I'm not so easily disturbed.'

She held out her hand. 'Very well, let's seal it with a handshake.'

'Without spittle, certainly?'

'No. There's no spitting in first class.'

He took her hand and gave it a good squeeze. 'Now, tell me my darkest secrets.'

'You are too easy to lure in.' She brushed a few crinkles from her lap and cleared her throat. 'You are unmarried. Quite unusual for a man in his thirties and of high social standing. The reason is rather unusual, too. Pride, aggression, arrogance. You are unable to share your life with anyone but yourself, and even this seems difficult for you. There is a darkness lurking behind your irises. A darkness that makes me wish to never again meet you alone at night. I believe you have what it takes to be a murderer — the will to control someone's life and death, and the courage and coldness to do so.'

Slowly, he exhaled. 'You are wrong on all accounts.'

'I believe I am not.' She blinked and changed the topic. 'Alexander Easy said he was a widower of six years. That he missed his wife terribly and had never before visited *a woman of my profession* — that's how he put it.'

Mary uncrossed her arms, unsure how to proceed. She watched how Sévère allowed a trace of expectation to show in his face, while remaining friendly and open. The impatience that must be twisting his insides was invisible. She wondered which mask he put on at court.

'I knew before reading your notes that he is...was a mortician,' she said.

'He told you this?'

'No, he didn't. I could smell it. In his hair and on his hands.'

Sévère's eyebrows rose.

'The hair on his head. Not the other,' she muttered.

'Who would have guessed.'

'Putrefaction and embalmment liquid, I believe. A mere whiff. He must have washed before he came to me.'

'Obviously. He'd worked on a bloated corpse only hours earlier.'

'You repeatedly attempt to rattle my composure. I wonder why that is.'

Sévère did not reply, so she continued, 'Alexander Easy arrived at my door in a fashion that suggested he came on a whim, that he didn't plan it in the least. He must have left his home, perhaps, and simply drifted in an...unexpected direction. I greatly doubt he read any of the city's nightlife guides. He's not a man of that...was, I mean... Anyway. He must have walked past the only billboard that advertises Madame Rousseau's. It's an old, tattered thing, at Charlotte's and York. He couldn't have seen it from a cab. The address is torn off. Your witnesses from the public house told the truth when they testified they'd seen Mr Easy that evening and had told him how to find me.'

Sévère's lips curled to a smirk. He gave a slight nod. 'Charlotte's and York, you say? Why would he walk through the slums?'

'And I keep wondering why anyone would advertise

Madame Rousseau's at that squalid corner,' she said, absentmindedly. 'Alexander got lost. And then he found me.'

'And then he died.'

'He died a happy man. He was extraordinary lonely. But when he died, he was happy. Or as close to happy as he could be.'

Sévère regarded her, his curiosity attempting to burn a hole into his stomach. But his main question had to wait a little longer. *Why dispose of him?*

---

'THERE'S one thing I don't understand,' Mary said when they exited Redhill station and walked up to a trap with an old donkey tied to its shafts. 'According to the inquest notes, you kept referring to the offender as male, although it might be more likely that the mother of the infants is the murderer.'

'Excuse me, sir,' Sévère called up to the man in the worm-eaten driver's seat. 'We are looking for a nursery.'

'Plants or children?' he barked, his long pipe precariously close to dropping from his mouth.

'Apple trees,' Mary provided.

'Fifteen minute walk that way.' The man jerked his brush of a beard somewhat ahead of him, or perhaps leftish or rightish, one couldn't be sure. He threw a measuring stare at the two town people before him and grunted. 'Or a three-minute drive. Costs a shilling, mind.'

Mary looked at Sévère and down his left leg.

'We walk,' he said.

'You are stubborn, Sévère.'

'And you have a death wish.'

Mary squeezed his arm and they set off. 'I merely keep my end of our bargain.'

Sévère looked up at the sky. 'You do indeed. You asked why I referred to the offender as male. Call it political reasons. Every jury comprises respectable middle-class men who seem to be unable to convict the *fair sex* for crimes of murder or manslaughter. They would wish to believe that temporary insanity was the cause, or that, despite the evidence, the victims were born dead. If I had referred to the offender as female, the jury would have likely arrived at the verdict "concealment of birth," and that won't do. In the past twelve months alone, two hundred thirty-five infants have been found dead in Middlesex, and barely a hundred women have been charged. Only five of them were charged with manslaughter, the rest with concealment of birth. The verdict here is unlawful killing in nine cases, which gives me the freedom to investigate further and find the murderer. Had the verdict been concealment of birth, the involvement of a coroner and his officers would be unlawful. It is even possible that the magistrate would then deem the inquest unnecessary and disallow my fees. He tries that as often as he possibly can.' Sévère showed Mary a sour smile.

'He can do that? I believed coroners were independent from the police.'

'Yes and no. The office of coroner is much older than the police. It dates back to the twelfth century. But — and this is the unfortunate part — since the invention of police, there have never been any statutory definitions on the intersecting responsibilities of police and coroner. Police believe they are modern and coroners are outdated. For decades now, magistrates have tried to exercise control over coroner inquests, which form the core of our work. If the magistrates and the Metropolitan Police could do as they please, I would be an anecdote in a museum.'

They came to a halt at a small stone house. A thin layer of snow covered the straw roof, a row of poplars waved their scrawny twigs in the wind. Smoke curled up from the chimney and was whisked away by the icy breeze.

'Here we are,' Sévère said and pointed at a wooden board nailed to the fence.

*MacDoughall's*
*Plant Nursery*

'Any preferences for a fake surname?' he asked, as he opened the garden gate for her.

'Jenkins,' she answered. 'He's the milkman.'

Sévère raised his cane and tapped the front door. His knock was answered quickly. The door creaked open and a wave of warmth touched Mary's face.

'Good day to you. I am Gavriel Sévère, Coroner of Eastern Middlesex, and this is Mrs Mary Jenkins, my assistant. We have questions regarding a recent case of infanticide in London Whitechapel. May we come in?'

The woman swallowed, and pressed the bundle she was holding closer to her bosom. A tiny fist stretched up and clutched a strand of her hair that had come undone. She stepped aside and beckoned them in.

As Sévère placed the flowerpot on the ground, Mary inhaled the scents of fresh, warm bread and melting butter. She smiled at the woman. 'Is smells very good here. Reminds me of my own home.'

The woman seemed to wake from her shock. 'Oh, yes, well. Um…'

A man rumbled through the back door, wiping his hands on his trousers. 'Celia, I saw someone—' His gaze fell on Sévère and Mary. 'May I enquire what two strangers are doing in my house?'

Sévère repeated his introduction. The man's expression darkened. He indicated a well-worn table with four well-worn chairs. 'Have a seat, please. Celia, bring tea. Give me the little one for the moment.'

Chairs scraped over polished floorboards. Sévère leant his cane against the table, sat, and folded his hands. 'Mister MacDoughall, I assume?'

'Are we suspects?'

'No, of course you are not. I was hoping you could provide me with information on this sapling. It is evidence in a crime we are investigating. Do the pot and the tree look familiar to you?'

The man threw a glance at the small tree. 'Well, I know what it is, if that's what you mean. It's an apple tree.'

'Would you take a closer look, please?'

With the child in one arm, he squatted down and ran his fingers up the stem and back down. He inspected the grafting knot and the bare roots. 'Why is it without soil?'

'The soil and what it contained is kept as evidence in London. Does the pot or the tree look familiar to you?'

'Not the pot, no. But the tree could be one of mine. The grafting looks quite similar to my own.'

'Quite similar or identical?' Sévère asked.

'Isn't that the same?'

'No, it is not. Similar indicates that it has not been done by you, but by someone who grafts in the same fashion. Identical means it has most likely or definitely been done by you.'

'Looks like mine, but I couldn't swear upon it,' the man said, and rose. The child in his arms squeaked.

Celia MacDoughall placed the teapot on the table, left, and returned with four mugs. 'The goat is dry and the honey harvest was poor this year,' she explained the lack of milk and something to sweeten the brew. She sat down next to her husband, who offered her the whimpering bundle. She unbuttoned her blouse. At once, the hungry complaints were silenced and replaced by small smacking noises.

'May I use your privy? I'm with child and, despite its smallness, I have the impression it sits on my bladder day in, day out.' Mary dropped her gaze to the floor.

'Oh. Certainly,' Mrs MacDoughall said, and nodded to the back door. 'Through the corridor, straight ahead and out into the backyard. You can't miss it.'

Mary thanked the MacDoughalls, and left the room. Through the shut door she heard the husband mutter, 'You employ a woman who is in the family way?'

She scanned the short corridor. There was a door ahead of her, one to the right and one to the left. She opened the one to her left and peeked in. A tiny room, clad with shelves that were filled with a number of small crocks. It smelled of lard, smoked meat, old wood, beeswax, and pickles. She retreated and opened the door behind her. A larger room that smelled of vinegar, dust, and, faintly, of urine. A bed with two blankets and a lamb skin. A bucket with a nappy in it. She stepped forward and sniffed at it. It was the source of the vinegar and piss smell.

Crammed between the bed and the window was a smaller pallet. A pile of blankets began to stir and two large, dark eyes peeked out. 'Hello. Are you an angel?' a faint voice croaked.

'Hello. Are you an owl? Your eyes are as big as an owl's.' Mary smiled and stepped closer. She dipped her index finger against the small nose. It was hot. The child coughed.

'Am I dying already? Mother said I won't. She said I have a cold, not the flu.'

'You will be all right in a few days. Will you keep our secret?'

'Secret?'

'That I came to visit you.'

A small nod.

Gifting him her sweetest smile, she brushed a strand of hair off his moist forehead. 'Rest well, dear.'

She left the family's bedroom and opened the last of the three doors. The cold made her cheeks tingle. She stepped out into the backyard and followed the narrow walkway. Left and right grew bushes of gooseberry, currant, and others she couldn't identify.

Next to the privy, a hawthorn held its red fruits into the winter wind. She touched the berries, their black, prickly navels and white snow caps. The sun stood low in the trees, its milky light seeping through the branches.

WHEN SHE WALKED BACK into the house, silence greeted her. The husband was bent over a journal filled with slanted handwriting. Sévère watched. The wife nursed her infant.

Mary sat, wrapped her frozen fingers around the tea mug, and pushed the hawthorn berry around in her mouth. With her teeth she scraped the thin layer of flesh off the pit and began to chew. The hawthorn berry turned into a bland mush, and, after a minute or two of chewing, it gave off a pulse of short-lived sweetness. Mary swallowed. The infant demanded the other breast, and soon fell into a satiated slumber.

MacDoughall turned the journal around and pushed it toward Sévère. 'There is no entry for the sale of seven apple tree saplings. Not for the past year, or the year before.'

Sévère scanned the journal, extracted his notebook and pencil and jotted down all bulk sales from the past twenty-four months. 'You have six regulars here who purchased a number of fruit trees from you. Would you mind writing down their full names, addresses, and where they sell your trees?' He held out his notebook. MacDoughall frowned, scratched his ear, and began to write.

While MacDoughall worked, Sévère addressed the wife. 'A very healthy child. How many do you have?'

'Two.'

'Where is the other one?'

'School.'

'A boy, then?'

'Yes.' She arranged her blouse and looked Sévère straight in the eye. 'You said we are not suspects.'

'You aren't. But I do consider every possibility. Do you know of a woman who appeared to have been with child several times, but was never seen with an infant of her own? Or a woman who's taking in infants for a fee?'

'Excuse me?'

'In which way precisely was my question unclear?'

'I don't know of any such woman,' Celia MacDoughall answered.

'My grandfather was a beekeeper, too,' Mary said, and all eyes were on her, faces unable to conceal the puzzlement. 'I saw the bee skeps in your back yard. I was little when he passed away.' She cleared her throat and dropped her gaze.

'We are no beekeepers,' Mr MacDoughall muttered. 'Well, weren't until a few months ago. Our neighbour, Mr Hunt, sold us his bees for very little money.'

'Why would he do that?' Mary asked.

'His wife died and he couldn't tend to the daughter all by himself. She's deaf and in a workhouse now, I believe. Hunt moved away. His property is for sale.'

'Mr MacDoughall, did you ever have a burglary? Did anyone ever steal trees from you?' Sévère asked.

'No. Not that I can recall. Oh, yes! Someone took a few of our prized roses. When was that, Celia?'

'Summer, six years ago. It was a very dry summer.'

'Hm. Yes. That it was.'

'No thefts in the past two years?' Sévère asked again.

'No.' MacDoughall scratched his ear. He'd been scratching that ear for quite a while. 'Well, some imbecile raided our herb garden last year. But no trees were taken.'

'Would you, without exception, know if a tree was taken?'

'Of course I would!'

'Hm,' Sévère nodded slowly. 'You don't happen to have Fuller's Earth on your premises, do you?'

MacDoughall leant back, blinked, and then began to holler with laughter. His wife kicked him under the table and he shut his mouth instantly. Wiping the tears from his eyes he said, 'Coroner, if I had found Fuller's Earth in my backyard, I wouldn't be sitting here.'

'You wouldn't?' Mrs MacDoughall asked, her brow knitted.

'I wouldn't. You and I and the bairns would be…would be…. Well, wherever we would be, we'd have plush pillows under our arses.'

Celia McDoughall's eyes shot from her husband's face to Mary's and Sévère's, and back to her husband again. She set her chin, looked down at her child and swallowed. 'You should tell them,' she whispered.

Sévère's tapping foot stilled abruptly.

'What about?' McDoughall asked, rather puzzled.

His wife sighed, whisked a stray curl from her eyes and said, 'The cledge.'

'Oh. That.' McDougall's hand shot up to his ear and he began to scratch it again. 'The Fuller's Earth deposit is located at eighteen to twenty-six yards depth. The mine-able portion of it, anyway. But, there are several overlying strata of clay and sand. And a very thin layer of Fuller's Earth, only about a foot thick, often less. The diggers call it the cledge. It's useless to them because neighbouring sands and clays insinuate themselves within it.'

'At what depth can one find this cledge?' Sévère asked.

'Four to six feet.'

---

'FOUR TO SIX feet is a nice depth to bury a corpse,' Mary said, as they walked down the street toward Redhill church.

'Do you have experience with burying corpses?'

'Not as yet.'

'I'm glad of it.' Sévère tapped his cane hard against the cobblestones. 'MacDoughall sounded very much like a miner when he talked about the cledge. "Insinuated" and "strata" don't seem to be terms a gardener would be using. And she lied about the older child. Wherever he or she was, it wasn't in school. Besides, what was that about? "I am with child and need to use your privy." And, "My grandfather was a beekeeper."'

She poked him with her elbow. 'Imagine, Sévère, that I got lost on the way to the privy and that, completely by accident, I peeked into the pantry, the family's bedroom, and around the backyard. And so, coincidentally, I discovered the bee skeps, and wondered why the skeps were exposed to wind and rain. No experienced beekeeper would allow that, most certainly not in winter. Oh, and by the way, imagine that the bedroom I accidentally stumbled into had a large bed for the parents and the little one, plus a small mattress for the oldest child — which was occupied.'

'By the child?'

'Yes. He's ill. A cold, I believe. He thinks I'm an angel. And I'm absolutely sure no one else lives in that house or on the premises, such as a sister of the wife or husband, or tenants. Celia MacDoughall is too young to have given birth to nine dead children plus the two she has. You'll have to look for the culprit elsewhere.'

Sévère refrained from commenting on the fact that he had not thought of asking about tenants or relatives living with the MacDoughalls, and that Mary had surprised him yet again.

'You are welcome,' Mary said. 'Where are we going now?'

'Public house,' he grumbled.

'May I recommend you treat me like the bad-tempered husband you are, while I make big, watery eyes at the innkeeper?'

'To extract all kinds of hearsay from the poor man?'

'Precisely. I expect I must tell him that I fear for the life of my unborn child, because my husband is a brute. I'll ask him if he has ever heard of such a thing as infanticide, because I read about it in the papers a few days ago.' She smiled at him. 'And I'm utterly and thoroughly upset. A hysteric attack is threatening.'

'Under these circumstances, you may.'

THE INNKEEPER, naturally, was shocked. Sévère treated Mary as though she didn't deserve to walk the face of Earth, and Mary treated the innkeeper as though he were her would-be saviour.

At some point, a constable entered and asked Sévère to follow him to the inspector's office. He obeyed without making a fuss, while his *wife* held on to the innkeeper's large and hairy paw.

---

'CORONER SÉVÈRE, why did you not come to us directly? We would have been able to answer all your questions regarding the nursery or any cases of infanticide in Redhill.' The inspector was still pacing up and down in front of his desk. His mutton chops stood out as if struck by lightning.

It had taken Sévère a good fifteen minutes to convince the police that he was indeed Coroner of Eastern Middlesex, and that his papers were genuine.

'What about this woman, then? Is she your wife?'

'She's my assistant and, at present, she is interrogating the innkeeper.'

'You have no jurisdiction here,' the inspector pointed out.

'The bodies were found in my district and the evidence shows that the offender might have committed the murders here in Redhill. Hence, I am fully within my rights to conduct an investigation in your district.'

'You could have notified us.'

'I was on my way to the police station,' Sévère lied. 'And now that I am here, I would greatly appreciate if you could provide further information on the quarry, and fetch your files for me. I need to know about all cases of infanticide, concealed birth, adultery, rape, or the death of a child by neglect.'

---

WITH A BELCH, the train pulled out of Redhill and huffed northward.

'You were not surprised when the police arrived,' Mary said.

'I saw the innkeeper slipping a note to one of his boys. Both were looking at me as if I were the devil. I was sure the boy would go straight to the local police office. What mysteries did the innkeeper reveal to you while you were squeezing the lifeblood from his hands?'

She pressed her palms to her tired eyes, and sighed impatiently. 'He told me to dump you, and marry him.' She dropped her hands into her lap and shrugged. 'Whenever I tried to direct our conversation to gossip or infanticides or women who might have been in the family way, but were never seen with an infant, he said that Redhill is so much prettier than London, that he's a fine specimen of a man, and that he's saved enough money to support a woman like me. We could give your child to a wet nurse and start anew. Gah!'

'Unfortunate,' Sévère noted and rested his elbows on

his thighs. 'Now the interesting information, if you please.'

'Alexander Easy died…beneath me.'

'I thought so. Did he scream?'

'He moaned. Clients do so quite regularly,' she provided. 'He did not scream. But he grabbed his chest, his face crumpled, and he died silently.'

Sévère scowled.

'You paid for my honesty. Did you forget?' she asked sweetly.

He doubted he would ever forget that. 'Ah. So that's where the peculiar burn in my backside comes from. How very interesting.'

'You asked for it, Sévère.'

'Mr Sévère, if you please. Or Coroner Sévère.'

'You asked for it, Sévère.'

His fist hit the window. 'I did not ask for being flogged senseless!'

'You did not lose your senses during the procedure. Not once. A lot more pain is needed for a man to lose his senses. Or a woman, for that matter. You asked for my honesty and I gave it to you. I still do. One word from you is enough to stop it. Do you want me to lie?'

His jaws tensed. His eyes gleamed with anger.

She shifted in her seat. 'I see. You do want me to lie. You want me to give you the feeling that you are stronger in body and mind and heart than I am. You would feel better if I allowed you to believe that I am a low human being because I sell my body to men like you. I should be ashamed so that you can go on feeling noble.'

Sévère cleared his throat. 'Why did you humiliate me?'

'Because *you* were planning to humiliate *me*. It's what whores are for: to receive humiliation. I merely showed you how it feels, allowing you to reconsider your plans.' Her cheeks and chest felt uncomfortably warm. She exhaled her tension, uncurled her fingers, and stared out the window.

'Tell me about Easy's death,' he said hoarsely.

Without looking at him, she said, 'Alexander Easy grabbed his chest. His face spoke of the pain he was in, but he said nothing. Spittle was dripping from his mouth. He didn't breathe. I put my ear to his chest, but found no heartbeat. He began to twitch, then.'

'Twitch? Did he fight?'

'The body always fights death. Have you never seen a living thing die? A beheaded chicken? A cow whose brains have been bashed in with a sledgehammer? Alexander Easy's body twitched, and I fetched Bobbie and the madam.'

'Who is Bobbie?'

'He takes care of clients who believe they don't need to pay. He hid when you and Inspector Height arrived.' She looked at him now, but found no surprise in his face.

'What happened then?'

'Well.' She leant back and crossed her arms over her chest.

'I warn you, Miss Mary. Stop traipsing around it. Spit it out already!'

'It's delicate.'

'The unlawful disposal of a body usually is.'

She narrowed her eyes at him. 'I retreated to another room, inserted a tube into my vagina and washed

Mr Easy's semen out of me with a caustic solution to prevent pregnancy. If you must know.'

Despite himself, Sévère blushed. 'Go on.'

'When I showed Bobbie and the madam the dead man in my bed, they asked what had happened. I told them the truth. They said I should swiftly take care of my business — meaning I should douche to avoid getting with child. It usually takes me a few moments only, but that night I was...a little beside myself. I spilt most of the liquid and had to mix it anew before rinsing myself with some difficulty. I don't know how long it took, but certainly not more than half an hour. When I returned to my room, Mr Easy was gone, the sheets were gone, and the madam said that Bobbie had taken care of things.'

'And of course you are completely and utterly innocent,' Sévère muttered.

She snorted. 'Little imagination is needed to know that Bobbie disposed of the corpse.'

'And you did nothing about it.'

'It was done. Reporting the incident to the police wouldn't have accomplished anything. The man was dead as a doornail and, most likely, already floating down the Thames.'

'What about his family? Did you not think someone might miss him?' Sévère asked.

'No. Alexander Easy told me he was a widower.'

'He could have had children.'

'He didn't. He said, "My house is empty. My arms are empty." This man was utterly alone. He had no one and no one missed him.'

'You surprise me, Miss Mary.'

She shrugged. It did not interest her.

'You can read and you seem to devour information. Knowledge. That's very unusual for a woman like you.'

'A woman like me?'

'I should have said, "unusual for a prostitute." But no matter your profession, it seems impossible to categorise you.'

'You are utterly and entirely wrong. Any dimwitted onlooker would place me into one of several categories in the blink of an eye: a female, well-dressed, in the company of a gentleman, and hence, untouchable. Let's remove you from the picture for a moment, and the categories begin to shift. She's pretty. Is she married? May I court her? Let's imagine I pull a strand of my hair down and let it rest on my shoulder. And let's imagine I tear a button from my dress. The upper-most one. She's a tad disheveled. Improper. Might she be a whore?'

With her index finger, Mary drew a face onto the fogged-up window. It had long, pinned-up hair, large eyes and a tongue sticking out of a full-lipped mouth. 'You see, Sévère, I am a woman and thus more subject to the stupid opinion of others than any man ever will be. So why should I regard opinions as worthy of my attention?'

'What about the opinions of your clients?'

'That is an entirely different matter. I want them to be satisfied, and not merely to have an opinion of me. I don't want them to say, "It was good," or, "it was boring." I want them to... I want them to sigh deeply and say, "It was... Oh, words fail me. I can't describe it. You have to see for yourself. You have to go to her, my friend."'

'And then you whip them?'

Mary burst out laughing, caught her breath, and demurely folded her hands in her lap. 'No need. More often than not, I tell them I can't see them. That's worse than receiving a good whipping.'

'Why would you say that?'

'I take only one client per night and make few exceptions to this rule. Alexander Easy was one. The quality of my services would suffer from too much a... um...productivity.'

'I can imagine,' Sévère muttered. 'Your right arm must hurt. The other thing that's surprising is the fact that you seem to sharply analyse your options. Almost like a man.'

She huffed. 'Please, Sévère! This discussion is ridiculous. You seem to be reading that idiot Darwin.'

His eyebrows shot up. 'Darwin? You read Darwin? Consider me utterly dumbfounded.'

'I can certainly do you the favour. However, I do know that you are waiting to sink in the knife. It is your style. You try to surprise me, to tip my balance by saying things like "you are more intelligent than I had supposed" or "I'm so utterly surprised by how much you think like a man." You want me to grow unsuspecting, to lower my defences. You will not succeed. So say what you have to say now. Without playing a game.'

The amused smile left his lips. 'You are a liar.' His face was once again a remote mask. He curled his fingers around the head of his cane. 'I will have to visit your establishment soon.'

'Why would you say that?'

'Alexander Easy was fully dressed when he was found floating in the river. If, as you stated, he was taken from your room while you only shortly left it, I wonder who put his clothes on so swiftly. Bobbie couldn't have done it all alone, and certainly not out on the streets or on a bridge before he tossed the corpse into the Thames. The madam could have helped him, perhaps. But again, you pretend not to have seen or heard anything of this. You pretend you had nothing to do with the transport and disposal of the corpse, other than not reporting it. You lie.'

Mary frowned, her gaze unfocused, her thoughts drifting. 'When I returned to my room, the sheets were gone. But that is normal. Rose takes care of those things. She's very good at that. She delivered fresh sheets a few moments later, as usual...' Mary cocked her head. 'Later than usual. But she cannot have...'

'What can she not have?'

'It's impossible. She's only eight. I doubt the madam helped. She doesn't dirty her own hands. Rose can't have dressed the corpse, even if Bobbie had held it for her. The limbs were too heavy.'

'And how would you know this?'

She regarded him sharply. 'Because I'm a whore. Men do occasionally lose consciousness on top of me.'

Sévère nodded once. 'Go on.'

'I don't know how many people are required to dress a corpse so quickly, but they couldn't have dressed him in the parlour. The risk of a client seeing it is too high. That leaves the kitchen and the basement. But I would have heard them going down the stairs. Bobbie's footfalls are heavy, they would have been even heavier had he carried Mr Easy.'

She stared out the window, watching houses and trees

rush by. Suddenly, she clapped her hand to her mouth. 'Could they've hidden him under my bed and taken him away after I left my room in the morning?'

'No. His blood was not coagulated at the time of the autopsy. Dr Johnston concluded that he'd been immersed in cold water around the time of his death.' He narrowed his eyes at her.

'Oh, right.' she said. 'Did the inspector find out if Easy was a bleeder?'

'They thought it unnecessary to find and question Easy's physician, because the death was deemed natural.'

'So the police lost interest in the case? And you have no jurisdiction. How lovely.' She clapped her hands together, looking very satisfied with herself. 'Sévère, if you must, you may visit me once more. But I've told you the truth. You know everything I know about my night with Alexander Easy.'

'If you say so.' He turned to gaze out the window.

She watched him for a long moment, knowing he didn't believe her, then joined his silent appraisal of the landscape.

'Didn't you forget something?' she asked.

'Excuse me?'

'You didn't tell me what you learnt at the police station.'

'You believe I planned to share this information with you but simply…forgot to do it?'

'I had hoped so.'

He waved a hand in dismissal. 'Redhill is a place of peace and harmony. Or so it appears. No rapes have been reported in the past ten years. Two cases of concealment of birth, both of which might or might not have been infanticides. I'll look into these further. No cases of murder or manslaughter, no cases of death by neglect. No one who could be suspected of baby farming. Three cases of adultery, all of which were resolved in a civilised manner.'

'Meaning no man lost his parts?'

'Meaning the accused pleaded guilty.'

'How boring.'

THE TRAIN ROLLED into Victoria Station and screeched to a halt. Mary bent close to Sévère's face, and whispered, 'This was a most enjoyable day. Thank you. But I have a confession to make: You are the first man who's received a thorough lashing from me, and I did not enjoy it as much as I probably should have. Better ask someone else next time you need your backside stroked.'

'I will try to remember your suggestion.'

He stood and grabbed his cane, and they alighted.

She bade him farewell with a mere quirk of her lips, and strolled across the street, mingling with the chaos of pedestrians, hansom cabs, and omnibuses.

———

'ROSE,' Mary called. 'Quick, the water, there isn't much time.' She hurried into her room, kicked off her boots, and shed her coat, dress, and undergarments.

She washed the dirt of the journey off. She was hungry, but supper would have to wait. Naked as she was, she opened the window, drew the curtains, and placed her hands on the reveal.

The door opened. The rustle of a coat. The clink of a belt. Thick fingers curled around her neck.

'Two weeks,' he growled and rubbed his groin against her bare arse. 'Two weeks you eluded me. For what? For another? Don't speak. I don't want to hear your excuses. What you need is a strong hand.'

He grabbed her neck harder, drove his cock home, and slammed her head against the wall.

# SLEEPING DRAUGHT

*M*ary followed the scents of scorched onions and cooked meat. Down the stairs and into the kitchen. Her stomach was grumbling. The ladies were already assembled around the table, someone had placed a beeswax candle and a few pinecones onto its kinked surface. Claire distributed punch into six mugs, Rosalinda picked lice from Abby's scalp, and Lily shoved blood pudding into her mouth.

Old Ava hoisted the pot with steaming potatoes onto the table. 'Merry Christmas, lassies! Eat up.'

'Is that gravy in there or—' Mary received a slap on her head as she approached the small pot, reaching with her spoon.

'Be quiet and say your grace,' Old Ava said.

'My *what?*'

'Thank you! Amen!' screeched Rosalinda. She wiped her hands on her dress, and tucked in.

'Use vinegar. Kills the buggers right off.' Ava pointed

the ladle at Abby, who scratched her head in response. Her red curls looked like a prickly shrub on fire.

Claire impaled a small potato with her fork, held it up, nodded importantly, and said, 'Did I ever tell you about this particular fella?'

A collective groan echoed through the kitchen.

'So he knocks on my door and I says, "Come on in," and so in he comes. He's awfully drenched with rain. And he has a cute little waistcoat on, checkered, with a gold chain dangling from the pocket. His right eye is pinched around a golden monocle that's all fogged up. He's half blind, mind, but doesn't take the thing off. And then he says, "Madam!" he says, and bows as if I was the queen or something. So he says, "Madam, I must warn you." And he fumbles on his trousers — doesn't even take off his coat or anything, but goes straight to his trousers — and then he...'

Claire scrambled up onto her chair, stepped onto the table, careful not to set her skirts on fire with the candle, and hollered, '"Madam, I must warn you. My tool may not fit."'

She yanked her skirts up to her ears and all she wore underneath were stockings and garters, and everyone could stare straight into her Garden of Eden.

'Was it remarkable?' Rosalind asked, only half-interested.

'Och, no.' Claire kept her skirts up, looked down at her audience, and moved her hips from side to side. 'He wiggled it a bit and then it grew.'

'Did you wash that before you put it on the table?' Mary enquired, pointing her spoon at Claire's pubes.

Abby snorted. Bits of blood pudding landed on the table.

Claire dropped her skirts and jumped back onto her chair. 'It was the size of this wee thing.' She held up the potato she had skewered with her fork. 'But he was convinced he would hurt me if he put it inside me.' She stuck the tuber into her mouth, bit down, and swallowed it in one gulp.

'Did you do him the favour of screaming a bit?' Abby asked.

'You think I'm a cold-hearted monster? *Begged* him to spare me...*oh, the torture...!* He promised to return, the little rantallion. I thought him quite sweet. Is there more of that blood pudding, Old Ava?'

'Where's Rose?' Mary asked.

'I saw her with a bucket earlier. She's probably scouring floorboards somewhere,' Claire provided, as Old Ava noisily slopped another serving of blood pudding onto Claire's plate.

'But she must be hungry.'

'She knows when it's lunch time,' Old Ava said.

MARY CLIMBED down the stairs to the basement, pushed at the heavy door, and entered to a loud creak. The room was as dark as a coal mine, and she regretted she hadn't brought a candle. 'Rose?' she called.

No answer.

She listened in the dark and heard a small shuffling noise just beneath the short set of steps. She peeked through and saw a dim light. 'What are you doing?'

Still no answer. Mary grabbed the banister and carefully probed for the steps with her feet. She made it down without falling, but knocked her head on a ceiling beam as she turned.

'Ouch!'

'Mary?'

'Rose? What are you doing here?'

'Celebrating Christmas. Want to join?'

'Oh! Yes. Thank you.'

Mary approached the small light, careful not to stumble over the clutter that had accumulated over the years.

Rose's outline was barely visible. The closer she got and the more her eyes adapted to the darkness, the more she saw of the girl: the tip of her nose, her chin, wisps of hair sticking out of a shawl she'd tied around her head and shoulders to keep out the chill. Her hands held a thin stick with which she pushed something about in a tub. The girl smiled, mesmerised.

'I made two. Want one?' Rose asked.

'One what?'

'A boat.'

Rose handed Mary a small wooden object. 'Hold it still,' she said, struck a match and brought it to Mary's hand. It was the shell of a walnut, a tiny candle stuck into it. Rose lit the wick. 'Put it in the water.'

Mary did as she was told, wondering what could be so special about a walnut and an old, battered zinc tub. When her ship touched the water, she understood. 'Oh!' was all she could utter.

'You are the captain of your ship.' She handed Mary a

thin stick. 'And I am the captain of mine. We are explorers.'

With their sticks, they began pushing their ships across the dangerous, wide waters. The small bubbles of light illuminated a magic underwater world, a new universe wherever they went: shiny black pebbles here, the house of a snail — yellow with black stripes — there. A handful of light-blue glass shards became a school of impossibly quick fish, the jagged neck of a green bottle became a treacherous sea monster. They explored the deep sea, fought through mighty waves, and wove about forgotten mangrove forests, all the while Rose softly sang a song she'd made up, a song of rough pirates, brave girls, and wild adventures.

---

ASIDE FROM THE pockmarks the mining company had gnawed into Bedfordshire and the piles of Fuller's Earth vomited out in the process, Woburn Sands could be described as an exemplar of picturesque. With its pretty homes and front yards that must all have won a gardening competition at one point or another, the hamlet sent chills down Sévère's spine. He wanted to get back to Whitechapel as quickly as possible, where the ugliness of mankind was apparent and not hiding behind lace curtains and perfectly-trimmed rose bushes (never mind the temporary nakedness of the latter).

He passed a bakery, a pub, a cobbler, a second-hand shop, and a school before he finally found the town council house. All of these were respectable red-brick buildings with elaborately carved, white-washed timber frameworks — masterpieces of traditional carpentry and masonry. Sévère rubbed the back of his tingling neck, and banged the knob of his cane on the door in front of him. It was opened by a thickset man in his fifties.

'Gavriel Sévère, Coroner of Eastern Middlesex. I need to speak with the inspector of the Woburn Sands police office.'

'That'll be me.' The man held out his hand. 'Peter Fenwick's the name. Come on in. You look like you need a hot tea. And biscuits, perhaps?'

'Tea,' Sévère managed to reply.

They entered a small room on the ground floor, which contained one chair, one largely-empty desk, three shelves with yellow-backed novels, and an armchair with a lace antimacassar. An abundance of immaculate doilies covered the polished furniture, and two shiny, lace-curtained windows were adorned with a flowerpot in each sill.

'Have a seat, please. I'll get the tea.'

Sévère pulled off his gloves and sat in the armchair, wondering if even Fenwick's undergarments were made of lace. He shook himself and blinked the image away.

When the inspector returned, Sévère said, 'I see you are alone.'

'I'm married, and father to five wonderful children.'

'I was referring to the police station.'

'Oh. Of course you were. Well, there isn't much policing to be done here. But my people keep me busy. You see, I'm also the mayor.'

Fenwick stirred sugar and milk into his tea, sipped

noisily and, with a soft *clink*, set the cup onto the saucer. 'How may I help you, Coroner?'

'I was hoping you could provide me with information regarding a case I'm working on at present.'

'I'll do my best to help. What is the nature of the case? I haven't heard of any unlawful killings in Bedfordshire.'

'I'm investigating multiple counts of infanticides. I have reason to believe the perpetrator lives here.'

Fenwick turned a pasty white. His hand gripped the saucer hard. The cup rattled. Droplets of tea spilt onto his trousers, unnoticed.

'It would help greatly if I were granted insight into all case notes of infanticide, baby farming, rape, murder, manslaughter, adultery, concealed birth, and death by neglect in the past ten years.'

'No such...' Fenwick cleared his throat with difficulty. 'There have been no such cases for ten, fifteen, probably twenty years. Not here or anywhere in Bedfordshire. Except...' Frowning, he picked up his cup and took a sip. 'A young shepherd was molested by a tramp who was never found. The boy was badly injured.'

'What kind of injuries?'

Fenwick coughed. 'Castration. The surgeon couldn't do much for him. But he found that the young man had been raped. Probably multiple times before his...his testicles were cut off. Happened in summer 1867. You must have read about it in the papers.'

'Yes, I did. Wasn't he found bound, unconscious, and with his testes stuffed into his mouth? An astonishing case.'

'Astonishing? I wouldn't call it—'

'And that's the only violent crime you know about?'

'That's one too many already, if you ask me.'

'Are there any women offering foster care for infants in your district?'

'Yes. Betsy Fouler. She's a good woman.'

'I need her address.'

'Coroner, I greatly doubt—'

'Until this case is solved, I have jurisdiction over the whole of Bedfordshire. Presently, I need to talk with Mrs Fouler.'

'I'll accompany you.'

'I would much prefer if you could go through all your files and find—'

'There's no need for this.' The inspector interrupted harshly. 'Woburn Sands has three hundred and twenty-two inhabitants. I know every soul here. I know who was born, when and where, and who died, when and under what circumstances, for the past ten years, and I don't need to consult my files to know this. In all my time as a policeman, precisely one crime has been reported, common brawls not included.' He poked his index finger into the air. 'A burglary which turned out to be a drunken neighbour trying the wrong door. I will accompany you to Mrs Fouler, Coroner Sévère.'

With that, Fenwick stood, screwed his top hat onto his skull, buttoned his coat, and yanked open the front door.

They walked down the main road, a gentle slope that allowed a view across woodlands. Upon Sévère's enquiry as to the Fuller's Earth deposits, Fenwick happily provided all relevant information, and much more:

'At the southern end are most of the mining pits. The

company has to dig twenty, twenty-five yards deep. There's even a thin layer of sandstone they have to break through. We export to—'

'Is there a shallow layer of Fuller's Earth? A cledge?'

'There is. Just beneath the sandstone. That would be...' He looked up at the sky, thinking. 'At twelve to eighteen yards depth. The major turning point for us was the Bedford-Bletchley Railway in 1846. The Duke of Bedford supported its development. Since then we've been exporting bricks and Fuller's Earth around the whole of Britain.'

'Hm,' said Sévère.

'Over there at Hogsty End and Aspley Hill...'

Sévère didn't listen. He scanned the houses and theorised as to what could possibly lay hidden behind the pretty facades.

'...developed into a holiday destination for the Londoners. Ah, what am I saying. A health resort! We have a hotel, guest houses, refreshment rooms, souvenir shops—'

'And despite all these strangers, one burglary, committed by a sot who couldn't find his own home, is that all that has ever happened to the good people of Woburn Sands.' Sévère's voice was brittle with sarcasm.

'Um...exactly. Ah. Here we are.' Fenwick opened a small gate and stepped into the front yard. The evergreen bushes were shaved into perfect egg shapes, the brick walkway was polished and void of weeds and mosses of all kinds, and the flowerbeds seemed to have been drawn with a ruler.

Fenwick knocked. The door was opened by a scrawny

woman in her sixties. She wore a stiff, black dress and a spotless apron. She appeared altogether freshly laundered, starched, and pressed.

'Oh hello, Peter. How are you doing? I see you've brought a visitor. How lovely!'

'Gavriel Sévère, Coroner of Eastern Middlesex.' Sévère tipped his hat. 'I'm investigating a multiple infanticide.'

'Oh dear,' she sighed and grabbed the door frame for support. 'Am I being arrested?'

'Should you be?' Sévère asked.

'Betsy, would you mind offering us a cup of tea?'

'Oh, where are my manners?' She bustled back into the house, forgetting to invite them in. Fenwick beckoned Sévère into the hall, and shut the door.

The hallway was rather small. Nonetheless, Mrs Fouler had managed to cram in a lot of furniture. Of the wallpaper, not one patch showed below waist height. Above that, much of it was covered by paintings — mostly romantic landscapes.

It took Sévère a moment or two to realise what was missing from the scene: noise. He dropped his hat onto a hat-stand and his coat onto a hook, and followed Fenwick through a corridor and into the drawing room.

'How many charges do you have at present, Mrs Fouler?' he asked when she had served the tea.

'Eight lovely little angels.'

He peeled back his lips. 'Where are they now?'

'It is nap time. They are sleeping upstairs.'

'Would you tell me more about the services you offer? May I see your registration papers?'

Her head swivelled toward Fenwick. 'Peter, tell me the truth. Am I a suspect?'

Fenwick leant forward and patted her freckled hand. 'No, you are not. I can assure you. Am I correct, Mr Sévère?'

'Quite so, Inspector.'

Reassured for the moment, Mrs Fouler left and returned with her papers a few minutes later. Sévère inspected them and found them to be genuine. 'Thank you, Mrs Fouler. How long have you been offering boarding for children and infants? I expect you keep infants, too?'

'Oh, exclusively. I am getting a bit too old to manage little rascals of eight, nine, or ten years of age. The wee ones are much easier.'

Sévère nodded. To him, all children were annoyingly difficult creatures.

'After my husband died, may the Lord rest his soul, I opened my home to illegitimate children. You see, the mothers don't know what to do with them. These young women have disgraced themselves. And their parents. Naturally, they give away their children soon after birth, and then they move to another town where no one knows them or their immoral history. They try to find work there, or even a husband.'

'Do they ever come back for their children?'

'Not before a child can earn its keep.'

'At what age?'

'Three years.'

'Do all your children go back to their mothers?'

'Well...no.' She crumpled her apron between her

hands. 'Often, the mother never returns. Sometimes a child dies.'

'How often?'

'Only two mothers have taken back their children.'

'How are you paid?'

'I'm paid twenty pounds for the first three years.'

'How can an unwed mother afford to pay twenty pounds, and how is this amount enough to feed and clothe a child?'

'It is enough. Just enough. It's usually paid by the bastard's father.'

'To keep the mother quiet,' Sévère mused. 'How many children have died in your care?'

She croaked something Sévère didn't understand. He asked her to speak more clearly.

'Six.'

'Out of how many?'

'Twenty-four.'

One in four. Sévère rose. 'Mrs Fouler, I wish to see your charges. Inspector Fenwick, the local practitioner will have files on the deaths of these children. I want you to fetch him for me. Including his files.'

'Coroner, I can assure you that—'

'You can assure me by delivering the practitioner and his files within the next quarter hour. Now, Mrs Fouler, if you please?'

They climbed the stairs to the first floor, and entered a dimly lit room. Sévère counted eight cots. A thin sheet of light fell through the curtains. The air was stuffy.

'Their boxes are made of wood, not ch...cheap cardboard,' she explained with a wobbly voice.

He walked up to the window, pulled aside the curtains, and bent over the box closest to him. A child of probably six months of age lay in it, eyes shut, mouth open, pale countenance. He put his ear close to the infant's face and was relieved to hear a quiet snore. He repeated this with the other seven boxes. All the children were alive and seemed comparatively well. Their faces showed no indications of malnourishment or abuse. The bite of ammonia and faeces in the air was normal, as far as he could tell.

'They've received a sleeping drought?' he asked.

'I allow them a spoonful of laudanum each. They are more restful.'

He walked back to the window and gazed out into the backyard. He thought of Miss Mary. 'May I use your privy?'

Certain that Mrs Fouler was watching from her window, Sévère strolled past the privy and took his time to investigate the garden. The lawn was trimmed and soggy, no obvious signs of digging activities within the past growing season. The flowerbeds, though, had potential. He'd have to return with a shovel.

The practitioner of Woburn Sands rumbled into the backyard as Sévère stepped out of the privy and shut the door.

'Dr Robert Potton,' he provided, and shot out his hand. Sévère shook it and introduced himself.

They went back into the house and settled down in the

drawing room. Potton extracted his files from his brief-case and handed them to Sévère.

'Two cases of gastroenteritis, one in 1878 and the other in 1879. A measles outbreak in 1876 that resulted in the deaths of three children in Woburn Sands, two of which were Mrs Fouler's charges.'

'What about the remaining two? She said six had died. Can you corroborate this number?'

'I could not determine the cause of death of the other two children with certainty.' He leafed through the papers and said, 'Both died in winter 1878. Twins, it appears.'

'I remember them well,' Mrs Fowler said hoarsely. 'They'd been only a few days old. The mother brought them in. They were very quiet and small. Looked sickly, both of them. I kept thinking that I shouldn't have taken them in. And sure enough, they didn't eat as much as they should. Only one week later, they died.'

'What did you feed them?'

Mrs Fouler tried to hold her head high; her eyes began to water and her chin wobbled. 'Naturally, all I could give them was white bread soaked in honey water. This is the normal practice for December and January. Goats give milk from February through November. Cow's milk is not good for children of that age.'

'Is that so, Dr Potton?'

'Betsy…I mean Mrs Fouler has done nothing wrong. She is licensed, she feeds her charges according to what is recommended, and she treats them well. I don't know what unlawful thing you could possibly find under this roof.'

At that, Mrs Fouler burst out sobbing.

'Now, now,' said Fenwick, patting her back.

She jerked away from him and stood. 'I have to attend to the children now. If my presence is not needed any longer, I would be most obliged if you would allow me to go upstairs.'

'You may go. Thank you for your hospitality, Mrs Fouler,' Sévère answered. 'Although I have one last question, if I may. You mentioned you take only infants until the age of three. What happens to your charges once they reach that age and their mothers don't want them?'

She scrubbed tears from her cheeks. 'I send them to Northampton Orphanage for Illegitimate Children.'

They watched her leave. Sévère turned his attention back to Dr Potton. 'Do you see each new child as it arrives, and do you examine her children regularly?'

Potton made big, round eyes. 'What for?'

Sévère frowned. He was grasping at straws. 'Let me ask this differently: When a mother gives her child into Mrs Fouler's care, would you always know it? Do you know which child arrived at what time?'

'Sooner or later I'll know.'

'How so?'

'We are a small community. People know each other. This isn't London, where one can do anything and no one knows about it.' Potton's ears gradually acquired a healthy shade of purple.

'Which means that no one would notice the death of a new charge.'

'Are you insinuating—' Fenwick jumped from his chair.

Sévère cut him off. 'Where were the children buried?'

Fenwick jerked his chin toward the window.

'The backyard?'

'Where else? Are you suggesting that bastards be buried in sacred soil?'

Sévère leant back, and regarded the inspector. 'I've never thought about it.'

Fenwick shrugged.

'Inspector Fenwick, Mrs Fouler's premises are now evidence in an infanticide case.' He rose, and grabbed his cane. 'I will return with my assistant to conduct an exhumation. The evidence is not to be disturbed and Mrs Fouler is not to leave Woburn Sands until a surgeon examines the bodies. Furthermore, she is to be present during the exhumation.'

'Are you jesting?' Fenwick croaked.

'It is not in my nature to be funny. I must leave now. I thank you for your help. Inspector Fenwick, Dr Potton.' Courteously, he lowered his head, and left.

---

STRIPLING FELT miserable in his waterproof. Rivulets of icy rain ran down the mucky garment and into his boots. He kept wiggling his toes to warm them up a bit, but it didn't seem to be working all that well. His upper body was warm enough, though. His arms ached. He'd dug five holes already. Not deep. Perhaps ten, twenty inches until his shovel would strike something that didn't feel like soil. More like soft, rotten wood.

While Stripling had been digging holes into the mucky and half-frozen soil, the coroner had been occupied sketching a map of the premises in his notebook, marking where Mrs Fouler had indicated the location of the graves, and labelling them with numbers. A corresponding number was later clipped to the rag that was wrapped around each corpse, before the bodies were placed into a crate.

Stripling resented this distribution of tasks. He was doing the crude, stupid work: dig until you feel there's something. Then Sévère, armed with his small shovel and a spoon, would scrape the body free, as carefully as though he were planning to resurrect the dead. Stripling thought of his armchair, a blazing fireplace, a good cigar, and satisfying paperwork.

'Did you find another?' Sévère called.

'Not yet,' Stripling grumbled, and continued digging.

---

WHEN SIX BODIES were safely tucked into the crate, Sévère walked along the line of graves. He gazed back at the house, where he could see Mrs Fouler standing behind a window, a swaddled child in her arms. She was bouncing it as if her life depended on it.

'Stripling, I want you to look at this.'

His officer walked up to him and Sévère pointed at the graves. 'What do you see?'

'A lot of work for one day.'

'And what else?'

Stripling shrugged.

'Dammit, Stripling. The pattern!' Sévère caught

himself just in time before wiping his face with his dirty hands.

'There's a gap between the fifth and the sixth hole,' Stripling supplied.

'Precisely. Dig there.'

'But—'

'As well as on either side of this row. I want to know if she buried more than these six. Also, check the flower beds at random places.'

As Stripling slammed his shovel into the ground between graves five and six, Sévère looked up at the house. Mrs Fouler was gone.

'Inspector Fenwick!' he called. 'Would you please see to Mrs Fouler?'

Fenwick, who'd waited at the back door, somewhat protected from the wind and rain, gratefully retreated into the house.

Sévère watched Stripling work, and when the shovel at last struck something, he bade his officer step aside. Sévère bent down and began to move the soil with care. A root. And another.

'Would you dig here and here, please?' he asked, and indicated the new sides of the hole. In went the shovel and the hole grew larger.

'I guess that explains it,' Sévère muttered after several long moments, and rose to his feet. He brushed the dirt off his hands, and rubbed his cold fingers.

'Explains what?' Stripling asked, tapping his shovel against an unearthed stump.

Sévère shrugged. 'A bush that didn't fit the scenery.' He

indicated the symmetrical lines running through Mrs Fouler's garden. Whoever had planted this bush or small tree had violated Mrs Fouler's desire for orderly aesthetic.

———

THE FOLLOWING DAY, an exhausted Dr Johnston arrived at the morgue. 'You are digging up too many bodies for my taste,' he told Sévère. 'And you must be the new mortician.' He nodded at a young, bespectacled man in a black frock coat, whose greased black hair was neatly parted along the middle of his skull.

The man nodded, stepped forward, and shook the offered hand. 'Alf Griggs is the name.'

'You wouldn't mind if I used your tools, would you?' Johnston asked. 'I left my bag in the hospital, and noticed it only when it was already too late.'

'It would be an honour,' said Mr Griggs. He hoisted up a large black leather bag with a white skull and the word "Mortician" in white capital lettering on its front, plopped it onto the table and took a respectful step back.

'Well, then. Tell me what you know about them,' Johnston said to Sévère, and began to carefully unwrap the corpses.

'Those were found in the backyard of a Mrs Betsy Fouler of Woburn Sands, Bedfordshire. She's been taking in illegitimate infants since spring 1876. These six children were examined by the local practitioner after they died. In four cases he was able to determine the cause of death. This one died of gastroenteritis in 1878 at the age of six months, this in 1879 at five months of age, also of gastroenteritis. These two were aged one and a half and two years, and died during a measles outbreak in 1876. The two smallest bodies are twins who died in 1878 at the age of two weeks. Cause of death is thought to have been malnutrition. Mrs Fouler's statement can be summed up as…' Sévère extracted his notepad. 'When the mother brought them to her, the children were very quiet and small. They appeared sickly and ate very little of a mixture of honey water and white bread. They died one week later.'

At that, Johnston looked up from his work, puzzled. 'Why did you call me?'

'Mrs Fouler stated that six out of twenty-four children in her care have died. A quarter. I found that to be a high number.'

'But from what you've told me, it appears that none of these deaths are suspicious. Or did I miss something?'

'No, you didn't. I had rather hoped you could tell me if there are any similarities between the two groups of dead children. I need to know whether or not it is likely that the person who buried these children also killed the other nine.'

'Ah, I see. Well, I can tell you that this one didn't die of a cut throat.' Johnston indicated a small, blackened body with bits of flesh and skin still clinging to its bones. 'That's the gastroenteritis of 1879. Do you see this?' He pulled at the decomposed tissues until the windpipe and oesophagus became visible. 'Intact,' he said. 'Until decomposition set in, that is.'

'Hm,' Sévère answered.

'I'll examine them, but I need an assistant. Would you

mind much?' Johnston pointed his dirty finger at Sévère's pen and notepad.

'It would be an honour.'

---

'VERY FOUL SMELL, I must say. Very foul indeed,' grunted Pouch when he poked a pencil at the corpse and the dirt attached to it. 'Material essentially comprising sand, gravel, clumps of clay and...' he bent closer and picked up a crumb of soil, rubbed it between his fingertips, but refrained from sticking it into his mouth. 'Peat.'

'You might want to compare that to the soil on the other skeletons,' Sévère said, pointing to a table in a far corner.

'No need. This here...' He pointed at the corpses in front of him, '...is very different. The soil over there comprises of types of loam and clay, while this is sand with a small amount of clay. That over there has a low permeability, and this here, a fairly high permeability. One cannot confuse these two.'

'Hm.' Sévère scratched his chin. 'How likely is it, in your opinion, that the bodies discovered in the pots and the ones here were buried in the same area?'

'What size area?'

'The size of a small village.'

'There is no possibility whatsoever.'

'Dammit,' Sévère growled.

'Oh, I meant to tell you. These babies,' Pouch walked up to the nine skeletons and pulled the cloth aside. 'I kept thinking about them. And so I visited a friend of mine who's working for the Mining Record Office. He allowed me to inspect his samples of Fuller's Earth. I must apologise for my previous lack of attention, but all Fuller's Earth deposits in Britain differ slightly, meaning one can identify where a sample originates. I should have said as much when I examined these.'

'I didn't know there were different types of Fuller's Earth.'

'There are four in Britain alone.' Pouch wiped his hands on a hanky, picked up a skull and examined it closely, and then another. 'Ah, wonderful. My memory and judgement have not failed me. This is Fuller's Earth from Redhill. No doubt.'

## STRENGTHS & WEAKNESSES

*G*avriel Sévère hurried along Leman Street. He was late for his appointment with the magistrate. He carried a list of issues he would insist on resolving. He would not step back. If the magistrate continued refusing to pay his fees, he would personally visit Home Office for every single invoice that was rejected until this problem was solved once and for all. In the past three months, his travel costs, fees for more than thirty postmortem examinations, and fees for jury and witnesses had been disallowed on no specific grounds. The situation had become highly unacceptable.

As he neared the top of the stairs to Division H Headquarters, the large front door burst open and nearly hit him in the face. Two policemen came flying through and knocked him over.

It was as if time stopped. Sévère felt a whoosh of air before the man collided with him. He felt his cane slipping over the thin layer of ice that had formed during the previous night. His left leg gave way. He heard a popping noise issuing from his knee and felt a pain unlike any he'd ever experienced. He almost cried out in agony as the side of his ribcage hit the stone steps. All he could do was hunch his shoulders and tuck in his head to prevent his skull from being cracked open like a raw egg.

'Blazes!' one of the men cried, and Sévère wanted to kick his balls like he'd never wanted anything in his whole life.

'Coroner! Are you hurt?'

Sévère pushed himself up. The cold bit through his gloves and trousers. He swallowed bile. Hands grabbed him under his shoulders, attempting to hoist him upright.

'Stop it, you blithering idiots!'

'Just trying to be helpful, Coroner. The steps are frozen over, and it's easy to slip.'

'Constables,' Sévère growled. 'One more word, and I'll lose my temper. You two brutes broke my leg.'

'Blimey, ' one man muttered.

The other didn't move. His knees trembled. 'Chief will kick me out. He will.'

'Goddammit! I will personally decapitate both of you if you don't summon a cab within the next two seconds.'

One constable was still frozen to the spot, staring at Sévère, the other constable took the remaining steps in three slithering hops, thrust his arm into the air and hollered, 'Cabbie! Cabbie!'

It did take longer than two seconds for an available hansom to arrive at Headquarters, and an eternity for Sévère — aided by the two policemen — to climb into the carriage and sit down. His left limb was painfully crammed into the limited legroom. 'Guy's Hospital,' he called to the driver.

He didn't know how to hold his leg so that it wouldn't scream with pain at every turn and every pothole. He clenched his teeth until his ears rang as they rode over cobblestones and wove in and out of the busy traffic. When they finally arrived, he was trembling and bathed in sweat.

'Would you please call for help? I believe I can't walk.' He said it loud and clear to pretend the feeling of helplessness was in no way humiliating.

Two men with a stretcher between them arrived and helped him onto it with surprising gentleness. 'If Dr Johnston is not too busy, perhaps you could bring me to him.'

'Leg doesn't look like it needs to be taken off,' one of the men muttered.

'Right now, I wouldn't mind too much,' Sévère answered, wiping his damp brow.

And so they marched off toward Johnston's ward. He'd have to wait, they told him when they placed him on a cot. He squeezed his eyes shut and tried to think of nothing, tried not to count the minutes.


JOHNSTON TOUCHED SÉVÈRE'S SHOULDER. 'Are you paying me a courtesy visit?'

'You smell of blood.'

'I usually do. How can I help you?'

'I believe my knee is fractured. The left.'

Johnston ran his fingertips softly down both sides of Sévère's left leg. 'What happened?'

'I fell down the stairs.'

'Why?'

A chuckle forced itself out. 'Well, mainly because of two factors. One: ice-coated stone steps to Division H Headquarters. Two: A police officer who is as blind as a mole and as large as an ox. At the moment, an appropriate comparison for his clumsiness isn't forthcoming.'

'At least you haven't lost your humour. Nurse!' Johnston waved at a woman clad in crisply-starched linen. They moved Sévère into the ward, and pulled off his trousers.

'Hum. Bruising and swelling of the knee joint. Did you hear a pop or a crunch?'

Sévère shuddered at the memory. 'There was a popping noise.'

'Hum. I'll examine your leg now to see if and where it is fractured. It might hurt a little. Let me know if you require morphia.'

Sévère nodded once and watched Johnston's hands probe and squeeze. He grew more tense the closer Johnston got to the injury.

'Does this hurt? Tell me where and when precisely it hurts.'

Sévère could only grunt.

'I doubt it's broken. It would hurt significantly more.' Seeing Sévère's raised eyebrows, Johnston added, 'You would have climbed up that wall had I shifted fractured bones, lad.'

'What's wrong with the knee, then?'

'Well, I believe you have an injury to the knee due to a hyperextension of the joint. We can only hope that ligaments and cartilage weren't torn. I'm not sure how this could have happened from a fall as you've described it. But you were limping before, and I can feel that your left leg is very slightly atrophied. Why is that?'

'I don't know. You're the surgeon.'

'You never took that to a physician?' Johnston pointed at Sévère's leg.

'No.'

Johnston frowned and pushed his spectacles higher up his nose. 'Might it be that you have a good idea what's causing the weakness of your leg?'

'A suspicion, but not a very good one.'

'Tell me, then.'

Sévère let out a sigh, and looked up at the ceiling. 'When I was ten I fell ill. My left leg was paralysed completely, the right leg from the knee downwards. Sometimes, for perhaps a year and a half now, there's a prickling beneath my skin, running up and down the left side. It reminds me of the pain I felt when I was paralysed. But it can't be coming back. I've never heard of such a thing.'

'Ah.' Johnston took off his spectacles, and methodically polished them on his lapel. 'I've heard it from several colleagues and seen it twice now. A surgeon up in Edinburgh is conducting a study on it. He's asked all major hospitals in Britain to send him data on infant paralysis: number of cases, name, age, gender, which limbs where affected, mortality. It appears as though one-third of the individuals who survive the disease will experience very similar symptoms some thirty or forty years later. It's as if the disease has a memory of where it first struck. When did you begin to limp again, Sévère?'

'About a year ago.'

'Did it come on gradually?

'Yes. First the prickling only, and later it seemed my knee was less…stable.'

'Hum… Let me look at your hip and your spine.'

Johnston took his time examining Sévère. He commented on the bruised ribs, asked a few questions as to his history of diseases and injuries, his eating habits, how much he sat and how much he walked, if he did any exercises. But mostly, Johnston was silently examining his patient's muscles and bones.

When he was satisfied, he straightened, pulled a blanket back up and said, 'It appears you are suffering from recurring infant paralysis. In fact, this is the only forthcoming explanation for your symptoms. Your muscles are losing their ability to stabilise the knee joint. The ankle and hip will probably be affected next, but I can't tell when. Another injury such as the one you've incurred today will become more and more likely without a proper walking aid. I'll get you a fitted brace so your knee can heal. You'll have to wear it for two to four weeks, together with a crutch.'

Sévère felt his eyes burn and his throat ache. He squinted at a tree outside the window, and fought for self-control.

'I meant to ask you something,' Johnston continued. 'I was rather hoping you might wish to consult me on all your future cases. I appreciate a man with a clear mind and sharp eyes. I've heard your predecessor was rather… dull. He and Baxter must have been a good fit.'

Despite the throbbing in his knee, Sévère couldn't help but grin. 'Johnston, you called me "lad" and I failed to object, now you want to exploit my weakness even further and sneak yourself into all my cases?'

'Precisely.'

'To be honest, I desperately need a surgeon with your skills.'

Johnston smiled broadly. His eyes twinkled. 'I knew that, lad. We are rare specimens, aren't we? Tell me, why are you interested in medicine?'

'Because I firmly believe that a coroner should be an expert in both, medicine and law. Unfortunately, neither is required to be called into office.'

'Is it not?'

'The only requirement is that the man must own property.'

'That is all?'

'That is all.'

'Hum. Why am I not surprised?' Johnston scratched the nape of his neck, and grew sober. 'One of our staff manufactures the most comfortable crutches. He'll need about a week after he takes your measurements. You'll certainly be needing a customised crutch in the future, even after your knee has healed. I would recommend using it at home even when you think you don't need it. It prevents you from tiring your leg too much. You might think you are doing fine with your cane, but the more you exhaust that leg, the faster the paralysis progresses. I don't like to say this, but… Sévère, in the best case, you'll need a crutch permanently in ten, fifteen years. In the worst case, you'll be sitting in a chair by next winter. I can't tell you what will happen, or when. No one can. But do me a favour and rest your leg when it tires you. You will make matters worse if you put too much strain on it. There will be pain in your joints most likely. Do you smoke opium?'

Sévère shook his head.

'You'll probably do so, soon. Let me know when your leg starts growing weaker. Invite me for a drop of tea in a week or two, and I will bring that fine crutch along. Use it only at home for now if you don't want to be seen with it. Exercise your torso well, because your body and your heart need to stay healthy, but avoid running at all costs. Avoid climbing stairs wherever possible. I'm sorry, lad. I wish I could be of more help.'

SÉVÈRE STARED down at his newly fitted brace. Four days after the injury and the pain in his knee had lost its knife-like quality. Now, a throbbing stretched from shin to thigh. He stared until he felt an itch in his eyes. This was the third time in his life he felt utterly devastated. He'd spent years conquering the deficiencies left by the disease. He learnt to walk twice, and now had to watch this ability gradually leave him again.

He wondered if he should bury himself in drink.

'You would walk even more awkwardly, lad,' he muttered to himself. Then he unbuttoned his waistcoat and his shirt, shed both garments, grabbed his temporary crutch, and hobbled to the doorway that separated his bedroom from his library. He balanced on his right leg, dropped the crutch and reached up, curled his fingers around a newly-installed metal bar and pulled himself up.

He didn't count the number of pull-ups. He pushed beyond the pain to free his fury. Growling, he worked until sweat rolled down his face and chest, then he dropped to the floor, and punched the doorframe.

He watched the beads of blood crawl in between his fingers. A knock disturbed him.

'Mr Sévère, sir? I heard a noise. Are you quite all right?'

'Yes, thank you, Netty. Would you please bring me water to wash?'

'Of course, sir.'

He listened to the tapping of her feet on the rug, fading down the stairs toward the scullery.

A drop of sweat hit his palm. He blinked down at it; the reflection of the oil lamp painted it golden.

A vibration crept through his body, and Sévère found himself wishing to see Mary lift her face to the falling snow once more, looking as if she were in love with everything.

'I'll be damned,' he growled.

---

SAMUEL STRIPLING LEFT Covent Garden with empty hands. Or an empty notepad, so to speak.

He hailed a hansom and climbed aboard. 'London is a madhouse,' he muttered to himself as the driver tried to manoeuvre his horse through the dense and chaotic traffic. Twenty minutes later, he arrived at the Cannon Street offices.

'Stripling,' Sévère called out. 'The Posgate case will be heard on February 28. That's in a little more than a month.'

Stripling entered the office, and sat down on an armchair opposite his employer. 'We don't have anything more to add to that case. The man was about the centre of the road—'

'I know my cases, Stripling. Thank you. I meant to ask you if you had spoken with the magistrate of Division H. He was to have paid our fees by January 2, and he still hasn't done so. A large part of the last quarter's budget was spent on this case. Posgate is to be tried for felonious killing. I fear that the magistrate might believe the verdict of an accidental death, which was returned by our jury a few weeks ago, justifies his disallowing of our fees. Yet again! I want this to be handled before Posgate's acquittal. So. Did you speak to the magistrate?'

'Yes, I did.' Stripling picked at his fingernails.

'And what did he say?' Sévère, trying to keep the edge from his voice, sounded unnaturally soft.

'He said that Home Office is delaying payment of Division H allowances and that he must wait for this money to arrive, else he would be paying you from his own pocket.'

'For Christ's sake!' Sévère's fist hit the desk. The fountain pen jumped from its holder. 'I don't give a damn about Division H's budget problems, or where the magistrate privately spends his money! How in all that is holy am I to do my work?'

Stripling grumbled agreement.

That noise irritated Sévère even more. 'And what was your reply?'

'Um…I bade him a good day.'

'As expected.' Sévère took a deep breath, poured himself a coffee without offering a cup to Stripling. 'How was Covent Garden?'

'I… Mr Sévère, there is no man who fits the description. No one sold seven apple trees to Mr Bunting. I believe we are wasting our time on this case.'

Sévère swallowed all further comments on the matter. All he said was, 'Write your report. I want it in an hour.'

'An hour?'

Sévère leant back and regarded the man sharply. 'Are you aware that the only reason you are still employed is that you excel at paperwork?'

He watched a spectrum of colours flicker across Stripling's face: red, white, and red again. The nervous darting of his eyes, the shuffling of his feet. Sévère had to admit to himself that he was, in fact, already damned.


CIGAR SMOKE CURLED up toward the ceiling. Sévère thought of his health that was once again betraying him, the poor intelligence of his officer that seemed to worsen the longer he kept the man employed, and the string of financial problems the magistrate deemed it necessary to create. The situation was unacceptable.

He pulled out a pen and drafted a letter to the Justices advising them that the magistrate was to be sued for unpaid fees due the coroner. As soon as he'd put his seal to the envelope, he felt better.

There was little he could do about his leg, but he would have to replace Stripling. He needed an assistant with wits and balls.

Balls?

He almost choked on the thought.

---

"NEED *your opinion on recent developments in our case. Come to my practice when convenient. G.S.*"

She re-read the telegram but it puzzled her still. *Our case.* She shook her head and gazed out the window. Drizzle hit the glass and ran down in small rivulets. The day was a foggy yellow. A while ago, the church bells had struck ten. She grabbed her coat, and told Bobbie that she was off for an early lunch.

---

A STRANGER ANSWERED her knock and offered to take her umbrella and coat. She thanked him and walked through the hall, stopping in front of a door that stood ajar. There he sat, behind a large desk, stacks of paper piling up on either side of him, a cloud of smoke rising from a cigar that sat on an ashtray.

When he lifted his head to find her framed in the doorway, his eyes lit up. For a moment she wondered why he would be happy to see her. But the expression disappeared in a heartbeat. Perhaps a trick of the light.

She took a step forward. 'Hello, Sévère.'

'Miss Mary, come in and have a seat. Tea or coffee?'

She took off her gloves and her bonnet, and sat. 'Coffee, please. No milk, no sugar.'

He frowned, stood, and bent forward. 'This scar is new.' His arm stretched over the desk, a finger touched the small scar at her eyebrow. She pulled back.

'How did that happen?'

She opened her mouth, then shut it. 'You need my opinion on a case. How can I help you?'

He sat back down and scanned her face. 'How did that happen, Miss Mary?'

'Are you still investigating who dumped Alexander Easy into the Thames?'

'Yes, I am. In my spare time. But as long as I'm not allowed to search a certain brothel for evidence, I can't get anywhere with my conclusions. Something, however, tells me that such a visit would result in arse pain.'

She threw back her head and laughed. When she looked at him again, he asked softly, 'How did this happen, Miss Mary?'

'Occupational hazard. I don't wish to talk about it.'

His expression darkened. He nodded once and said, 'I have to apologise. I forgot to wish you a Merry Christmas when we parted.'

'You've thought about this for weeks? Do Jews celebrate Christmas?'

'I'm neither a Jew nor do I see any reason to celebrate Christmas.' He pushed a folder toward her. 'The case notes. I will summarise them for you in a moment.' He rose, grabbed his crutch, and limped slowly to the door, called for fresh coffee, and returned to her side. 'Shall we sit by the fire?'

She nodded, and they relocated.

'What happened to your leg?' she asked.

'A small injury to the knee. It looks much worse than it is.'

She tipped her head at him. 'You could have said instead that you don't wish to talk about it.'

'I could have.' He picked at the armrest and flicked a speck of lint toward the fireplace. 'It is an automatic response. You are correct, I don't wish to talk about it.'

He looked into the flames, lost for words.

'The summary of the case,' she said softly.

'Ah, yes. Thank you. The short version is this: There's no suspect. I don't have the faintest idea who could have done it, nor where I could find additional clues. The long version... Well.' He inhaled, and began to recount the past five weeks of investigations. The coffee was brought in and they emptied their first cup, and then a second. Mary remained silent until Sévère signalled the end of his speech.

Mary wiped a drop of coffee from her upper lip and slowly shook her head. 'You were hoping I would see something you don't? I am very sorry, but I can't help you. There's nothing I can possibly add.'

'Read the case notes. Return them to me in a few days. If you have questions, send a telegram or find me here. I will pay you your usual fee.'

She gazed at the folder, felt across its edges with her fingertips, and said, 'You are a queer man, Sévère.'

MARY PLACED the case notes on her bed and opened the folder. She read for hours, but all clues led to a dead end. The nine newborns must have been buried in, or near, Redhill — the soil indicated as much. But there was no suspect, nothing that pointed from the Redhill-type Fuller's Earth found in one of the skulls to a person, an event, or a specific location in Redhill. These nine children seemed to have never existed. As did the vendor who had sold the trees to Mr Bunting at Covent Garden, in summer the previous year.

All the men who had regularly purchased plants from MacDoughall to sell off elsewhere had been located, and none of them could recall selling seven apple tree saplings to an elderly man at Covent Garden. But then... If the vendor had been the murderer or an accomplice, he would certainly not have volunteered this information...

There was no other plant nursery in the area between Redhill and Limpsfield. No vendor had sold MacDoughall's apple trees to someone who in turn had sold them at Covent Garden.

Woburn Sands was a hamlet of hobby gardeners with two semi-professional nurseries, neither of which exported their plants to London. Mrs Fouler had been the prime suspect for two days, but the whole of Bedfordshire lacked a shallow cledge, and its Fuller's Earth deposits were located at below twenty-five yards depth — too deep for someone with a shovel and the need to hide a corpse quickly. Besides, the findings of Johnston and Pouch showed that the six bodies buried in Mrs Fouler's back-yard had not suffered violent deaths, and they had nothing in common with the nine skeletons found in seven flowerpots.

Mary sighed. The church bells struck six in the evening. She had to do her homework. She rose, hid the notes under her bed, and dressed in a deep burgundy dress.

'Rose?' she called down the stairs.

The girl stuck her nose around the corner, and showed a toothy smile. 'Bite to eat?'

'I'm perishing.'

While she ate, she opened a fairly new volume of "Anatomy. Descriptive and Surgical," by Gray and Carter. Simon had lent it to her months ago. She wondered which section she should choose for tonight. Something complex, perhaps? Smiling, she turned the pages to "Muscles and Fasciae of the Foot."

After she had eaten, she washed her mouth, face, and feet, and settled on the armchair. The bells struck seven.

He would be early tonight, he'd written. His letter had contained a short poem he claimed to have penned. It was Whitman, though. She liked it anyway.

A rap at the door. 'Come in, please,' she called.

A young man in his twenties entered, swept off his hat with a grand gesture, and crooned, 'My princess!'

'Good evening, Simon.'

Simon dropped his coat, scarf, hat, and gloves. 'I'm parched,' he said, placed a gold coin on the table, and poured them wine.

'How was your day?'

'Gory anatomy practice. But next year I'll have my first

patients.' He eyed her dress, obviously searching for a clue as to what she might have planned for tonight.

She placed her feet into his lap. 'Muscles and fasciae.'

'Are you sure?' he asked.

'Do you find it too difficult?'

He blew through his nose. 'No, not at all. First, second, or third layer?'

She leant forward. 'Can one even reach the third layer without a knife?'

He gazed at her ankle. How neatly it fit into his hands. 'I doubt it.'

'Well, then. Do the first. Bones, too, if you please.' She nodded at him, and leant back.

He pulled off her boots, and let his hands slide up her long legs. His fingers unhooked her garters and pulled down her stockings.

His eyelids sunk lower as he gingerly probed her flesh with his thumbs. The soft, inside portion of her sole. *'Flexor helices brevis,'* he muttered.

He drew a line to the outside of her foot, down toward her heel. *'Fibularis longus.'* His index and middle finger traced the arch of her foot and he looked up at her, whispering, 'First *cuneiform* bone, second *cuneiform* bone, third *cuneiform* bone, *cuboid* bone. Are we doing the foot or all lower extremities?'

'There are more than a hundred muscles in the foot, and you've identified only two. Does that answer your question?'

'Damn.'

Some time between caressing her *Abductor digiti minimi* and the *distal phalanx* of her small toe with his right hand, he managed to extend his explorations with his left hand all the way up to the soft hollow of her knee. When he muttered, *'semitendinosus,'* and, *'gracilis,'* she moaned and slid down in her armchair, offering him access to her thighs.

*'Mons pubis,'* he said softly, and then, *'Labia minor.'*

'You forgot something, Simon.'

*'Clitoris,'* he sighed.

SIMON LEFT PAST MIDNIGHT. Mary curled up in her bed, exhausted. Before she fell asleep, the strings of evidence seemed to tangle her mind. She pictured the case like a ball of yarn a cat had used as a toy.

What did one do with such a chaos?

Undo it.

'We have to begin anew,' she whispered.

'SÉVÈRE, I've examined it from all angles. It's the only option left.' She blushed and added, 'I believe.'

She emptied her cup and placed it back on his desk. Cigar smoke curled up thickly from the ashtray.

'Do you ever smoke it or do you just leave it smouldering there?'

'I never smoke.' Frowning, Sévère opened his pocket watch. 'Half past eleven. Do you have any plans for today?'

'Not before seven o'clock in the evening.'

'Let us visit Mr Bunting, then.' He stood, and grabbed his crutch.

'BUT I'VE TOLD you this already. All of it.' Mr Bunting spoke a little too loud, his eyes wide open as if to compensate for his poor hearing. His ear trumpet was directed at Sévère, then swivelled to the housekeeper, who stood at the door, kneading her apron. 'Mrs Hopegood gave you the exact same information under oath as I did. What else could we possibly help you with?'

'I was hoping that time had stirred up a piece of memory. A small detail that might seem unimportant to you. Something about the man who sold you the trees.'

'Stirred what?' Bunting said.

Sévère scooted his chair closer to the man, leant forward and said loudly, 'I hoped that time might help your memory. Do you recall something more about the man who sold you the trees? A detail that you haven't mentioned previously. Something that might appear unimportant to you.'

'Coroner, I am an old man. Time doesn't stir up my memory, it muddles it.'

Mary felt as though Bunting had kicked her in the gut. 'May I use your privy?' she whispered, trying to control her excitement. 'My apologies, but...I suffer from a... weakness of the bladder.'

'Excuse me? What did the lady say?' Bunting shouted.

Mary walked up to Bunting, lowered her mouth to his ear trumpet and repeated her request.

Bunting turned a shade of burgundy, and flicked his hand at Mrs Hopegood.

Mary was led downstairs and through a corridor.

'Poor Mr Bunting. Suffering from rheumatism all these years,' she said.

'It didn't used to be this bad. He was much better this past summer, when I entered his employ. The chilly weather has made it worse. To the right, please, Mrs Jenkins.'

They walked through the back door, and toward the servant's privy. 'Thank you, Mrs Hopegood. I am really sorry about this, but I simply can't help it.'

'It's all right,' Mrs Hopegood said. 'Will you find your way back?'

'Oh most certainly!' Mary pulled the door closed and hoisted up her skirts. She listened to Mrs Hopegood's exceedingly slow retreat. Mary suspected the woman to be eavesdropping, so she squeezed out what her bladder contained, added a few relieved sighs, and muttered, 'Christ! Not my guts again!' Then she wet her lips, pressed her palm against them and produced a very crude sound.

Mrs Hopegood shut the backdoor noisily.

Mary counted to twenty and left the privy. She quietly pushed down on the handle and pulled open the back door. Sévère's low voice trickled down the stairwell.

Her eyes scanned the corridor. There was a door to her right; she tried it. It opened. Bookshelves on the left, two windows on the opposite wall. A fireplace, a desk, an armchair. No flowers. She stuck her head back out into the hallway and pricked her ears. No one was descending the stairs.

Mary took a deep breath and disappeared into Mr Bunting's office.

'Are you feeling better, Mrs Jenkins?' Sévère enquired upon her return.

'I am, thank you.' She sat, squeezed his arm, and slipped a note into his hand.

Sévère gazed down at the crumpled paper and unfolded it. For a long moment, he said nothing.

'Will that be all, Coroner?' Bunting enquired.

Sévère looked at Mary and whispered, 'Do you have it on you?'

She nodded, and patted her skirts.

Sévère grabbed his crutch as if to leave, stopped himself and looked at Bunting, 'That will be all, Mr Hunt.'

Bunting nodded and smiled.

Sévère leant back.

Bunting frowned. 'You have another question?'

Mary waited, hoping that Sévère would repeat the test, because Bunting might believe he'd misheard, or, indeed, had not heard the name "Hunt" properly.

'I forgot to ask your age. A mere formality.'

'Three-and-sixty.'

'Thank you, Mr Hunt.'

Mary threw a glance at the housekeeper, who was looking at the scene in puzzlement. A cough pulled her attention back to Bunting.

'My name is Bunting. Rupert Bunting.'

'You lived in Redhill until summer the previous year, is that correct?'

Bunting paled, blinked, and shook his head slowly.

'Mr Hunt, assuming a fake identity and failing to

reveal the truth when interrogated by the police is fraud. If you do not cooperate with us, I must ask the magistrate to issue a warrant at once. If you are found guilty, you will spend up to two years in prison.'

Bunting unstoppered his ear and placed the trumpet on his lap. Then he muttered, 'I love her.'

'Excuse me?' Sévère said.

Bunting looked up at his housekeeper. 'I believe our guests wish to leave now. Would you show them to the door, Mrs Hopegood?'

'Mr Hunt,' Sévère bent forward. 'You will answer my questions here, or in the House of Detention.'

Bunting looked out the window.

Mary touched Sévère's elbow, and gave a slight jerk of her head.

'Show it to me,' he said.

She stuffed her hand into the folds of her skirts and extracted a small, red volume with a bee printed on the cover.

### *THE BRITISH BEE-KEEPER'S GUIDE BOOK*

Sévère took it from her and opened it. A receipt was tucked into the book.

BRITISH BEE JOURNAL. THE BEEKEEPERS' RECORD:
23, BEDFORD STREET, STRAND,

*London, W.C. 2, 4. July 1879*

*Received of ___ Rupert W. Hunt ___ the Sum of*
*___ Three Shillings ___*
*for The Beekeepers' Records, June 1878 to July 1879*

---

ON the inside cover an inscription read:

*Property of Rupert W. Hunt. Redhill Apiary*

SÉVÈRE ROSE AND SAID, 'I will keep this as evidence. Mrs Hopegood, may I speak with you in private?'

She paled, and staggered back onto the landing. Sévère followed.

'I must ask you to not leave your lodgings, else you'll both be sent to the House of Detention until your case is heard. I doubt Mr Hunt's rheumatism will take lightly to a cold cell.'

'B…but…'

'At the very least, you are an accessory to fraud.'

'I… He said he forgets things. When he saw the…the skull. He said he's afraid the police will detain him if he can't give a clear statement.'

'He told you to lie for him?' Sévère was shocked about his own lack of skill. How could he have missed the dishonesty of the housekeeper?

She shook her head violently. 'No, he did not! When I began working for Mr Bunting, I asked him about the trees on the balcony. He told me he had purchased them a few days earlier at Covent Garden. Even mentioned how nice the man was who'd sold them to him. And then in December...' she heaved a sigh. Her fingers twitched on her crumpled apron. 'I found the skull and I screamed, and he asked, "What is it?" So I told him — showed him — and he looked like he was about to faint. He stammered something I didn't quite understand, and I said he mustn't worry about the police — the vendor must have put the skull there. He looked all flustered at me and said, "What vendor?" So I told him what he'd told me in summer, and he nodded and said, "Yes, yes, I believe that is correct. My mind is all muddled these days." And then he asked me to repeat it once more, so he could give a clear statement.'

Sévère, relieved that he'd not been entirely blind after all, huffed. 'You withheld information, Mrs Hopegood, and you interfered with a murder investigation. Did it never occur to you that your employer might have put the bodies there?'

Her eyes grew wide. 'No! Not Mr Bunting. He cannot have... No. He's no murderer. I am absolutely certain.'

'Be that as it may, your employer is now the prime suspect in my infanticide investigation. I have to remind you that neither of you is allowed to leave the house until the police take your statements regarding the identity fraud. I will issue a warrant for Mr Hunt, and my officer and I will return shortly and take him into custody.'

---

WHILE SÉVÈRE WAS SPEAKING, Mary kept her eyes on

Hunt. He let his gaze stray toward her, and, seeing that he was being watched, flicked it back out the window.

From the corner of her vision, Mary noticed Sévère waiting behind the half-open door. It was time.

'Mr Hunt?' she said, approached, and knelt in front of him.

He blinked at her in puzzlement, snatched his trumpet, and put it to his ear.

'You must miss your bees,' she said. 'Your rheumatism must be so painful. Did you let them sting you? Did you snatch one or two, and rub them over your joints?'

A smile flickered across his face. His gaze lost its focus for a moment.

'The scents of honey and wax and resin during a hot summer day. You must have loved it.'

'I did,' he croaked.

'I saw your bee skeps at MacDoughall's. There was no roof protecting them from the rain. I was sorry to see them half soaked.'

Hunt dipped his head. A tear welled up and lost itself in the wrinkles of his face.

Mary waited.

Hunt's chest heaved, his gaze connected with hers and he said. 'She gave me no choice.'

'Who?'

A deep, rattling sigh. 'I will say no more.' He jerked his head toward the door. 'He can arrest me. I don't care.'

'Did you kill those nine children, Mr Hunt?' Her voice was clear and strong, but to her it seemed vulgar to speak so.

Hunt gazed at her, then at Sévère who had stepped

from the landing back into the room and now leant against the doorframe.

Hunt seemed to brace himself, inhaled, and said, 'Yes, it was me.'

A squeal issued from the landing. A heavy thump followed. Sévère limped back to Mrs Hopegood's side to pat her cheek and mutter her name.

Mary stood. 'Thank you for your patience, Mr Hunt. I believe the coroner will arrest you now.' She walked up to Sévère and said, 'I will see to her.'

'Thank you,' he said, and entered the room. Mary held Mrs Hopegood's head and felt for injuries. There was a slight bump on the side of her head. Her lashes twitched and her eyes opened. 'Will he be arrested?' she said hoarsely.

'I expect so.'

'What about me? Will he take me too?'

'I honestly don't know. Don't fret now, Mrs Hopegood. Try to sit. Slowly. There. Would you like something to drink?'

'Yes, that would… Yes, please.'

Mary went down to the kitchen, fetched a mug, filled it with cold tea she found in a pot, and brought it to Mrs Hopegood who seemed to recover with every sip.

She heard the two men approach the landing. When she looked up, she saw a trace of horror in Sévère's face. Climbing the stairs with his crutch hadn't been too hard, but descending it with a suspect who could barely walk himself was outright impossible.

She rose and scanned first Sévère: one crutch, an

injured knee. And then Mr Hunt: two canes, a bent body, clumsy feet.

'Perhaps the gentlemen might offer me an arm?' she asked, and held out both elbows.

Sévère frowned at Mary's slight figure, and shook his head.

'Mrs Hopegood,' he called over his shoulder, 'would you be so kind as to help Mr Hunt down the stairs?'

Mrs Hopegood grunted, 'Of course,' but didn't seem to be able to rise.

Mary leant close to Sévère and whispered. 'Swallow your stupid pride. I'll help you down the stairs, and then I'll bring you Mr Hunt.'

She grabbed his elbow and took the first step down. Sévère followed, trying to put as little weight as possible on his left leg.

During their slow descent, he spoke with a low voice so as not to be overheard, 'Did you accidentally stumble into his office and happen to see a beekeeping book falling off a shelf and opening all by itself and you picked it up to put it back?'

'Well…nearly. Mr Bunting's statement about his muddled memory got me thinking about the pastries I bought at Regent's Park last spring.'

'Pastries.' Sévère said as though he believed Mary had just lost her mind.

'Yes, pastries. I remembered it was a woman who had sold them to me. They were extraordinarily delicious. A remarkable experience. I should remember the face and clothes of this woman, but I don't. So I wondered how it was that Mrs Hopegood and Mr Bunting could recall the colour of the clothes of a man who had sold them seven apple trees several months earlier. Then I needed to use the privy, of course, and accidentally entered Mr Bunting's office.' She smirked at him.

'And quite by accident,' she continued, 'a book fell from the shelf, just as you've said. When I read the inscription, I realised that the "H" of "Hunt" could rather easily be changed into a "B" for "Bunting" in any identification papers the man might wish to have modified. And that bee-stings alleviate rheumatism, and that Bunting deteriorated after summer.'

'After he moved to London.'

They arrived in the hallway and Sévère grumbled, 'You seem to fancy having two invalids on your hands.'

'I've had worse days.' She shrugged and went to help Mr Hunt down the stairs. Sévère clumsily pulled on his coat, and held Mary's coat out for her.

When the three were dressed, Sévère called up the stairs to remind Mrs Hopegood that she was not to leave the house, that he would have more questions for her later.

'Are you ready?' he asked Mr Hunt.

'Excuse me?'

'Are you ready?' Sévère spoke loudly into Hunt's ear.

Mr Hunt set his jaw, and opened the front door.

They hailed a cab, and the two men climbed into it awkwardly.

'I take it you are not coming, Mrs Jenkins?'

'No, thank you very much.' With a glance at Hunt, she lowered her voice. 'I remember the House of Detention and its damp prison cells well enough. That dreadful building should be torn down.'

'The city is planning to demolish it,' Sévère supplied.

'Excellent. Goodbye, Mr Hunt, Coroner,' Mary said in a clipped tone, and shut the door. She felt strangely empty. The case was solved, and yet, something didn't sit quite right with her.

# SECOND ACT

IN WHICH A BARGAIN IS STRUCK

## ASYLUM

*A* sharp gust tore at Sévère's coat. He unfurled his umbrella, and immediately regretted it as the wind turned it inside out and kicked his hat off his skull. He watched the clumsy trajectory of his accessory as it bounced off the back of an old lady and rolled several yards before it was picked up by a conductor.

'Sir?' he called to Sévère, and waved the hat at him.

Sévère held on to his crutch, growled something about February being too wet, stormy, and cold for anyone's taste, and retrieved his hat from the conductor.

He stuffed the bent umbrella into his shoulder briefcase, and, holding onto his hat, left Sevenoaks train station as swiftly as his leg allowed. He made his way to a nearby cab and called, 'To the asylum!'

A sheet of drizzle hid the driver. The horse shivered as the whip struck its back. And off it went, neck bent against the wind.

Sévère took little notice of his surroundings. He

thought of Hunt and how the man had collapsed when he'd been identified by MacDoughall. Sévère had made sure that MacDoughall did not know why, precisely, he'd been summoned. All MacDoughall had been told was that more evidence had come forth, and a few issues needed to be clarified. When MacDoughall entered the room he found several detectives in plain clothes and the suspect, sitting around a table. As soon as he laid eyes on Hunt there was a look of shock and perhaps a trace of disgust in his expression, as though MacDoughall had suspected Hunt all along and this suspicion was now confirmed. But Sévère wasn't quite certain if he'd observed correctly, and MacDoughall had refused to elaborate on his relationship with Hunt. They'd simply been neighbours who talked on occasion, that was all.

Since his arrest, Hunt's lips had remained sealed. 'I did it,' was all he kept saying. Fortunately, an earlier telegram to the Redhill police station had resolved the whereabouts of Hunt's daughter within a few hours. She was an inmate at Sevenoaks Asylum for Women.

Sévère turned up his collar. His knee ached only a little. He wondered when he could dump the crutch.

*Swallow your stupid pride.*

A low, 'Ha!' burst from his mouth.


THE ASYLUM WAS SMALLER than he'd imagined. It stood on a slope, an aged mansion clad in thick ivy, and surrounded by large, fenced-in premises.

Sévère, who'd announced his arrival via telegram that

morning, was a little surprised when he was received by a flustered nun.

'My apologies, coroner. Dr Faulkner has had an emergency. I'm Sister Grace. Please do come in.'

They entered a lobby, and Sister Grace offered Sévère an armchair at the window.

'You've come because of Miss Hunt, I expect?'

'Indeed. Can you tell me something about her?'

Sister Grace inhaled deeply. 'It will be problematic to interview her, for you especially.'

'How do you mean?'

'Men distress her. And she is deaf, we believe. It appears her family misinterpreted her hearing impairment. You see, they believed her to be an idiot. I detest this word, but it's the term used by most people.'

Sévère pulled his notepad from his briefcase, and asked about the age and medical condition of Miss Hunt.

'She is thirty-three and in good physical health. She was brought to us by her father this past summer. It seemed to pain him greatly to leave her here, but he said he couldn't take care of her anymore. He said he was getting too old.'

She stared at her knees, frowning.

'There is something else?' Sévère asked softly.

Sister Grace shook her head, a jerk of the neck that appeared to shake off something repellent.

'How many patients do you have here?'

'Seventeen women, aged between twenty-one and sixty-four.'

'What emergency is Dr Faulkner attending to?'

'Oh.' She waved her hand in dismissal. 'Mrs Lewis

shaved off the tip of her big toe down in the vegetable garden. She was turning the earth, you see. A trifle, really. But she faints at the sight of a single drop of blood, and there was rather a lot of it.'

'She ran the spade through her boot?'

The Sister smiled. 'No. She wore only stockings.'

'Why had she been committed to your house?'

'Uterine derangement.'

Sévère could only imagine what that meant. 'I see. Your patients are free to roam the house and the premises?'

'Our patients are not dangerous in the least. Their diagnoses are all linked to disturbances of the female sexual organs, such as insanity caused by child birth, by excessive menstruation, uterine derangement, masturbation, or fornication. We, that is we of the Religious Sisterhood of the Church of England, guide them back onto the path of Our Saviour. Once they find peace here, they are allowed to return home.'

'Will Miss Hunt be allowed to leave?'

Sister Grace lowered her head. 'I doubt it.'

'But didn't you say that her ailment is merely deafness?'

'We believe that…that a man had relations with her without her consent, and that it was this that caused her insanity.'

'Excuse me?'

'Marks,' slipped from Sister Grace's mouth. 'On her stomach. From the stretching of the skin.'

Sévère sunk heavily against the backrest. 'She'd been with child? How often, in your opinion?'

'I cannot tell. Perhaps twice. More than once, I'm certain.'

'What makes you think so?'

'Experience.'

'I expect you found a way to communicate with Miss Hunt?'

'Well, yes. But it is limited. We knock very loudly to let her know that we are about to enter her room. She feels it. The vibrations in the walls and the floor, I expect. It doesn't help to call out to her. But knocking on the door or on the wall does. We found that hand signs work well enough.'

'She can neither read nor write?'

'Unfortunately not.'

'Can't you teach her?'

'How? If I speak a word, she doesn't hear it. How would she know what it means when I write it down for her? Besides, I also have other patients to oversee.'

'Well, you could point at the wall and write down "wall," for example.' Sévère lifted his eyebrows in puzzlement.

Sister Grace opened her mouth, not quite sure how to reply, and was saved by approaching footfalls. Soon, a hatless and rather ruffled man appeared. 'My apologies. You must be Coroner Sévère? I am Dr Faulkner.'

They shook hands. Faulkner leant against the windowsill and inhaled deeply. 'Your telegram said you wish to see Miss Hunt. I'm afraid it is not possible.'

Sévère eyed Faulkner sharply.

'Miss Hunt gets upset if a man enters her room. Besides, it will be futile to ask her anything. She's deaf.'

'What do you make of this fear of men?'

Faulkner pushed away from the window, and crossed the room. Sighing, he stuffed his hands into his trouser pockets. 'Sister, you have a talent for explaining such matters. If you don't mind?'

'It is rather clear, I expect,' Sister Grace began. 'A woman wouldn't need explaining. But a man does, it seems. Men scare her. She has learnt that men can't be trusted. She's had a child, if not two or three. This woman has seen years of suffering under the hands of a man. I thought I had made that clear.'

'If you are so sure about that, why didn't you report it to the police?'

Sister Grace snorted. 'What good would it do to summon policemen who would ask questions she cannot answer? What good is it to call for a physician to examine her for signs of abuse, if she claws out his eyes when he attempts to touch her?'

Sévère grabbed his crutch and hoisted himself off the chair. 'I need to take her statement. A case of unlawful killings hinges upon it.'

'I cannot allow it,' Dr Faulkner said.

Sévère leant demonstratively heavier on his crutch, and put on the kindest of expressions. 'You can see I am a cripple. In no way am I a threat. Sister Grace will accompany me. If Miss Hunt protests, I will leave her room at once.'

'No. Under no circumstances—'

'We can try,' Sister Grace said.

The doctor sighed. 'Very well. She is your patient.'

THEY WALKED down the corridor and stopped at a door. Sister Grace slammed her fist against the wood three times. She pushed Sévère gently aside so that he wouldn't be visible. Then she opened the door, and said, 'Hello Miss Hunt, I have brought a visitor.' She was gesturing with her arms, pointing to herself, then she made a wave-like, searching movement with her arm toward Sévère, her hand groping for him. He took a step forward into full view. He made sure he looked smaller, friendlier, and very much crippled.

A woman was seated at a desk. She had a beautiful face, a straight, small nose, full lips, and high cheekbones. Her hair was pinned up in a simple knot. When her eyes met his, she shook her head, and pointed at him. Her mouth opened, producing a low, odd cry. He lowered his head a fraction, but kept his eyes on her.

Sister Grace approached the desk, speaking softly although everyone knew Miss Hunt could not hear her. But the movements of the Sister's lips seemed to pull her attention away from Sévère.

He wondered if he should risk a step forward, but decided against it. One doesn't catch a bird by flinging oneself at it.

Sister Grace signed and talked to Miss Hunt, and Miss Hunt signed back, her mouth moving, issuing strange noises.

'She wants to know what happened to your leg.'

'Recurring infantile paralysis,' Sévère answered. He'd purposefully chosen the complicated words. It didn't escape his notice how Miss Hunt squinted to follow the movement of his lips. She blinked, turned to Sister Grace, and shrugged.

Sister Grace tried to explain it as best she could, but after a few attempts she settled on injury or partial amputation. Sévère wasn't sure which.

'Would you ask her how many children she's had and what has happened to them?'

This time, he couldn't read Miss Hunt's reaction. Her face was a mask of naïveté, painted with shadows. Sister Grace was translating, signing at her stomach, and pretending to rock a child in her arms, then pointing at herself and signing, 'Zero.' She pointed at Dr Faulkner and signed, 'Three.' Then she pointed at Miss Hunt.

Miss Hunt shook her head.

When her gaze met Sévère's he said quietly, 'You had nine children, and among them were two pairs of twins.'

Her face crumpled and she threw an ink bottle at him. Her scream was utterly inhuman, a howl that seemed to come from deep in her chest.

Sévère stepped back and out of view. He had only guessed that she might be able to read lips, and then had gone a step farther in suggesting she'd been the mother of the nine infants. A little stunned, he leant against the wall. Faulkner eyed him with suspicion.

When the shouting had lost its shrill intensity, Sévère called into the room, but avoided showing himself so as to not cause more screaming. 'Sister Grace, would you please let Miss Hunt know that her father is in custody. He has confessed to the wilful killing of the nine infants. The trial will be held in three days in London and

Miss Hunt's statement is of utmost importance. In fact, I can apprehend her if she is not willing to cooperate.'

'This has to stop now!' Faulkner barked. 'Sister Grace, leave Miss Hunt alone.'

'Are you attempting to influence a witness, Dr Faulkner?' Sévère warned. 'Sister, please tell Miss Hunt what I said.'

With a voice that fought for self-control, Faulkner growled, 'This woman has suffered enough, can't you see that?'

'Has she?'

The crash of what Sévère guessed was a chair told him that Miss Hunt had received his message. Her wail chilled his bones. Sister Grace screamed for help and Dr Faulkner rushed into the room, ignoring the onslaught of protest and flying items. A book skidded to a halt just outside the door.

Sévère peeked into the room. Faulkner and Sister Grace had wrestled Miss Hunt down on her bed, and tied her thrashing arms and legs. Three more Sisters hurtled down the corridor and entered Miss Hunt's room, one of them carrying a cloth and a bottle of what Sévère suspected to be chloroform. A minute later, silence fell with a sigh.

# INQUEST

*S*évère tapped his crutch against the wooden floor. The sound was dull. He much preferred the sharp, echoing knock of his cane. 'The inquest is herewith opened. Officer Stripling will make the case for the prosecution.'

Stripling stepped onto the witness stand — improvised from a table and a chair — and placed his hand on the Bible.

'I do solemnly and sincerely and truly declare that I will speak the truth, the whole truth, and nothing but the truth.'

'Thank you, Officer Stripling. If you would now outline the case for us, and read the witness statements that would justify the committal to trial of the accused, Mr Rupert Hunt.'

Stripling smartly snapped open his folder, smoothed the first page, and began with the seven flowerpots on a balcony of a house on Whitechapel Road, the statements of Mrs Hopegood and Mr Bunting/Hunt, the results of the postmortem examinations, and the statements of the naturalist, Mr Pouch.

Stripling was reading slowly and without enthusiasm. Nothing he said was new to anyone in the room. They had all heard it during the first inquest, and, if not, they had read it in the papers. People stifled yawns. The newspapermen, who were sitting at a long table before the jury and who had been scribbling away during the first few minutes of Stripling's speech, now stretched their shoulders and checked their watches.

Sévère observed the struggles of a one-winged fly on the floor in front of him.

Stripling didn't pause once, not even to take a sip of water.

Vestry Hall grew stuffy.

Anticipation rumbled through the hall when Stripling neared the end and read Sévère's statement on the identity fraud of Mr Bunting/Hunt and his confession to the wilful killing of nine infants. Stripling shut the folder. A small cloud of dust rose in the murky light.

'Is the jury satisfied with the evidence against the suspect to justify keeping him on remand until a verdict is given?' Sévère asked.

The men of the jury looked at one another; all of them nodded. The spokesman stood and said, 'The jury is satisfied with the evidence. The accused may be kept in custody.'

Sévère tapped his crutch against the floor. The *fomp* irritated him. 'The inquest is adjourned until after lunch.'

AN HOUR and a half later the jury moved back into Vestry Hall and took their places, the audience shuffled and pushed into their benches and chairs, and Sévère took his accustomed position at the centre of the spectacle. When the room became hushed, he stepped onto the witness stand, swore upon the Bible to speak the truth and nothing but the truth, and read the statements of Dr Faulkner and Sister Grace on Miss Hunt's whereabouts and condition. That she was deaf and had been deemed insane by her own family. That she had been with child, likely multiple times. He then read his own statement: that, when confronted with the facts, Mr Hunt had confessed to having had relations with his own daughter, physical relations of the kind between husband and wife, and that she had given birth seven times, twice having twins. That he had killed the newborns with his own hands. That the abuse of her own person and the deaths of her children had driven his daughter, Charlotte Hunt, into insanity, which made it impossible for her to give her own statement.

The silence was total. Sévère could hear the faint, irregular buzzing of the one-winged fly.

When he stepped off the witness stand, the audience roared with anger. Someone threw an umbrella at Mr Hunt, but the missile missed its target. Several gentlemen broke through the masses in an attempt to throw themselves at the accused. Inspector Height did his best to wrestle them down, boxing their ears and calling for enforcements. Sévère knocked an especially rude man on the head with his crutch, and threw the Bible into his face. Stripling shouted at the crowd. All to no avail. When, finally, Height pulled his service revolver from his pocket and fired a shot at the ceiling, people screamed and froze in place.

Sévère roared his disapproval, and banned them all from the hall. Height and two other policemen escorted the audience outside.

The sweat-bathed news reporters scribbled away, not without a gleam of happy excitement in their faces.

Stripling helped Hunt up into his chair, and dabbed at a scratch on the man's brow.

'We will now hear the statement of the accused, Rupert Hunt,' Sévère said loudly, his voice a little hoarse from the shouting.

Hunt was led into the witness stand, confessed to fathering and killing the nine infants, and was led back to his chair.

'All statements have been heard. The jury may now retire.'

When the men of the jury had left, Sévère sagged onto a chair, needing a brandy rather badly. But none was forthcoming.

'How is Hunt doing?' he asked Stripling.

'He's got a scratch on his forehead, but otherwise he seems to be doing just fine.'

Sévère wasn't sure if he'd ever seen a serial murderer sitting through his trials *just fine.*

It didn't take long for the jury to come to a decision. When the door to the anteroom opened, Sévère checked his watch, and raised his eyebrows. They had needed only eight minutes.

They filed in and took their place on the benches.

The spokesperson of the jury stood and read the verdict. 'We, the jury, find Mr Rupert Hunt guilty of the wilful murder of nine infants.'

Sévère raised his voice. 'The accused will be committed to trial at the Old Bailey.'

He kept his eyes on Hunt. The old man sat bowed, his head in his hands. Gradually, the jury and the news reporters packed up and left. Someone must have told the waiting crowd outside what had occurred. Whoops where heard, and the knocking of umbrellas against the pavement.

When the hall had finally emptied, Hunt gazed up at one of the large windows. The sun had begun to set behind a veil of thick clouds. He looked as though a great weight had been taken off his shoulders.

---

SÉVÈRE WATCHED the cigar slowly transform into a cylinder of compacted ash. His leg was propped up on a chair; the ache had softened, the swelling and bruising had subsided.

The doorbell rang. He heard Netty rushing across the entrance hall, her heels clacking on the marble. She admitted the guest, fussed with his coat and hat, and led him up to the drawing room.

Johnston entered, followed closely by the housekeeper. She carried a long package, wrapped in brown paper. Johnston thanked her, took it, and placed it next to the door.

'May I serve tea or coffee, sirs?'

Sévère looked enquiringly at Johnston, who politely declined.

'You may retire. We won't be needing you further tonight, Netty,' Sévère said, and rose to his feet.

'Extraordinary,' Johnston said, looking around the room. 'I never expected a man of your standing to live quite so spartan.'

'May I offer you a drink?'

Johnston nodded toward the bottle on the table, and Sévère poured the brandy. They raised their glasses and Sévère said, 'With this your accusation of me leading a spartan lifestyle has been disproved.'

Johnston's moustache twitched. 'You seem to detest knick-knackery. Rather refreshing, I must say.'

'As well as a crowded house. I very much like my privacy. People believe I'm a miser, because I employ only a cook, a housekeeper, and a daily woman for the roughs, not the common gaggle of servants.'

Johnston leant back in his armchair, and looked up at the ceiling. 'It is quiet here. I like it. A man's den.'

'A one-man den.' Sévère sipped on his brandy and enjoyed the warm, soft burn in his throat.

'So you caught the murderer. He even pleaded guilty. How unusual. Do you know why he did it, why he confessed?'

'Unfortunately not. He confessed to having fathered and killed all nine children. Other than that, he spoke very little. His daughter is an inmate at an asylum of the Religious Sisterhood of the Church of England. Her condition doesn't allow questioning by me or the police.

That leaves me with Hunt's meagre statement. I hope he'll provide more information to his attorney.'

'When will his trial begin?'

'March twenty-fourth.'

'Hum. I don't wish to intrude, but you seem unsatisfied by the outcome of your inquest.'

Sévère rolled the glass between his fingers. 'I don't believe he did it.'

Johnston nodded slowly.

'Worst of all,' Sévère continued. 'I've caught myself growing complacent. Despite my instincts telling me that Hunt is innocent, I've felt indifferent to it. I've wanted the case to be done with. Because of this.' He jerked his chin at his left leg.

Johnston chuckled. 'It is the same with old age, lad. I tire faster than my young colleagues. My joints and muscles ache sooner now than they did twenty years ago. I catch myself thinking I should retire. And then I laugh at myself.'

Sévère emptied his glass. 'I expect all men have a sense of honour. But what makes one man pursue honour and another man pursue comfort?'

'It's all in the priorities. When a man comes to a cross-road, he has to be alone with himself and decide what it is that is most important to him. If he never takes the time to deeply think about this, he might always choose the easy way.'

Sévère leant back and gazed at Johnston. He'd never considered him old, despite the shock of light-grey hair, his salt-and-pepper moustache, the furrows spreading from eyes and mouth. Now it felt as if his friend — for somehow he'd come to consider him a friend the moment he'd entered the drawing room — had, in a fatherly gesture, lifted a veil from Sévère's eyes.

'Because, you see,' Johnston continued, 'if a man doesn't take the time to think, he might never know *why* he does this thing, or that. It is the cause, the worthy cause, the *why* that is essential. Never the pain and sweat of how he might get there. It's not success that makes a man great. It's his courage to fail.'

———

SÉVÈRE HELD a match to the cigar, and pulled at it until its end glowed bright red. He placed the smoke onto the ashtray, and spread out the plans of his town house on his desk. He'd bought it when he'd been called into office. A modern, five-storey house with enough space for a family and an army of servants. A man of his standing wasn't supposed to live in a small apartment somewhere off Whitechapel Road. For some time, he'd been wondering if it hadn't been a mistake to purchase this monstrosity of a building.

He pulled out a notebook and began jotting down annual allowances for his servants, and potential future costs. He might need a manservant at some point, someone strong enough to help him up and down the stairs. He was unwilling to move his private rooms to the ground floor and be cut off from the rest of the house.

A private coach, perhaps? There was a two-stall stable across the terrace. He'd bought it together with the house, and had never known what to do with it.

And what then, lad? What are you going to do when you have to use a chair? Sévère dropped the pencil. His gaze fell on the package Johnston had brought. His new, customised crutch.

*It's not success that makes a man great. It's his courage to fail.*

Well, he wasn't a great man, but failing without ever daring wasn't his style.

He picked up his pencil, wrote "Personal Assistant" and put the pencil back down. Stripling was useless as an officer. He would have to fire him, or perhaps offer him a position as a clerk. The man would feel mightily downgraded.

His thoughts strayed to Johnston, and how he felt like an essential part of his team. Inspector Height was… acceptable, but an outsider. Police would never be part of his operation, that much was clear to him.

Still, the essential man missing was an officer, a man whom Sévère could trust to make intelligent decisions when he wasn't around to make them himself.

An ad in the papers, perhaps? Sévère snorted at the thought. That would result in a horde of applicants who wouldn't even be able to find their own nose, if it came to it.

Sévère slammed his fist onto the desk. Cigar ash dropped into the crystal bowl.

'I'll be damned!'

# PROPOSITION

'Good evening, Miss Mary.' He rose, limped around the table, and pulled back the chair for her.

She noticed the deepened triple lines between his eyebrows. His voice and posture appeared different tonight, reminding her of the first day they'd met, the interrogation and her arrest.

She sat, carefully avoiding physical contact.

'Good evening, Sévère. Thank you for your kind invitation. I see your leg has improved.'

'Thank you for accepting my invitation. I hope Pagani's is to your liking.' He gifted her a smile that didn't reach his eyes.

Wondering why he was so tense, she let her gaze travel through the restaurant, though she'd inspected it when entering. For his sake, she appraised the pretty wallpaper, large windows, and the heavy chandeliers once more. The satin cushion she sat on and the engraved silverware in front of her.

'It is to my liking,' she said in her most pleasant tone.

'Excellent.' He drummed his fingers on the edge of the table, and after a short moment of consideration, he pulled an envelope from his waistcoat and pushed it across the impeccably white tablecloth. 'I wish to make a proposition. To demonstrate my sincerity, I took the liberty to prepare a draft of the contract.'

She narrowed her eyes at him, and then at the letter. Was this the reason for him to be so different tonight? Her heart sank at the thought he might wish to keep her as a mistress. Most prostitutes would be delighted by such an offer. But not Mary. Not with this man. Dread prickled in her palms as she reached for the paper.

His long fingers kept the letter pinned to the table. 'It contains the details of the agreement we struck some time ago. More or less.'

She opened her mouth to ask what agreement he could possibly mean, because the only agreements they had ever struck had concerned her honesty to him, and her opinions on the infanticide case. The latter had been solved, had it not?

'Good evening, Madame, Monsieur. May I take your orders?'

Startled, Mary looked up at the waiter. 'Ah...' she said, and only then spotted the menu in front of her. She flipped it open, found it to be in French, and pointed her finger at something random. 'My husband will choose the wine.'

*Husband*, she thought bitterly. Should he propose some

kind of bedding contract, she would... She'd have to think of what to do. Because if the man demanded her honesty, her wits, *and* her legs wrapped around his waist, he was up for a surprise, that much was certain.

Sévère addressed the waiter in French, and Mary smiled down shyly at her folded hands. It was something fine ladies ought to do: mouth shut, with the corners slightly curled upward, eyes avoiding looking at anyone in particular, especially when men were in conversation with one another.

When the waiter had disappeared, she crossed her arms over her chest. 'Sévère, what agreement are you talking about?'

He lowered his voice to a soft murmur. 'I offer you a position as my assistant. However, I must ask that you abandon your current situation at once.'

Her gaze grew cold, and she, too, lowered her voice. 'And with what specifically do you need assistance, *Coroner?* Do you need me to bring you to bed every night?'

He leant forward, and whispered, 'Abandoning your present situation includes you stop playing *anyone's* whore.'

She swallowed all acrid comments that constricted her tongue.

'May I?' She indicated the letter, and he nodded consent.

Her knife slid into the envelope, fraying the thick paper. She extracted the contract, unfolded it, and began to read:

*MISS MARY (REPLACE by real name) will be employed as a personal assistant to Mr Gavriel Sévère, starting (insert date here, 1881). Her basic annual payment will be one hundred pounds sterling, paid in quarterly instalments. Bonuses will be paid according to additional services rendered.*

'ADDITIONAL SERVICES RENDERED?' she muttered and looked up, but he didn't reply, only nodded at her to continue reading.

*THE AGREEMENT IS RENDERED void at once should the assistant violate the following regulations:*

*Mr Sévère's assistant is not to:*

*1.) take clients other than Mr Sévère, unless parties agree otherwise;*

*2.) lay hands on her employer, unless parties agree otherwise;*

*3.) break the law, unless parties agree otherwise.*

'EXCUSE ME?' she squeaked.

'You will need to supply your real name to make the contract legally binding.'

'Shouldn't you at least explain what this assistantship is all about?'

'Various…services.'

'Sévère, you have to use your pretty mouth to convey relevant information. Did someone hit you on the head? This…' She waved the letter in his direction, careful to avoid the candle flame. 'This is a poor draft of a contract. I doubt it is legally binding anywhere in Britain, with or without my real name on it. You'll have to specify the services required, period of validity, work hours, *etcetera*.'

He clicked his tongue. There were traces of surprise and incredulity in his expression.

'You believe I am a simpleton,' she said before he could speak. 'You believe I will sign anything to get away from the life I'm leading. You are a fool.'

'I know perfectly well that you are not a simpleton. In fact, this is the main reason I'm offering you the position. But I do wonder how you can doubt the validity of our contract.'

'You believe I have no clients proficient in legal matters.'

'Some might be. But I do believe they grunt and moan, and do not talk about legislation.' He peeled back his lips.

She gifted him a sweet smile until his began to falter. 'You are wrong about the latter, Sévère. Now, tell me what services you require of me.'

He cleared his throat. 'You will work as my eyes, legs, and brain. You will be something akin to a private detective, although a detective who works for me alone. Basically what you have done already, but on a permanent basis. And there'll be a few extensions and diversifications.'

Mary leant back in her chair. Her fingers, suddenly trembling and clumsy, dropped the letter to the floor.

'Excuse me,' she said, and bent to pick it up.

Her thoughts were racing around the life she led, the

plans she'd made of leaving London, her savings, and now…this.

It's a lie. Or a game. It must be, she thought. 'I am hungry. And I have questions.'

'I expected no less.'

The waiter brought the wine and poured a sip for Sévère, who tasted it and nodded approvingly. Mary remained silent and tense while their glasses were filled and the waiter enquired if he could do anything else for them.

Once he'd left, she asked, 'You expect me to give up my current situation, find an apartment, and meet you in your office every day?'

'Monday through Saturday, eleven o'clock to four o'clock, and then again from eight o'clock to ten o'clock. Plus the hours needed to interrogate suspects, informants, witnesses, and so on. These are my working hours. Yours might differ somewhat. You will meet me every morning in my office and we will discuss cases, or I will send you to gather information. In the beginning.'

'And after the beginning?'

He frowned. 'I might require your assistance to walk from my office to crime scenes, mortuaries, inquests, and so on.'

'Excuse me?'

'You will have noticed my limp.'

She nodded.

'Come Monday next week, I will close my present office and re-open it at my own lodgings to accommodate for my…increasing infirmities.'

He lifted the wine to his lips and drank. Her gaze

followed the liquid as he swallowed it, the movement of the throat, the bobbing of the Adam's apple, his tongue darting out to lick his upper lip.

'Impossible,' she finally said.

He cocked an eyebrow, and placed the glass back on the table. A drop of wine surrendered to the white table-cloth and formed a burgundy semicircle.

'If your social status were much lower, and your position not that of an official of the Crown, a young woman could go in and out of your house without causing so much as raised eyebrows and a little gossip. If your offices were not in your own home, it might be possible, also. But this? No. There is no reasonable way for you to explain why a prostitute is frequenting your private quarters.'

'Prostitute or not, employing a young and unmarried woman as my assistant will cause a scandal, and damage my reputation.'

'I am well aware of this. But it was you proposing it, not I.' She flicked her hand at the paper. 'This…mess. I can only assume you have a plan to solve it.'

'Well, we have limited options. Two, to be precise. You must live under my roof and I will introduce you to my household as my servant, or…' He swallowed. 'Or as my wife.'

Her skin grew cold. Her fingers curled around the stem of her wineglass, and her mind calculated how to best throw it at Sévère's head. 'You do believe me a simpleton after all. How often will I have to share my bed with you, Coroner?' she asked through clenched teeth.

'You shouldn't have a problem with that, should you now?'

Mary felt the blood pounding in her temple. She managed a dazzling smile, one that seemed to fool even Sévère, because his posture relaxed.

She pushed back her chair, stood, and announced, 'My coat.'

He opened his mouth to reply, but was interrupted by her soft, 'If you dare utter another word, I will cause a scene of such proportion as you don't dare dream of. And please do remain seated. After all, I have two healthy legs with which to fetch my coat by myself. Good evening, Coroner.'

SÉVÈRE BLINKED at her retreating back, wondering how and why this conversation had gone so wrong. He'd expected her to be, if not happy, then at least relieved by his offer.

The door to the restaurant swung shut and the waiter, who had helped Mary into her coat and accompanied her to the exit, threw him a quizzical glance. In reply, Sévère lifted his glass to his lips and slumped back in his chair.

'I'll be damned,' he muttered, and after a moment, he groaned, and made for the door.

He found her on the other side of the street, waving at a hansom. He didn't call out for fear she might run away or pick up horse manure and throw it at him. When a cab halted in front of her, Sévère had just reached her.

'We'll not be needing you,' he called up to the driver.

Seething, Mary curled her hands to fists. Sévère took her elbow gently, bent closer, and said, 'I know you enjoyed yourself playing detective. And that's all I ask of you — to keep doing it. But society demands a facade. I doubt you can move freely if you are not under the protection of a gentleman. See it as an offer. The protection of my name in exchange for your assistance. A marriage is the most practical solution to this problem, and it will exist on paper only. Trust me on this, please.'

'On paper,' she said, her eyebrows at a dangerously sarcastic angle.

'As I said. Should my *prick itch,* as you so poetically put it the other night, I will leave the house like the gentleman I am to return a few hours later and a few shillings lighter. Do you believe I have the slightest urge to share your bed after what happened during my first attempt?'

'I do know quite a bit about the tenaciousness and stupidity of men. You can trust me on that. Why do you offer this to me? Why now and…why offer it to a whore?'

'Might we continue our negotiations inside? I find it rather chilly here, and I'm hungry.'

She stared at the pavement and, after a long moment, nodded. 'For now.'

She handed her coat, bonnet, and gloves back to the bewildered waiter, and sat down at their table. 'You were saying?'

Sévère picked an invisible crumb off the tablecloth. 'I have several reasons for offering this position to you. For one, I need an assistant with a brain. Stripling has none whatsoever, but he is useful in his own ways. You, Miss Mary, are brilliant, ruthless, and, when the need arises, coldly analytical. You have no mercy with me. I offer this to you because I need help, not pity. Do not believe for a moment I'm offering this out of charity. I do not function that way, and I do see that you are doing rather well in your profession. But I have to warn you. I would have been more of a gentleman had I let you run away just now, because it is *you* who will hold the wrong end of the stick. I am twice your age, I might be bound to a chair before the end of this year, and I'm neither well-mannered nor patient in my own home. View my behaviour tonight as a reference point.'

'Bound to a chair?' Her gaze slid to where the table-cloth shielded a view of his legs.

'We will discuss it once you've signed the contract.'

'Nonsense! We will discuss it now.'

He leant back, arms crossed, and shook his head.

'For the moment, let us pretend I'm considering your proposition. I will not be your housekeeper,' she said.

'I have a housekeeper.'

'I won't be your cook, either.'

'You can cook, Miss Mary? Never mind. I have a cook.'

'Maid?'

'Yes. I mean, I employ a maid. You will have your own, if you wish. I don't need you to wait on me. I need your wits and your legs.' He groaned and rubbed his brow. 'I will say this only once: I am still the same man you came to know.'

'Sévère,' she bent forward and whispered, 'I am not quite sure what you mean by "still the same man," but I must tell you this: you *cannot* marry a whore. My presence in your house will utterly ruin your reputation. Among my clients are men who will know you. The Chief Magistrate of Bow Street Office, to name but one.'

Blood rushed to his cheeks; his eyes flickered. A

wicked grin spread across his face. He scanned the restaurant. They were alone in a secluded corner; the next occupied table was at a great enough distance to grant them privacy. He wondered, for the first time, if he'd invited a witch into a business partnership.

He shook his head, irritated and amused with himself, pulled up the chair next to him and beckoned her closer. She abandoned her chair and settled down on the one he offered.

He leant toward her until his shoulder brushed hers, and said softly, 'Is that so? How very interesting. Are you aware that this might provide me with a certain amount of leverage? He will believe I know all his dirty secrets.'

'You presuppose that he's told me all his dirty secrets.'

'Did he not?' Sévère asked.

'No. But I know them anyway. They are very dirty. The question is, do you require me to reveal them to you?'

'Hum… Perhaps. The question is, do I really want to know?'

'You might,' she said softly.

'Anything unlawful?'

She smiled. 'How much time do you have?'

'Excuse me?'

She nodded toward his legs. 'How long—'

'You think I'm dying? Don't get your hopes up, Miss Mary. I'm not dying. Although I might be perishing from hunger if that wretched waiter doesn't bring our food in the next two minutes.'

'It takes more than one missed meal to die of hunger, Sévère. Drink a sip of water. As long as you don't feel compelled to eat your expensive boots, you don't know what hunger means.'

'You believe me spoiled.'

'I believe you always fell on the soft side, if you ever fell at all.'

'That might be true.' He searched her face.

Distraction arrived in the shape of the waiter, laden with two large plates.

'Ah, the famine has ended.'

Mary looked down at her food. 'Oh no.'

'What is it?' Sévère's knife was half stuck in his steak, blood oozed from the cut.

'Little ballerinas.' She pointed at what appeared to be a dozen pairs of very small, very muscular legs attached to a dozen flat and muscular buttocks.

Sévère choked on his food. She slapped him between his shoulder blades.

'Frogs' legs,' he explained and nodded encouragingly. 'They are delicious. Taste them.'

She picked up the fork and impaled one of the small ballerina-halves through its behind. She held it up to her mouth, unsure how to proceed. 'Well, dammit,' she grumbled, salvaged the morsel from her fork, and pulled meat off bones with her fingers.

'The ladies will surely faint,' Sévère commented dryly on her inappropriate eating style.

'They can toughen up. This tastes like very young chick. Is this an appetiser?'

'No, this is a full meal for ladies whose intestines have been constricted by too-tight garments. Very fashionable. Will you consider my offer, Miss Mary?'

She took her time to answer, calculating the offered income into the time she would need to spend with a man she had entirely misjudged, until she could finally leave London.

'It's not my real name,' she said after a moment, dismembering another of her ballerinas.

'What a surprise.'

She chewed and frowned, and abruptly emptied her wine. The waiter appeared from nowhere and refilled her drink. Once he'd disappeared, she wiped her hands on the napkin and said, 'I will enter your proposed agreement under three conditions.'

Sévère coughed. 'You will enter it? I thought you'd think about it for days, if not weeks.'

'I am generally disinclined to wonder for days whether or not I should consider an option. If I ever feel undecided, it's usually because it's not a good idea to do it at all, whatever it is. Besides, this proposition of yours requires good planning, which can only be accomplished by first taking the endeavour seriously. I will, however, retain the right to reject your proposition, should we find ourselves unable to draft a contract agreeable for both parties.'

'Go on.' Sévère, rather surprised by the quick turn of events, hastily washed down his food with his wine. His fingers pinched the slender crystal stem, and slowly turned the glass, the chandelier light reflecting off it and throwing small rainbows across the skin of his hand.

'I agree that a marriage would be the most practical solution. But as your wife, I am your property and I can't possibly accept that.'

He grinned widely, and she hissed an irritated, 'What's so funny?' at him.

'Oh, Miss Mary, you cannot imagine how endearing you appeared just now, despite your violent tendencies. I flinch in horror every time I recall you flogging the living daylights out of me. You must know that I've met a number of young women who have wished nothing more than to be my property. The prospect bored me to death. Now, what do you suggest? Revolution? Funding all suffragettes in the country?'

'You may continue to make an ass of yourself, Sévère, but you will gain little with such behaviour. If you want this negotiation to proceed, you will learn to behave yourself.' She emptied her wine in three unladylike gulps and set the glass down with too much vigour. Lightheadedness crept in.

Gavriel Sévère produced a smirk that made her wish she could slap the arrogance off his face.

'You will draft a marriage contract which clearly states that I am free to go wherever I may choose, that I am not to be locked in your house or in any other property you own, that I am entitled to manage my own finances in a bank account which you will set up under my name, but which you cannot touch without my consent. That you own nothing of me. Should there be any children—'

He paled. 'Children? I told you this marriage will exist only on paper.'

She shook her head. 'You are a man. I am a woman. You may choose to take me against my will, and I could do little to prevent it. The law is on your side. Should a marriage contract, an assistant agreement, or any other written statement contain any mention of us agreeing to an unconsummated marriage, any marriage that we may have entered into is void, as would be this proposed assistant agreement.' She tapped at the paper before her.

'Why do I get the impression a law student is hidden in this dress of yours?'

'I am a business woman. I sell my body for profit, and I make sure my assets and services remain in the best possible shape, before, during, and after the business transaction.'

While she spoke, a blush spread from Sévère's throat to his ears and his cheeks. 'I've never heard a woman speak about these matters so…unabashedly.'

She shrugged. 'Should a shoeblack feel ashamed for scraping dog shit off his client's boots? Of course not. Why should he? He's an integral part of this society. Now tell me, why should I feel ashamed for cleaning cocks and dirty minds? Perhaps you believe that what I do is humiliating for a woman?'

She dipped her index finger against his sleeve. 'Now tell me this: if one person humiliates another, who is to bear the shame?'

'I see your point,' he answered.

'I am glad you are not one of those men who believe that little girls wake up one sunny morning and dream of making a living as a prostitute. I will tell you about one of my regular clients. He is a barrister and visits me quite frequently. He is in his sixties and one of the few friendly and humble men I've come to know in my profession. He is incapable of obtaining an erection. He can't perform, so instead, he watches me. I lie on my stomach, sometimes my skirts are bunched up around my waist; at other times I'm completely naked. My legs are spread. Wide. My left hand is tracing down the page of a statute book as I read it to him. My right hand is fingering my cunt. And then I switch hands. He's the happiest man when he leaves my rooms with his code of law reeking of my sex. One cannot read statute books on a regular basis without learning something.'

She leant back, still smiling, and knowing from Sévère's expression that his trousers must be somewhat constricting at the moment.

'This barrister will serve as my attorney and make sure our marriage contract is to my best advantage. No, you cannot meet him, and yes, I will pay him the way he wishes to be paid. To finish what I was saying before: should there be children, they will, independent of their sex, inherit equal parts of your money and property.'

Sévère slowly recovered. 'That barrister will get apoplectic when he reads the contract. But that's none of my concern. Your other conditions?'

'First, do tell me why you believe you won't be able to walk by the end of this year. As long as you whisper, no one but I will hear.'

Sévère took a sip of wine, collected his thoughts, and decided to take a plunge, despite a feeling of undressing himself emotionally before this woman. But the sheer number of words that had been spoken so freely that night made him care less about the danger of being pitied. He threw a sideways glance at Mary who, he told himself, didn't seem to have the faintest streak of pity in her.

'At the age of ten, I succumbed to infantile paralysis.

My left leg was completely paralysed, my right leg only slightly and only from the knee downward. I recovered after a few months and learnt to walk again. The symptoms completely disappeared with time. A year ago, my left leg began to weaken. A surgeon I trust told me that the paralysis is returning. The symptoms will worsen gradually. There will be days I won't be able to leave my bed. These days will become more frequent. Hence, I need an assistant with brains, and a talent to find and interrogate informants who would rather have remained anonymous, someone who can track down suspects when I can't leave my house. Someone who can run for me and use her brain while doing so. As I've said already, your services to me can be described as those of a private detective.'

She leant away from him, and looked him straight in his eyes. 'I've made it worse by beating you.'

His gaze softened. 'I wish I could say that. What a wonderful revenge that would be. But no, you did not. The weather has not been very kind to me these past months.'

'Is it life-threatening?'

'The death question again. Why are you so fascinated by impending death?'

'If you die before I've collected enough funds for an independent life, I've made the wrong decision. If there's a great chance of you dying in the ensuing two or three years, the contract must state that I'm entitled to a dower.'

Ah! No pity at all. He felt strangely refreshed and delighted by her response. 'The law entitles you to a dower no matter what. And my condition is not life-threatening, not to me, not as far as I know. People whose breathing was affected by infantile paralysis — those who survived the disease — do experience breathing difficulties when or if the paralysis returns. It seems the disease remembers where it hit the first time. As I've said, my left leg was affected and the right calf, not my ribcage.'

'I am sorry,' she whispered.

Displeased, he huffed and gazed up at the chandelier. 'Don't worry yourself. I had not expected you would be in favour of this...idea.'

'I didn't say I'm in *favour* of your proposition. It's a stupid plan you've brewed up. What I meant to say was that I am sorry I hit you. It was excessive. Ten strokes would have sufficed.'

His nostrils flared. 'Ten, you say? How disappointing. Ah! I see our dessert is approaching.'

They ate in silence. Every once in a while, Mary stopped chewing, pointed her spoon at Sévère, swallowed, and shook her head. After a few more moments of this, she finally said, 'The other two conditions will need a bit of explaining.'

He lowered his head, inviting her to continue.

'When I was little...' She stopped herself, frowned, collected her thoughts and began anew. 'Every afternoon I took my brother in the pram to the park just in front of my parent's house. My mother walked with me often, other times she watched from the house, or from the small front yard. I loved how my brother's little button nose stuck out of all the frills. In fact, this is all I remember of him...'

Mary put the spoon aside and drew circles with her fingertip on the tablecloth, trying to remember her family better. But her mind seemed unaccommodating. 'One day, a nice lady said hello as she walked past us. We'd never seen her before, but from that day forward, we saw her frequently. She introduced herself as Mrs Gretchen. She gave me little chocolates, sometimes an apple, a piece of candy. I liked her very much, and mother liked her, too. Then came the day father fell ill. A simple cold, I believe. Mother wasn't feeling well, either. She asked me to take my brother out for a quick stroll in the fresh air; he and I had been inside the house the whole day. It was a Sunday. I remember it because we didn't go to church that day, for mother and father were unwell. Mrs Gretchen said hello and I said hello, and… She offered a piece of candy and asked where my mother was. I told her I was alone… I should have lied.'

Mary picked up her spoon and scooped the last of what tasted like vanilla ice cream from the finely crafted porcelain bowl, let it melt on her tongue, and swallowed. 'Mrs Gretchen told me she could get medicine for my parents, but that I must come with her. "Why don't you leave the pram in front of your parent's house?" she said. "It will certainly take only a few moments; the baby won't even wake up before you return." She called a cab and helped me in. We went to a house and she told me to go up to a room and warm myself in the bed. She would fetch the medicine for my parents. And so I did. I was nervous, because I thought of my brother. Would the maid or the housekeeper find him quickly? I kept thinking that I shouldn't have left him there without notifying anyone. I kept thinking of his small nose turning red from the cold.'

She cleared her throat. 'Is there more wine in the bottle?'

Sévère refilled her glass and then his own.

With a hoarse voice, Mary continued. 'A man entered the room and locked it from the inside. I screamed, "There's a man in the room!" and he said, "Yes, of course there is."'

She looked up from the tablecloth. 'Mrs Gretchen delivered maidens when and where they were requested. She earned five to ten pounds for each maidenhead, depending on age and prettiness of the girl. Most of these girls never returned to their parents, either because they were kept prisoners, or because they believed themselves to be soiled goods, that no man would offer for them in marriage for they'd already seen a man. Mrs Gretchen made twenty pounds selling me to a rich man who had asked for a very pretty, very young girl. I was nine.'

Sévère opened his mouth to say something, anything, but Mary held up her hand. 'Over the years, I've learnt. I've learnt that a man can call the police if something has been stolen from him and taken into a stranger's house. The police will help him enter that house and retrieve whatever is his. Not so with abducted children. The madam only has to keep the door safely locked to defy the father. Why is that?'

Sévère replied in his typical, professionally detached tone, 'The father would have to obtain *habeas corpus*. The process is costly — thirty to fifty pounds sterling or more. Not everyone can afford it. Before the case would be heard, a week might pass, sometimes two. In that time, the girl will have been abused ten times over. By law, abduction is no offence unless the child is in the custody of the father at the time of her abduction. You spoke about a house, a front yard, and servants. Your parents must have had the funds necessary to obtain *habeas corpus*.'

Mary looked down at her dessert bowl and absent-mindedly stuck a finger into it, swirled it around, and put it into her mouth. 'They did not know where I was, I believe. And the police did not investigate what was not considered a crime. During my first three, four years as a prostitute, I changed owners several times. I learnt that the more knowledgeable a man is, the more power he wields. So I thought: why can't a woman? I could read and write well; my mother had taught me. So I read whatever I could put my hands on. Books were like a world far away from my own. But I also needed to educate myself about my own rights and opportunities. I learnt they were very limited.

'I calculated how long I'd have to stay, how much money I would need to buy my freedom.' She laughed at herself. 'But women are never free. Not entirely, anyway. Now, I need to work one more year at Madame Rousseau's or two to three years as your assistant, depending on the bonuses I might receive. The pay may be lower, but so is the risk of being slit open by a madman. I will accept your offer under three conditions. The first you heard already. The second is this: You must change the law. Enable parents to get their abducted children back at once.'

Sévère looked confused. He held up a hand. 'Are you aware that changing a law might take years?'

'I am.'

'Very well, then, I'll do my utmost.'

She huffed.

'You must understand that I'm in no position to *change* a law. I must convince the men who *can*. It's like winning a long and difficult trial. And I will do my utmost.'

She lowered her head in assent, inhaled deeply, and said, 'I will not quit my current situation before the contract is signed.'

'You will quit it at once. This is one of my conditions,' he growled.

'You can't make conditions. You are asking me for help. Besides, I would show poor judgement if I trusted you to provide for me before our contract is legally binding. Entering a business agreement without securities is bound to result in catastrophe.'

'How long?' he asked through his teeth.

'Approximately two weeks. You might wish to arrange for the parson and the witnesses while I consult my attorney.'

Sévère nodded once.

Mary tapped her fingers against her wine glass. 'How much do you pay your officer, Stripling?'

'One hundred and fifty pounds annually.'

'Well, in that case you'll pay me one hundred and eighty, because I'm more capable than he is. And I need to clarify one more thing. You touched upon the issue earlier, but it was not to my satisfaction. You will refrain from courting me, from treating me like your whore, from any attempts of bedding me. Use other prostitutes for that. From this day forward, you will refrain from calling me Miss Mary. My name is Maria Olivia Kovalchuk. I prefer Olivia.'

'That's the third condition?'

'Yes.' Then she shook her head. 'Why in God's name did you not offer this position to a man?'

'I have an assistant. Stripling. You've met him. There is also the occasional runner boy. Neither is suitable for what I need. Miss Mary… Olivia. My apologies. You seem to have no idea how unusually full and sharp your mind is, do you?'

'I do have an idea.'

A smile curved his lips. He waved at an imaginary dust mote and continued. 'I must warn you: we will clash frequently, I am certain. But once you have entered our agreement, signed the contract, and the marriage contract and papers, you are bound for three years. Although I would prefer a longer period, five years at the least. After the initial three years, we will file a divorce or renegotiate the terms of our agreement.'

'Acceptable,' she said and her brow crinkled. 'Won't you lose your position as a coroner?'

'Because of my leg? No, the office of coroner is an appointment for life. The Home Office can only replace me should I be struck by mental illness or commit a crime.'

'And you ascertained that Home Office will not interpret your marriage to a whore as either?'

'Indeed I did.' He gazed at her hand that lay flat on the

table. He looked at his own, then held it out to her. 'Do we have an agreement?'

'We will probably regret it,' she said.

'Most likely.'

She took his hand into hers and squeezed it.

'Agreed,' they said in unison.

## THE FOURTH CONDITION

*M*aria Olivia Kovalchuk pulled a case from beneath her bed, brushed the dust off its cracked leather surface, and packed her money, her papers, her undergarments, and two dresses — one simple, one fine. The lid refused to close, even when she sat on it. She pulled the dresses back out and looked around the room for something to wrap them in. Her gaze fell on the velvet curtains. One of those would do. She searched for her knife and remembered that Sévère had taken it when she'd been arrested.

She rubbed her brow and gazed out the window. The bells struck seven o'clock. Gas lamps spit yellow light into the fog. Dark silhouettes moved about, hunched against the evening chill. She turned and scanned her room, told herself not to grow sentimental, and made for the door.

Bobbie sat in his usual spot — the green armchair in the entrance hall — awaiting the clientele. He raised both eyebrows at her. 'Anything the matter?'

'No,' she said with innocence, entered the kitchen, and returned with a long knife in her hand.

'And what do you need *that* for?' Bobbie said, eyeing the weapon.

'You wouldn't want to know.'

'Um?' The large man was torn between arguing with her and snatching the knife from her hand directly, but Olivia was already half-way up the stairs before he could make up his mind.

She shut her door, and sliced a curtain clean off the rod.

When her things were packed and wrapped up, she poured wine into two glasses, and settled down on her bed.


HER CLIENT ASCENDED THE STAIRS, wheezing and heavy footfalls announcing his arrival. Olivia opened the door before he'd had time to knock.

'Good evening, William.'

He caught his breath, tipped his hat at her, and entered. Once the door was safely shut behind him, he mopped his brow, and said in a low voice. 'Olivia. Such a beautiful name.'

'Wine?' she asked, and he signalled assent.

She handed him his glass and retreated to lean against the wall, her own wine glass clasped between both hands.

He looked around her room as though he'd never seen it before. When his gaze got stuck at the sawed-off curtain, he grinned.

She scanned his face, took a sip of her wine, and approached him, reaching out to help him undress.

He patted her hand. A grandfatherly gesture. 'Come, sit with me. Let's talk business.'

She sat on the armchair opposite him. He shed his coat, disrespectfully threw it behind him, and extracted a folder from his briefcase.

'This one...' he tapped his knuckles against the thick paper. 'I've never seen its like, as I've already said. I'll probably say that every time we talk of this thing. There are several potential pitfalls — all stemming from the conditions you've set — which I couldn't entirely smooth out. The paragraph that regulates your own finances is more than three pages long, and I doubt anyone will understand it fully. But it's binding. Everything is. And your future employer has accepted all my edits and addenda without protest.'

He looked up at her, and shrugged. 'Not that I can be entirely certain, of course. The man might have wept, for all that I know, but his letters to my office hinted at no qualms on his side.'

William held up a threatening finger. 'I made sure he didn't modify either of the two copies before signing them. However, if that man ever tries to trick you or break your agreement, call me, and I'll turn him into pulp.'

'I doubt that will be necessary. May I?'

He handed the contracts to her. She opened the folder. Her head snapped up as she remembered something. 'Perhaps, I should do this on the bed?'

He blushed. 'Mary...I mean, Olivia. I'm here as your attorney, not as your client.'

'You can be both, if you wish.'

He shook his head. 'No, you have been very kind to me in the past... What has it been? Two, three years? I owe you this.' He nodded at the papers.

'I meant to pay you.'

'There is no need. You've made me feel young and appreciated. Or at least remember being so. This was more than you had to do.'

'You have always been appreciated, William,' she said. 'I've enjoyed your company.'

He laughed nervously. 'Come, now. Don't lie to me. It insults me.'

'You underestimate yourself. You were one of the few men who kindly asked before taking what he believed to be his. In fact, you never took anything by force or coercion. You are a very charming man. I would have preferred all my clients to be like you.'

He blushed, coughed, and muttered, 'Now, now.'

She dropped her gaze to the papers in her lap. Sévère's initials were at the bottom of every single page, except the very last one, where his sweeping signature and the seal of the Coroner of Eastern Middlesex decorated the paper. Both copies were identical. One was for him to keep, one was hers.

William handed her a fountain pen and witnessed her signatures. Her fingers trembled as she handed back his pen.

'Satisfied?' he asked.

'Yes. Very much. Thank you.'

He nodded, and his expression turned somber. 'There is something I must caution you against. You told me that one of your verbal agreements was that he never beds you and refrains from all attempts of doing so. All this might do well for a normal business agreement. The partners not bedding each other, that is.' He chuckled. 'But, my dear Olivia, much of your contract hinges upon you being married to Gavriel Sévère. Your husband might choose to annul the marriage due to non-consummation any time he wishes.'

'We can draft a statement on the successful consummation of the marriage. Both parties sign after the wedding night,' she said.

'Well...I've thought about that, too. You see, legislation is a piece of text on paper. Judges, attorneys, and lay people may interpret it any which way. If, as you say, you two fashion such a statement, and a time comes when you need to prove your marriage legal, then I, as an attorney, would wonder why you've made this statement in the first place. I would grow suspicious as to the nature of this marriage, and heavily doubt it was based on mutual attraction. I would likely arrive at the conclusion that the marriage is, indeed, not based on anything physical. And since the marriage was also clearly not to ensure a lineage, my verdict would likely be to the annulment of the marriage due to non-consummation.'

'Hum.' Olivia grabbed her wine glass and emptied it.

'Is the man so repulsive?'

'No. No, he isn't. Quite the opposite.'

'Why is the thought of bedding him so difficult for you? You've had many men.'

'I have indeed,' she answered. 'If I allowed him to bed

me, he might see this as an invitation to treat me as his property.'

'I doubt that. The man who doesn't see what a force you are must be blind. This was one of the reasons I asked politely every time I wanted something from you. You should seriously consider adding the consummation of your marriage to your list of conditions. A verbal agreement, of course. And then make sure the servants hear your moans.'

'You wicked attorney!'

His grin widened. 'I am well aware of my qualities.'

'I will consider it.'

'Now, I see that you have packed. Do you require the protection of a gentleman?'

'I might. But my escape should be rather unspectacular.'

'Should it?'

'I've blackmailed the madam.'

His reddened face glowed like a lantern. 'Please do tell me the dirty details.'

'Well...' She paused for effect, the corners of her mouth quirking.

William bent forward, eyebrows travelling higher and higher in excitement and expectation.

'I told her that I had proof she and Bobbie had unlawfully disposed of a body. And if she didn't let me go, I would pay a visit to Division H and they'd be locked up for two years at the least.'

'How lovely! Might this even be a case of murder, do you think?'

'No. The man died of a heart attack.' She flicked her gaze at the bed. 'Beneath me.'

William huffed, and leant back. 'What an epic end! I regret I'm unable to die like that man. Was he a good lover?'

'William, we can either attempt to make you die like this, or we leave now. It is getting late for fine ladies to be roaming the streets.'

'Ah, well, yes. Do you have a room?'

'I do. In a boarding house not far from here.'

With some difficulty, William pushed himself from the armchair. He pulled on his coat, and reached out to her. A card was pinched between index and middle finger. 'Call for me should your husband give you trouble.'

'You are too kind,' she said, pocketed his card, grabbed her case, her bonnet, and her wrapped-up dresses.

They descended the stairs. The madam was nowhere to be seen. Bobbie narrowed his eyes at the pair. She winked at him, and stepped through the brothel door.

They walked a few yards along New Road and onto Whitechapel Road, and hailed a cab. William held her hand to his lips and kissed her gloved knuckles. Before she climbed in, she tipped her head up at the sky, smiled, and inhaled deeply.

'It is done,' she whispered.

<hr>

'YOUR ATTORNEY SUGGESTED THIS? The one whose law books reek of cunt?'

'My cunt.'

'Olivia, you may do what you wish. If you believe the marriage needs to be consummated, we'll consummate it. I don't see a problem here, considering that I've had a multitude of women in my life, and you've had a multitude of men in yours. So why the bloody hell are you fidgeting?'

She cleared her throat, and looked Sévère square in the eyes. 'This is my fourth condition: I want a proper wedding night. I don't wish this to be a mere client-whore transaction. I want a night where the man gives his best to please his woman. I will not ask for this again, and it will be only this once we share a bed. It is…an experiment, perhaps. I want to know how it feels — the respect paid by a husband to his wife. Lie to me, Sévère, you excel at that.'

He swallowed. Perhaps, this was the first time he'd seen her clearly. Perhaps, he wondered, he might even know what she was talking about. He decided to steer into shallower waters. 'What if I get you with child?'

'Unlikely. I take precautions. Very few clients got me pregnant in the past seven years.'

'Very few? You have children?' He was aghast.

'Of course not. An abortion was performed. Three, to be precise.'

He frowned and looked down at his folded hands, his desk, his ashtray with the cigar that smouldered away peacefully. He thought of the women he'd had, many of them paid for their services — not because he was so unbecoming, but because he preferred bedding them without the complications of attraction. The young, naïve ladies of high social standing, whose parents sought a good match for them, and kept them in complete darkness as to human mating behaviour, those women bored him to death. Few knew how to kiss; they knew only how to peck with pursed, dry lips, as if the exchange of any kinds of liquids would spoil their so-called purity.

He groaned. Not once had he been asked to make an effort. The couplings he'd been involved in had been sweaty, noisy affairs that required little but stamina, the urge to mate, and a few coins.

Dammit! What was so complicated about asking a woman how she wished to be rogered?

Nothing. It was all in the technique.

Sévère looked up at Olivia and said, 'Agreed.'

# A PARTNERSHIP BEGINS

*S*évère stared down at his shiny patent leather boots, his sharply pressed trousers, his impeccably crisp cuffs. He flexed his fingers, commanding them to not compact into fists. As he did so, he followed a rather chaotic discussion of several different personae inside his head. So far he'd failed to exert the least degree of control over what was being said.

His internal ramblings proved to be extraordinarily ridiculous, and, if the situation hadn't been so serious, he'd probably have laughed at himself. Or perhaps he would have got drunk. But as neither humour nor drink were forthcoming, his mind went on and on:

I have never seen her naked. Not from the waist up. What if her breasts sag down to her navel as soon as she takes off her corset? She's had a hundred men. Or more? Oh God. Certainly more. What if she's all worn out? Don't be ridiculous! She's young. Besides, women can give birth to six, seven, eight children and still look like women. Somewhat. But what if... Surely, she will compare me to all the men she's had. How could she not?

Inside of Sévère's mind, carnage ruled. Men with over-large phalluses mounted his soon-to-be wife. She moaned and screamed with pleasure. Then he came limping along. And she laughed and laughed.

He shook his head and squeezed his eyes shut for a moment. His gaze strayed down along the aisle. Again.

The aisle was empty.

Still.

He pulled at a gold chain and the watch slipped out of his waistcoat pocket, and dangled back and forth. Back and forth. It felt heavier than usual. He flicked his wrist and caught the small instrument. He opened it. Eleven o'clock. Sharp. She should be here now. They had agreed on eleven o'clock, hadn't they?

The aisle was still empty.

Why was she not here?

She'd had second thoughts. Yes, that must be it. She must have lied to him when she'd insisted on buying her wedding dress with her own money. She'd outright refused his pleas to let him pay for the gown. Why would a woman do that to her future husband if not to demean him or to lie to him? She must have planned her escape days ago. No woman in her right mind would wish to part with her meagre funds just to...

No. Her funds must have been sufficient. When they'd visited the bank the previous day, and he retreated a few steps to give her privacy to deposit her money, the accountant had thrown him a nervous glance as if to say, 'All this?'

This made no sense whatsoever.

He snapped his watch shut, dropped it back into his waistcoat pocket and turned to the witnesses. They didn't seem to share his worries. His assistant and his housekeeper stood there quite relaxed, waiting. The one rocking on his heels, the other with her hands folded behind her back. Both smiled pleasantly, perhaps stupidly. The priest smoothed nonexistent hair over his skull. Behind him, a fly buzzed around Jesus's crotch.

This is ridiculous.

His hand hurt. Which one. Ah, the left. He looked down at it and was surprised to find something pale, claw-like. He could barely loosen his grip around the head of his cane. That was when he realised he was about to panic.

He cleared his throat. Why the panic? Because it's my wedding, dammit. Why did I even... Ah, it was my own stupid idea. My own. No one to blame but myself.

A creak yanked him from his thoughts. He looked up and saw Mary, no, *Olivia*, stepping through the large double-winged door. The first thing he noticed was that she was alone. He had two witnesses, a priest, and even Jesus protecting his back. Not that he needed protection. But she walked alone, and that wasn't right. There should have been her father there, leading her to the groom.

Get a grip on yourself, man! This is not a happily-ever-after wedding.

And yet.

Seeing her walk alone made him feel uncomfortable.

The second thing he noticed was that, despite her solitude, she held her head high and her back straight. A queen walking to her own beheading.

*How do I bed a prostitute without giving her the feeling she's doing her duty?*

He almost laughed. Wives were supposed to fulfil their duties to their husbands. Whores were supposed to fulfil their duties to their clients.

*Where was the difference?*

*What a twisted situation.*

The third thing he noticed was that, today, she shone. An otherworldly creature. Her gown was made of white silk with white beads or pearls forming delicate patterns. Sunlight and dew on a butterfly cocoon. Her hair was elaborately braided and pinned, white pearls on black hair. Her gaze was directed at the altar, not straying left or right. He didn't even know if, to her, he existed. All of a sudden, he felt old. Old and incapable.

*What was I thinking, offering her this? Ha! Offer! I blackmailed her into it. Marry me, or die a whore.*

He blinked, and told himself to stop it already.

She came to a halt next to him, still looking straight ahead, and wrapped her gloved fingers around his elbow. He'd forgotten to offer it to her, so now he jutted it out a little too much to compensate for his previous lack of attention.

She tugged at his arm, and he bent toward her.

'You are nervous,' she whispered into his ear. 'It was your idea. However, you may run if you wish. I promise, I won't weep.'

He pressed his lips together and cleared his throat. It was all he could do to muffle the snort that was threatening to rip through his nervousness. He sucked in air, exhaled it, and smiled at her. 'Thank you, my dear. Should we run together?'

'A very romantic offer,' she whispered into his ear. 'But this is a business transaction. Treat it as such.'

'I should have courted you.'

'What for?' she asked, puzzled.

The priest announced the beginning of said business transaction with a pointed, 'Erhem!' then rattled down his speech. Sévère didn't hear much of it. It must have been what the man usually said on such occasions. At some point, Sévère said his vows and Olivia said hers.

Then, everyone looked at him expectantly. He wondered what they wanted from him.

Stripling wiggled his fingers.

The ring! Where was the bloody ring?

Ah! In his waistcoat pocket. He pulled it out and almost dropped it, then attempted to slip it onto her gloved finger. He cleared his throat yet again, and pulled off her glove, finger by finger.

A flicker of sunlight caught on the golden band.

Sévère inhaled, exhaled, grew calmer. Sign the papers, he told himself. Don't forget to sign the goddamn papers.

The priest said something and when Sévère didn't react, the stout man repeated, a little louder this time, 'You may now kiss your wife.'

Sévère knew he'd forgotten something essential. He looked down at Olivia and Olivia looked up at him. She took a step forward, rose on her toes, and pecked him on the cheek.

Pecked him!

'I'll be damned,' he murmured, and grabbed her waist with his right hand — he didn't dare let go of his cane, else his body might fail him entirely — and yanked her against his chest. The position forced her to tip her head upward.

There might have been coldness in her eyes, something that told him that she was used to being taken, that she couldn't care less.

As if.

Well, then, he thought. Here I come.

He softened his grip and ran his hand up along the silk which so deliciously hugged her body, trailed his fingers up to her neck, and rested his palm against her face, drawing circles on her temples with his thumb until her eyelids fluttered a little. He leant in and softly kissed her forehead, her nose, and the corner of her mouth.

He felt her stiffen under his ministrations, so he whispered against her lips, 'Later, perhaps?'

And that was when she stepped on his toes, grabbed his cravat, and parted his lips with hers in a no-nonsense kiss.

'Erhem!' the priest said again and Olivia let go of Sévère and answered, 'Erhem.' Sévère couldn't not say 'Erhem!' now, and so he did.

The priest's throat reddened over his whatever-this-collar-was-called-again, they signed the papers, and walked down the aisle together.

Sévère's new brougham awaited them.

'Are your shoes comfortable?' he asked Olivia.

'Quite.'

He shrugged off his coat and dropped it over her

shoulders, tucked her hand tighter into the bend of his elbow, turned on his heel, and marched her away from the four-wheeler, away from church and witnesses and priest. 'I've had enough of this circus. Let us have pastries and coffee. And perhaps a brandy.'

'Are you abducting the bride?'

'Precisely.'

---

'Allow me,' he said.

She dropped her hands and straightened her back. In the vanity, her eyes were watching him. 'You are nervous,' she said. 'Still. But why? Neither of us is a virgin.'

'I've never done this before. Tell me if I hurt you.' His fingers gingerly extracted the first pin from her hair. A strand was caught in the small metal loop and he struggled to remove it without causing her pain.

'Only ninety-nine left.' Her voice wobbled. A twitchy smile slipped off her mouth.

'You are nervous,' he copied her. 'Why? Neither of us is a virgin.'

'I've never been nervous. Before.'

'Neither have I.'

'I've never been married,' she said.

'Perhaps that's it? Neither of us has ever been married, let alone to each other. We are justified in being nervous together.' He managed to extract a second pin.

'It's growing dark outside,' she said.

'Are you in a hurry?'

She inhaled as deeply as her stays would allow. 'I want to know how it ends.'

'Do you read books like that, too? From back to front?'

She shook her head, pulling a pin from between his fingers.

'Did you always know how it would end when you received a client?' he asked.

'I usually did, yes.'

'I am not your client.'

Fifth pin! He almost blurted out his triumph. Were there really a whole of ninety-five left?

He began to count but stopped when she said, 'You are my employer.'

'It was you who asked to be bedded, not I.'

'True. Maybe that's why I'm nervous. I've never asked for this before. I don't know what to expect. Let me do this.' She raised her hands and impatiently picked one pin after the other, not caring about pain and ripped-out hair.

He watched until he couldn't take it any longer. 'Olivia, stop!' He covered her hands with his, pried her stubborn fingers off, and continued pulling her hairpins. One by one. 'Lean back,' he said softly.

She sank against the backrest.

He felt her eyes on him and wondered how he appeared to her with his clumsy fingers that would surely need another hour or so to free her hair of pins and needles. His age. His odd gait. Did they bother her?

He wondered if a man had ever served her this way — undoing her hair without making demands. His eyes strayed to her slender neck, her shoulders, the delicate sweep of her clavicles pressing against her dress.

He looked up at her reflection in the glass and saw that her gaze had softened.

'I am nervous,' he said quietly. 'Because you are young, and I am older. Because you are healthy and strong, and I am weakening. Because your social status is so much lower than mine. You've been coerced into taking my offer if you want anything better in life than what you've had. This should make me bold, but I am not. I'm afraid of breaking you, although you are the one who's laid hands on me. I've fancied myself experienced. Until now. I've fancied myself a man who could easily show any woman the pleasures of the marriage bed. "Look, this is how you do it. And here is how you touch me and this is how I touch you. You like it, don't you."'

He smiled a bitter smile. 'I know precisely what to do with a woman whom I've paid to give me pleasure. I might even know what to do with a woman who knows little of such matters. But I am at a loss for what to do with a woman who knows too much, and asks me to please her.'

'I intimidate you?'

'It's odd, isn't it.'

She nodded, and looked down at her hands. 'One hundred strokes,' she whispered.

'Excuse me?'

'One hundred strokes.' She held out the brush to him.

'Shouldn't I unbraid it first?'

Her hand sank back to her lap. 'Yes.'

His fingers wove through her braids and undid them. One by one. Her heavy hair spilt onto her shoulders, the straight black now in waves. He thought of a raven's wing ruffled by the wind.

He began to brush her hair, combing with his fingers, then running the bristles through the strands. 'Is this how you make it so beautiful? With one hundred strokes?'

'Yes. Twice a day.' Her voice was low, the timbre of it drew his eyes to her reflection. He felt a pull inside his chest, and the wish to lay his lips on hers.

'What is it?' she asked.

'I need to sit for a moment,' he lied. He felt surprisingly bad about the lie. But wasn't he supposed to lie tonight? She'd asked that of him. Didn't he lie with ease? Usually?

She rose and took his hand, led him to the bed and sat him down. Without a word, she slipped off his shoes and pushed them beneath the bed.

'Olivia,' he said hoarsely. 'Are you certain you want this? We can simply sign a paper that states we consummated the marriage.'

'As long as you are certain you can lie well, I am certain I want this to happen. Can you, Sévère? Lie well?'

'Have I ever treated you without respect?'

'Yes, at the beginning you did. But that does not matter now. What I'm asking of you is to pretend you love me. I ask you to make love to me as a husband does to his beloved wife on their first night together.'

'You owe me your honesty, Olivia.'

'If I lied to you, I wouldn't be so complicated.'

Frowning, he dipped his head.

'You have my honesty, Sévère.'

He gazed down at her slender fingers that rested on

his knees. 'Then I will make love to you as a husband does to his beloved wife on their first night together.'

She reached out to unbutton his waistcoat. He caught her hands and said, 'There are only three buttons on my garments, but hundreds on yours. Allow me to undo yours first.'

'Hooks,' she replied, as she sat on the bed, offering her back to him. 'Forty-five, I believe.'

He began to slip small metal hooks through small metal eyelets and peeled the gown off her shoulders, arms, waist. Silk pooled around her hips.

'And lace,' she whispered. 'And twenty-two eyelets. Whale bone. Silk. The word silk needs to be spoken softly, a brush of warm breath against skin, don't you think?'

'Hmmm. Lace needs to be whispered, too.' His hands trailed over her back and pulled at the narrow silk ribbon, loosening it at every eyelet. He watched her inhale deeply, and wondered how she'd been able to breathe in this constricting garment.

She stood and her gown fell to the floor as she peeled off her stays. Her breasts sprung free. Only the faintest sheen of silk covered them, her stomach, the dip of her navel and the swell of her hips. The black triangle between her legs.

She stepped out of her wedding gown, dropped her stays onto the floor, and put her foot up on the bed.

'Thigh, too, needs to be spoken softly.' He unclipped the garter, slipped a finger beneath the silk and pushed down the stocking. How can there be enough silk in this world to clothe all the beautiful women?

She offered the other leg and he repeated the procedure, leant closer, brought his lips against her skin, and whispered silk and lace and thigh. He smiled and told her that she was right, these words needed to be sent softly across skin. Her skin.

She raked her fingers through his hair and gently pulled him back. 'May I?' she asked and touched his waistcoat.

He signalled *yes* and so she slipped silver buttons through silk buttonholes. 'Four buttons,' she said, pushed the garment off his shoulders, and flung it aside. It flew through the room and landed next to a chair.

'You need target practice, dear.'

A smile flickered past her lips as she touched his shirt. 'Twelve buttons. Plus two at each sleeve.'

When he lifted his hands to untie his cravat, she pulled them away.

She took her time with shirt, cravat, and collar — starched, fine cotton, supple silk. She lay his skin bare until only the glow of the fire clothed his chest. The cold air drew his nipples to hard nubs. She licked her finger and touched one, then the other.

'I wonder…' she said and ran her fingers along his crotch. 'Ah, four buttons. I guessed as much.'

He huffed.

She unbuttoned his trousers. He lifted himself off the mattress, and she pulled them down his legs. His drawers were slipped off, too. His socks and sock garters.

His breath stopped when she placed her hands on his bare thighs. Worried she might be repelled by the appearance of his weaker left leg, he followed her gaze. Right thigh, left thigh.

Did she compare them? Surely she must?

Her hands travelled up, brushing past the nest of dark blond curls. Up her fingers went, up his stomach, his chest. The line of hair on his breastbone. Up to his collarbones, his throat, jaw, the side of his head. She buried her hands in his hair.

'I want to kiss you,' she said and he remembered to breathe. His lungs ached when she bent closer and stopped a mere inch before his face. He felt her warm breath on him, smelled coffee, brandy, pastries, and the sweet scents of her hair and skin.

He leant closer, halted a hairbreadth short of her mouth. Her lids were lowered, pupils wide open. He smiled and touched his lips to hers. As she opened herself to his imploring tongue he felt an urge to fall into her and lose himself.

Then he remembered that she was a prostitute. He drew back and looked at her, wishing he could dissect her reactions to him, her heart, her mind, so as to know and be certain that she was sincere.

'What is it?' she asked.

'It's chilly. The fire is dying. I'll put more coals onto it.'

She scooted back and lifted a blanket. 'This wonderful item has been invented to keep out the cold. Come. I'm warm enough for both of us.'

He hesitated for a moment, then slipped under the offered blanket, careful to leave a gap between himself and her.

She bent to the nightstand and blew out the candles. Then she tapped her fingertips onto his left leg and asked, 'Are you comfortable?'

'Yes, thank you, I am quite comfortable. As you will have noticed when I led you down the aisle and abducted you only moments later, I'm far from being disabled. But I think I might be growing blind. It's rather dark. Why did you blow out the candles? Am I not handsome enough?'

She hesitated. 'You are handsome. But I don't want you to see me.'

'Why?'

'I don't trust my face, my expression. I don't know what to do with it now that...'

'Now that you don't have to pretend you are the bawdiest little thing in London? Ouch! Why did you punch me?'

'You once said you fancied my ruthlessness, so...'

They both fell quiet.

Could it be? he wondered. Is it possible that she doesn't know what to do with herself, here in her own bed with him in it?

The silence seemed to wedge itself in, forming a wall between them.

'You don't know what to do with yourself,' he ventured.

'Yes. I mean, no. How would I know what women do on their wedding night?'

She sounded sincere, and yet, he found it hard to believe that a prostitute... He told himself to stop seeing her as a prostitute. He hadn't paid her for this. She wanted this, for whatever reason.

Doubt nagged at him.

'Well, how would *I* know?' he said. 'Would you do it

like all other women do it? Do you think they do it all in the same fashion?'

'I'm sure that whatever they do, it's proper.'

'And certainly very un-outrageous.'

'Why do people even get married?' she asked half-heartedly.

He decided to push all doubt aside. He would deal with it tomorrow morning. 'I don't care about other people's reasons for marrying. May I touch you, Olivia?'

'Yes, Gavriel.'

He was shocked by how softly his name rolled off her tongue, slipped past her lips. He wished to hear her say it again. Often. His fingertips found her throat, slid up along her jawline and into her hair. Sighing, he bent closer, inhaled the scents of rose and lavender and soap and Olivia.

'The other reason for the darkness is that…'

'Hm?' he hummed into her hair.

'I don't want to see you. No, shhh. Don't speak now. When I find arousal in your face, I'm afraid you'll look like a client.'

Sévère froze at her words. *This* was most certainly honesty he'd heard. And it scared him. He pushed himself up and reached across her to the night stand. A rustling, a match was struck, light flared.

'You will see me and I will see you. Arousal and all,' he said.

'I can't do it like this.'

'Then you don't. It's your wedding night. You do as you please.'

'It's your wedding night, too,' she reminded him.

'It was your condition, not mine. I never asked you to share my bed.'

'You did.'

'Ah. Yes. I did.' Lines formed between his eyebrows.

'I know which games a client wishes to play the moment he enters my room. When I look into his eyes, I know at once why he came, what he needs, and if he plans to hurt me. And then I adapt. A simple reflex. To tell me to refrain from doing so, is as if I tell you not to blink when I poke you in the eye. Prostitutes who never acquire this reflex are the ones who find themselves at the bottom of the Thames, sooner or later.'

'What do you see in my face?' he asked.

'I can't tell you.'

'You don't know?'

'I do know,' she replied. 'But it scares me. *You* scare me. You...look at me. I can't describe it any better. *You look at me.* Me. As though you want to know what's going on behind my eyes. You are very good at this, Sévère. At creating the illusion you care about me. You look at me, and you refrain from rubbing yourself on me, from grabbing my legs and spreading them to push yourself in. I find that disturbing. It is as though, tonight, not your arousal comes first, but mine. Not your pleasure, but mine. As an experienced whore I wonder what's wrong with you, are you incapable? Which game could it possibly be that you're playing? But I'm not a whore tonight and I'm at a loss as to what role I'm to play.'

A tear rolled off her cheek, and she stared down at the darkened spot where the teardrop had surrendered to the sheet, wondering why the bloody hell she was weeping.

Shocked, he placed his fingertip onto the small, wet spot. He swallowed, and tried to collect himself. He tried to think like an attorney at court whose every word counted.

'That is the point,' he said softly. 'You're not playing a role tonight. If I douse the candle, I will not know whether or not you enjoy me. When I do this…' He brushed a strand of her hair from her face. '…your lids quiver and sink a little lower, but your shoulders tense. What does it mean? I don't know. It's as if two Olivias are here with me. If I douse the candle, how could I tell the two apart?'

'Which one of the two do you want?' There was mischief in her eyes, as though she was testing him.

'The one who doesn't believe she has to serve me. The one who punched my ribs a moment ago.' He smiled at her and poked her stomach. 'Is she here?'

'She is. She never appears when a client is around. The other one is there, too. She's a seasoned warrior and an excellent liar. You won't get rid of her. You'll have to get used to both.'

'Hum. May I ask the seasoned warrior to watch over the other, while I touch you?'

'You may,' Olivia whispered, leant toward him, and smiled against the silky hollow where his neck touched his collar bone.

'I might ask a lot of questions,' he murmured. 'But I don't want you to think I'm interrogating you.'

'What questions?'

'May I touch you here, Olivia?' he whispered and curled his hand around her neck.

'Yes.'

'And here? May I touch you here?' His other hand ran down along her side to rest against her hip. A shiver spread from there all across her back. It warmed his palms and begged him to proceed.

'You may,' she said, and reached out to him. 'If you stop interrogating me.'

'Let me learn you,' he whispered and took her hand into his, kissed it, and placed it between the two of them.

'This?' he asked again when he touched her face, her throat, her chest. 'And this?'

She closed her eyes as he caressed her breasts. 'Kiss me there,' she said hoarsely.

He bent his head and closed his lips around her nipple, ran his tongue across it. Her flesh pulled into a tight bud, goose bumps raced over her skin. He drew small circles with his tongue until she writhed and giggled beneath him, then traced kisses down to her navel until she tensed.

He pushed himself up to lie next to her. His palm rested on her stomach.

She turned toward him. 'May I touch you now?'

'If you wish.'

Her warm caress was a shock of pleasure to his body.

She closed her eyes, her lips quirked, and she learnt his contours in her chosen blindness. Fingertips felt along the ridges of his abdomen, the sharpness of his hipbone, the slight trembling in his left leg, the soft fuzz that covered his skin there.

He held his breath.

Up her hands went, up along the inside of his thigh,

skirting his bollocks and his cock. She touched his chest, raked her fingers through the hair that covered his breast-bone, and flicked his nipples. He drew in a sharp breath. She leant in and kissed him where her nails had abused the sensitive flesh. Her hands ran around his ribcage, down his spine and found his buttocks. She drove her nails into the soft flesh until he hissed.

She opened her eyes and said, 'Turn on your stomach.'

'Not again,' he huffed, half smiling.

She frowned at him and rolled him over. He allowed her hands to guide him. Her long hair tickled his skin as she bent over him and covered his backside with kisses.

He shut his eyes and revelled in her touch, moaned his delight and suddenly remembered that his role tonight was that of a liar. He wasn't entirely sure where his lies began and where truth ended.

'You are torturing me,' he said gruffly.

'Oh! You want me to stop?'

He pressed his face into the pillow and grumbled, 'I don't want you to stop. Never stop. But, please, allow me to hold you for a moment.' He turned over and abruptly caught her, held her to him, his face in her hair, his breath heavy. He hoped his embrace did not feel like a prison cell.

'May I kiss you here?' he asked and touched her lips with his fingertips.

'Be gentle,' she said, and he answered, 'I am,' and bent to lay his lips onto hers.

'There is a war,' she whispered into his mouth, 'inside me. The old and the new. Expected and unexpected.' She bit his lower lip gently, and he moaned against her tongue.

'I am hungry, trembling here,' she continued, and led his hand to the juncture of her thighs.

His palm soothed her soft skin, his fingers teased her sex.

She sighed, tilted her hips toward him, and said, 'If you were to bed a murderess, would you think of evidence, victims, postmortems, and inquests, or would you give yourself to her without a second thought?'

'Why would I...'

She touched his erection. 'When I've touched a man, I've done so only as a prostitute. My mind has always been at work. When you are at court, are you able to put aside your professionalism?'

'Hardly. I see what you mean. What do you suggest we do now?'

She smiled against his mouth. 'Try to fit the expected and unexpected together. Perhaps...'

'Perhaps...' he interrupted, pushed himself down along her body, and blew against her thighs. '...We might try something else?'

He parted her legs. 'Expected, I assume?'

A wry smile.

He turned his attention to her feet, caressed them, then her ankles, knees, and thighs. He brought his lips to her skin, kissing up along the inside of her thighs and flicking his tongue across her vulva.

'Eeh!' she squealed, jerked away, and laughed.

'Did no one ever kiss you there?'

'No. Yes.' She laughed again. 'My cunt has been licked,

kissed, ravaged. But with you...here... I find my own reactions, those of body and mind, puzzling.'

'Unexpected,' he said with a smirk and brought his mouth down on her.

She grabbed his hair and wrung his neck with her thighs. He growled her name against her flesh.

'Stop!' she cried, and yanked his hair so hard his skull was on fire.

'Am I too heavy? I didn't bite! Or maybe I did?' he asked, confused.

'No, no. I'm...I...' She hid her face in the crook of her arm, then threw up her hands in frustration. 'Give me something expected, else I think I might fall.'

A satisfied grin spread across his face. He scooted up and kissed her mouth. 'I want you to fall, my dear. A sharp drop, and then you'll fly.'

Gently, he sank two fingers into her sex and rested the heel of his palm against the small and deliciously swollen button just below her pubic bone. Then he began a slow and steady rhythm.

He watched the blush rise to her cheeks, the flutter of heavy eyelids, the heaving of her chest, and how she tried to hide her face in the pillow. The movement made her back arch more, and brought her harder against him. She bucked and he felt her wetness soaking his hand, the heat she emanated.

The candlelight reflected off the small droplets of perspiration on her stomach, just below her navel. He bent to kiss her there.

She shivered and cried out, 'No! I need you closer. Cover me. Hold me.'

And he gathered her in his arm, the other still stroking her sex. 'I can't,' she whispered. 'Not like this. Not yet.'

'Next time, then?' he asked.

'No. It's complicated. Not yet. I want to touch you.'

'Touch me, Olivia. Touch me wherever you wish.'

She arched into him and curled her arm around his neck. She pulled him into a deep kiss, a mating of tongues and lips, a collision of teeth. She straddled him, received him with a growl.

They froze.

She huffed a deep breath, clung to him, and pulled him deep inside her. 'Hold me!'

'I'm holding you.'

'Kiss me.'

'I'm…kissing…you,' he whispered between kisses.

When she began to rise and fall, he felt every fibre of her body, the rolling of her muscles, her hands in his hair. The slide of skin against skin. The small, wet noises. Her ragged breath and his own. A trembling that began in her shoulders, travelled down along her sides, the small of her back, and over her buttocks and thighs.

He felt the tell-tale burning in his cock, and tried to direct his thoughts to a case. Whichever case.

He couldn't think of one, couldn't even find a name, date, location. He pushed himself up and held her to him.

'Olivia, you have to stop for a moment, else I'll…'

'Shhhh,' she breathed into his ear.

'Olivia?'

'Hm?'

He took her face into his hands. 'I look at you.'

'You do.' She smiled. 'Unexpected.'

He kissed her mouth and softly bit her lower lip. 'You think too poorly of me.' With that, he sank back onto the mattress and pulled her with him.

Sprawled atop of him, her hair was a curtain of thick black silk, shielding their faces from the soft light. Only the glint of his eyes was visible to her.

'You can't see me.' She began to move against him.

'I can see you with my hands,' he replied, and learnt the curves of her hips, the ripple of her spine, the soft down at the nape of her neck.

He pushed back her hair, gathered it, and wrapped it around his wrist.

His eyes held hers as they exhaled with every slow thrust. He sensed how she opened up to him — not only her sex, which already accommodated him, but all of her. Her expression that turned from slightly shut and perhaps a bit bashful, to softening, and then, to open-mouthed and low-lidded, to surprise, and finally into something that looked like fury.

'Faster!' she cried. He bucked and she gripped the bed frame so as not to be thrown off.

He was mesmerised by her letting go so freely, by the clenching of her muscles around his cock. By the force with which she rode him. He couldn't hold on to his own control any longer when she sank onto his chest, shuddering. He grabbed her hips and drove into her with abandon, felt fire rushing down his spine and into his balls. He cried her name, trembled, and took her face into his and kissed her hungrily, whispering against her lips that she was beautiful.

# THE MORNING AFTER

*S*évère sipped at his tea and unfolded the morning papers. Netty slunk through the door, carrying a tray with fresh muffins, butter, jam, eggs, and cream. She cleared her throat. 'Sir?'

He looked up from his reading. 'What is it, Netty? Are you all right? You seem…upset.' He'd almost said that she appeared dangerously close to explosion.

She cleared her throat again. 'Sir. I…We…'

'Is it the new maid?'

'No it's…it's…' More throat clearing.

'Spit it out, Netty. I don't have the entire morning to decipher your mutterings.' He emptied his cup.

'The Misses left at dawn. She had a large bag with her.'

The tea spurted from Sévère's mouth onto his empty plate. 'What?'

'She… Mrs Sévère—'

'What did she say when she left?'

'She said she'll return before breakfast is served.'

Sévère's gaze swung to the place opposite him. A plate, cutlery, a cup on a saucer, a napkin. No Olivia. He pulled himself together. 'She is a grown woman,' he said, and waved Netty away.

As soon as the housekeeper had shut the door, Sévère let out a long breath. Could Olivia have had enough of him already? Had she had second thoughts that he'd been too blind to see? Had he hurt her in some way?

She'd sent him away before daybreak. To attend to women's business. That's what she'd said. Too proud to protest, he'd only nodded. But she'd seen his hesitation.

'If I don't wash your seed out of me, I risk being with child,' she'd explained.

Perfectly reasonable. He'd thanked her for her honesty.

Should he have said something else? Something more? What was it one normally said to a woman after a wedding night?

'Thank you for lying,' she'd whispered as he took his leave. 'You were very convincing.'

That wasn't necessarily what one said to a man after a wedding night.

He'd made an effort to please her. A novelty to him, and, as it seemed, to her, too. He'd... Had he lied?

Abruptly, the door was pushed open.

'Olivia!' he barked.

Her expression darkened. She took a step back, held her hand out through the door, and pulled a scrawny something into the room. Sévère wasn't quite sure if it was a boy or a girl beneath the layers of grime. His eyebrows rose.

'I've abducted my maid,' Olivia said. 'Sévère, may I introduce Rose to you? Rose, this is Mr Sévère, the master of the house.'

The girl put a sweet smile on her face — a flash of white teeth amidst black soot. She swiftly walked up to him and pushed herself onto his lap, her face tilted upwards to meet his gaze. 'Hello, Mr Sévère. How do you do?'

'Rose!' Olivia cried. 'We've talked about this. Come back here.'

The girl pecked his cheek, hopped off his lap, and strolled back to Olivia.

Flabbergasted, and unable to utter a word of rebuke, Sévère picked up a napkin and rubbed the soot off his face and trousers.

'Go down to the scullery. Ask one of the maids to show you to my room *after* they've thoroughly bathed you and checked your head for lice.'

'Yes, Mary!' Rose squeaked. 'I mean, Yes, Sir, Olivia, Sir!' And she darted out the door and down the stairs.

Olivia toed the bag into the room and shut the door.

'Dare I ask what this is all about?' Sévère said, slowly recovering his composure. 'You've abducted a child. You've broken our contract on the very first day. I am amazed, to put it mildly.'

'I did not break the law. Hence, I did not break our contract. The girl was not in the custody of her father when I took her. In fact, it would be an extraordinary feat to identify her father, let alone to locate him.' Olivia sat down opposite Sévère and poured herself a cup of tea. 'Tea?'

He blinked. She took this as a yes, and rose to fill his cup.

'I am sorry I presented her to you all covered in soot. She'd been assisting the chimney sweep before I took her. She's usually clean and neat. And she's eight,' Olivia said when she'd seated herself. Her expression was forbidding.

'She can't be your maid.'

'It's in our contract. Do you want me to show it to you?' A sharp glittering in her eyes. Ready for battle.

'She can't be your maid. She needs to attend school.' Sévère calmly spread butter on his muffin. 'But she may attend to you in the early mornings and afternoons as long as it doesn't interfere with her education.'

A *clonk* drew his gaze away from his breakfast. He saw his wife swiftly bend down to pick her butter knife off the floor.

'There are no day schools for girls, except if you count the ones in the workhouses,' she replied once she'd taken control of her expression. 'And those aren't safe. There's only one alternative: I will teach her to read and to write.'

'Which would break our contract, which clearly states that you work for me and I employ a lady's maid for you. Neither of you two will have time for what you are supposed to do.'

Olivia picked at a muffin and stuffed a crumb into her mouth. 'I don't need another maid. I don't need to be serviced around the clock. She can help me with my dresses in the mornings and evenings, and I'll find a tutor for her. I will, of course, cover the costs. Would you pass the honey, please?'

'Very well. You will receive her allowance and decide

what to do with it, how much of it is to be given to her directly, and how much is to be spend on her education and clothing.'

Olivia coughed and lowered her gaze. 'Gavriel,' she said softly. 'Thank you for your kind offer. But I will use my own money for her tuition, clothing, and food.'

'You may do with your funds what you wish, but the allowance of the lady's maid will be given to you, whoever said maid might be. What did this mean, anyway? Why the blazes did she hop on my lap?'

'Her mother has taught her from an early age on, to be forthcoming with gentlemen.'

He paled. 'Her mother?'

'The madam.'

Sévère, who was about to decapitate his breakfast egg, smashed it. 'I hope this swine didn't force the girl to take a client!'

'She was planning to wait another year or two.'

He grunted in disgust. 'Teach this girl some manners. She can't take a tutor if she behaves like this. I don't even want to think about it.'

'Wouldn't *that* be entertaining?'

'No, it certainly wouldn't.'

'Would you pass the butter? Thank you. Now, do tell me whom I may chase down for you today.'

'It is Sunday. You may chase a church pew, if you wish.'

Olivia snorted. 'Tell me about the cases you are working on.'

'Nothing too exciting at the moment. Elizabeth Parker allegedly murdered her five month-old daughter, Rosina Alice Parker. The inquest will be held on Tuesday. The case is as clear as bright daylight. The woman will be charged with murder or manslaughter. The Temple case is quite an interesting one. Catherine Temple is accused of feloniously killing Annie Holloway.'

Sévère washed down his muffin and smacked his lips. 'You wouldn't believe it: Catherine Temple and Annie Holloway were both drunk and had a brawl. Frail Catherine hit sturdy Annie over the head. A little too often, as it turns out.'

'The fair sex,' Olivia mumbled.

'Indeed.

'And then there's the Burns case. I want you to work on it. Patrick Burns was indicted for the manslaughter of Mary Ann Hennessey. Evidence points to him having struck her behind the ear, which resulted in a haemorrhage of her brain. She died soon thereafter.'

Olivia cracked her egg and sunk her spoon into the soft yolk.

'I will give you the respective files tomorrow morning, before you take the train to Redhill. I expect it to be a short trip. There should be plenty of time to take a detour over Sevenoaks on your way back.' He opened the papers and continued to read where he'd left off.

'Isn't the case out of your hands now? Hunt has been committed to trial at the Old Bailey,' Olivia said.

Sévère dipped his head, and frowned.

'What is it?'

'My instincts tell me that Hunt is lying,' he said.

A soft knock interrupted their conversation. One of the maidservants — what was her name? — stepped into the room. 'You've received a message, sir, ma'am.' She held out a small silver tray; Sévère picked the letter from it. The girl curtsied and left.

'My face hurts from all this...' Olivia waved her hand at the door. '...stiff etiquette.'

'You'll get used to it,' Sévère answered, and slit open the letter. A calling card fell out onto his palm. 'I hope you'll get used to it within the next few days. News of our marriage has spread. Lady Anne and Sir Peter Berk have invited us to dinner.' He made a retching noise at the back of his throat.

Olivia tut-tutted and, a moment later, almost gagged on a spoonful of egg. 'What will your parents think?'

He looked at her sharply. 'You believe I told them all about you?'

'No. No, that would be idiotic.' She shook her head. But curiosity got the better of her. She leant forward and pointed her spoon at him. 'What did you tell them?'

'Nothing. They are dead.'

Olivia's ears reddened. 'I am sorry.'

'If you wish, I'll let the Berks know that we are unable to attend.'

'Thank you. But I prefer to face my enemies head-on. All I have to remember is to say "napkin" instead of "serviette" and "lavatory" instead of "toilet." And that I must refrain from blowing my nose on the tablecloth.'

'Keep in mind that the resulting uproar would save us from another such invitation,' he said, and spread butter on his second muffin. 'Tell me, why did you never run away from Madame Rousseau's? Why did you never go back home? Your parents must believe you dead.'

Her face fell and all colour drained from her cheeks.

She turned away and gazed out the window. Shoulders squared. Jaw set. After a moment, she turned back to him. 'It is none of your concern. But I will humour you anyway. Had I gone back to my parents, they would have been deeply dishonoured and shamed by their own daughter. A prostitute can't be married off to a suitable man. She would be the cause of slander, making her parents suffer until they moved far away from London, or died. So tell me, Coroner, would you truly expect me to have no honour whatsoever, and to do such a thing to my own parents?'

'I was merely curious. Curiosity is in my nature. However, you might wish to contact your parents now that you are married to a suitable man.'

With precision, she placed the spoon next to her plate, brushed two muffin crumbs off the tablecloth, and stood. 'If you don't require my assistance today, I will help my maid settle in. I will probably see you later.'

The door closed with a snap and Sévère stared at its bleak surface, wondering how and why this conversation had turned sour so thoroughly.

---

'NO...MORE...HOPP...ING...ON...TO...MISTER...SÉVÈRE'S... LAP!' Rose screeched with every bounce.

Olivia watched the girl's trajectory. The bedsprings were howling pitifully beneath her, and she had to hold onto the headboard so as not to be rocked off their pirate ship. The rug was strewn with pillows. The sea was merciless tonight.

Rose stopped bouncing. Her braids hung limply down the sides of her flushed face. 'Can I be a detective, too?'

'Hum.' Olivia stroked her imaginary beard.

'Please?'

'Well, I might need your opinion on a case from time to time. But you'd have to learn to read and write.'

'What...for?' The girl picked up her hopping again. This time, she flung out her legs, flashing her garters.

'Secret messages.'

'Oh!' The sea calmed at once. 'I can't be a pirate, then. Pirates don't know the alphabet.'

'Captains and first mates do.'

Rose plopped down next to Olivia, her breath whistling through her small windpipe, her brow sweaty.

'Is your cabin to your liking, First Mate?' Olivia asked.

Rose stuck a braid between her teeth for lack of appropriate facial hair, and looked around the small room as though seriously inspecting it yet again. She pulled her eyebrows together and nodded. 'Not bad, Captain.' Then she collapsed flat on the bed, and put her head on Olivia's shoulder. 'It's *really* my room, is it?'

'It is. It's the lady's maid's room. All fine ladies have a personal maid and every respectable lady's maid has a room like yours, all to herself.'

'Can I leave the door open?' A small voice. One that was afraid of the dark.

'You must, for what would happen should I wake up at night and need your services, and you couldn't hear me, because the door was shut?'

'What services?'

'Tie my corset. Button my dress.'

'At night?'

'Certainly. I might have to go on a mission. I might have to catch a murderer. You see,' Olivia said, her voice resonating dramatically, 'the most famed villains prefer the night. The moon is like the sun to them. Dense fog is their dearest friend, and the squelch of rain under their boots is their...their...um.'

With a heavy sigh, Rose rolled onto her stomach and blew her bangs out of her face. 'I want to be a detective.'

Olivia poked her ribs. 'Brush my hair, First Mate, and I'll brush yours. Then it's time for bed.'

The girl jumped off the mattress, screeched 'Aye, aye, Captain!' and flitted through the connecting door into Olivia's room, and stood at attention before the vanity.

Olivia sat down and watched the reflection of her First Mate, the seriousness and concentration of the girl, and she wondered if, one day, she would miss her mother.

'Rose?' she whispered. Their eyes met in the looking glass. 'If you ever want to go back. Back home, I mean. You are free, you know. This is not a prison.'

Perplexed, Rose frowned, then she turned her attention back at the strand of black hair she held in her hand, and gently pulled the brush through it.

In three years, Olivia thought. Three more years and then I'll be free. Rose will be eleven, old enough to make her own decisions. Should I take her with me? Would the girl even wish to leave London? Rose had time. Enough time to find out what suited her. If she decided she wanted to go back to her mother's, she'd be free to do so on her own terms.

# FINAL ACT

## IN WHICH NEW YARN IS SPUN

# NEIGHBOURHOOD

$\mathcal{A}$ fickle spring was upon Greater London. The morning sun dashed in and out of hiding, until it finally succumbed to a thick wall of clouds. The sky darkened.

Sleet nipped at Olivia's cheeks and she unfurled her umbrella hastily. Tapioca snow whirled on the pavement. The budding vegetation was shaken by angry squalls. Shivering, Olivia hurried past MacDoughall's Plant Nursery and pushed open a wooden garden gate with a neatly carven sign that read:

*Rupert Hunt*
*Redhill Apiary*

The whitewashed stone house hadn't been sold yet, a circumstance that made a search of the premises less bothersome. She pulled a skeleton key from her coat pocket and pushed it into the lock. The key was courtesy of Mrs Hopegood, who, after having heard the verdict, appeared to have shrunk to half her original height.

Olivia stepped into the hallway and shut the door. Darkness closed in on her. She should have brought matches.

Gradually, her eyes grew accustomed to the lack of light and she saw a pale, white strip a few steps ahead — a crack under a door. She set one foot in front of the other, careful so as not to run into something and knock it over.

She pushed at the door. Sharp white daylight cut through a gap between thick curtains, and blinded her for a moment. The air was stale. She coughed and came to a sudden halt as a thought hit her: what if this Sir Peter Berk was one of her former clients? And if not him, then some other man she and Sévère would happen to meet, sooner or later? No man in his right mind would mention in front of his own wife that he'd lain with a whore. But what man wouldn't try to blackmail her? Let me take you in the broom closet, else I'll tell your husband who you really are. Oh, he knows already? Even better. You'll serve me every night, else I'll ruin his reputation.

She grabbed the door frame for support. What was she to do? Had Sévère spent even a single thought on the consequences? He must have. But they'd never discussed it, never agreed on tactics. Had he evaded the topic when she'd asked him about it at Pagani's?

Olivia lifted her gaze. Behind the window, the sky cleared and sunlight hit the lawn. She wondered who'd cut it since Hunt's departure. MacDoughall, perhaps?

Briefly, her thoughts drifted to Chief Magistrate Frost. He was a man who would not take prisoners. What will I do when I meet him? Chills rippled down her arms. You won't get to me, you bastard. I will strike first.

She stepped through the door into the parlour.

THE HOUSE ECHOED HER STEPS. Not a cupboard, a picture frame, a lamp left. It was only the pale patches on the wallpaper and skid marks on the floorboards that told of former inhabitants. The outline of a headboard in the room where Mr and Mrs Hunt must have slept, a smaller outline in a smaller room that faced the garden. Was this what Charlotte Hunt had seen, day in day out? The line of apple and pear trees, the walkway with shrubs on either side. A small, overgrown pond.

Olivia opened the window. The forsythias were in full bloom. A gust tore petals off a wild plum tree; it looked as though the tree wept snow. MacDoughall's plant nursery was to her left, a pasture to her right, a farm building nestled against a group of larch trees farther off. She scanned the lawn that lay inconspicuous before her. Nothing indicated burial sites. Sévère had sent her here to locate the original graves of the infants, hoping she'd find clues as to why Rupert Hunt would plead guilty to a crime he had not committed.

She wondered if Sévère's instincts were fooling him. Surely, he didn't want her to spend days digging up Hunt's premises? She wondered if Rupert Hunt had been a rapist and murderer before his mind grew muddled and soft with age. Wasn't it common for old men to be entirely different from their younger selves? An arrogant wife-beater could turn into the most charming grandfather once strength of body and mind left him. They simply forgot who they were. Or they realised what it meant to be weak.

For a short moment, she wondered if it was justified to hang an old Rupert Hunt who seemed so different from his middle-aged version: a man who had repeatedly forced his own daughter, and then killed their babies.

Or had he?

Olivia turned on her heel and scanned the empty room. There was nothing of interest. She took two steps and lay down on the dusty floor where the bed must have been. She looked up at the ceiling.

The room was silent. As silent as Charlotte Hunt. Olivia was undecided as to how to approach the problem of the silent victim. She'd left the folder with the case notes on the parlour floor. It was of no use to open it yet again. The most curious fact hadn't been written down.

'If Miss Hunt is unable to read and write, what use does she have for book and ink bottle?' Sévère had asked earlier this morning.

'What indeed,' she muttered as she sat up. Something creaked under the pressure of her left palm. She lifted her hand and noticed two floorboards that were shorter than the others. Someone had cut a board in half, as though to repair damage.

'Dammit,' she growled. Sévère still hadn't returned her knife. She'd forgotten to ask him about it.

She rose and left the room.

She found MacDoughall in his garden, moving piles of twigs.

'Good day to you, Mr MacDoughall,' she called across the picket fence.

He straightened up and blinked against the light. 'Mrs Jenkins?'

'It's Mrs Sévère now. We got married two days ago. Isn't it a bit late for pruning?'

He narrowed his eyes at her. His gaze slid to her stomach and up at her face again. 'Congratulations,' he said, and tapped his foot against the twig pile. 'Pomaceous trees are customarily cut between January and March.'

'Ah,' Olivia said. 'I was wondering if you could lend me a knife. I forgot to bring my own.'

'A knife? What for? And why are you here? Mr Hunt confessed, didn't he?'

'Indeed he did. But a few things need clarifying.' She waited until MacDoughall had approached the fence and was standing a short distance from her. 'We need to know if there are more than the nine victims, and where they were buried before he put them into flowerpots and took them to London. You wouldn't know, would you?'

MacDoughall's throat seemed to swell. His carotid artery visibly throbbed. 'I do not.' He flipped a pruning knife in his hand and held it out to her, handle first. 'Be careful. It's sharp.'

'Thank you. I might ask you for a shovel later, if you don't mind.' She turned toward the house and walked away.

'What do you need the knife for?' he called after her.

She looked back. The sun caught on MacDoughall's

face. 'To move a floorboard. There seems to be a secret compartment.'

A sharp nod and he turned away.

THE MYSTERIOUS COMPARTMENT WAS, after all, rather un-mysterious. It was simply a damaged floorboard that had been cut to replace half of it. Olivia sat down heavily. She looked up at the ceiling, and said, 'What would I do?'

She stood and began pacing the room. 'I give birth. There's blood. I attend to myself. I need to protect my child. What do I do?' Her gaze drifted to the window. 'I would ask for help.'

She inhaled deeply. 'Slow down,' she told herself.

How much blood was in a newborn? One pint, perhaps? Where did it all go?

There was no mattress, no blanket or rug she could examine. Only the floor, the wallpaper, the window, the door. She knelt, put her nose close to the polished wood, and inhaled. Dust. She sneezed.

She picked up the knife once more and ran it along the edges of the repaired floor board, worked a long splinter out and inspected its rim. Nothing but dirt.

She looked at the pale patch that indicated where the headboard of the bed had covered the wallpaper. She sat right where the bed had stood. That's not where the blood would be, would it? Soaking its way through the mattress? No.

But why would the board beneath the bed be broken, and not the ones closer to the door where everyone walked in and out?

She couldn't find an explanation.

She chose other floorboards on either side of where the bed must have stood, and ran the tip of the sharp knife along the edges. She couldn't lift the boards, for they'd been nailed down fast. But she managed to extract slender pieces of wood from the edges. A side of one piece was covered with a dark-brown substance. She scraped it off. It looked almost black on the shiny metal blade. Wouldn't the floorboard itself be stained, if blood had spilt on it?

She went back to where the bed must have covered the floor and repeated the procedure on several boards there. The knife came away with a greyish substance. Dirt, rubbed into the cracks as one scours the floor?

Again, she sat down, thinking. If it *had* happened here, what would have been done with the blood-soaked blankets and rags? Where would I put them?

I would burn them. Or bury down.

Again she looked toward the window.


'MR MACDOUGHALL?' she called across the yard.

He looked up and leant on his rake.

'May I ask you something?'

He pushed up his hat and cleared his throat. 'I can't give you no shovel, Misses. How would I know the coroner sent you? For all I know you're with child.' He looked her up and down and added, 'Mrs Sévère.'

'Thank you for your concern, Mr MacDoughall,' Olivia said brightly, and extracted a piece of paper from her jacket. She unfolded it, and held it out for him to read:

LONDON AND SOUTHWARK AND LIBERTY OF THE
DUCHY OF LANCASTER IN MIDDLESEX AND SURREY.

*By virtue of my office and in the name of our Sovereign Lady
Queen Victoria, my wife and assistant Maria Olivia Sévère, née
Kovalchuk, shall be given full charge and responsibility on
behalf of said Lady the Queen to investigate the death of nine
infants, and for her doing so this shall be her warrant.
Given under my hand and seal this 12th day of March in the
year of our Lord 1881.*

*Gavriel Sévère*
*Solicitor at Law, Coroner of our said Lady the Queen
for the City of London and the County of Eastern Middlesex
and the Liberty of the Duchy of Lancaster.*

---

'HUM,' said Mr MacDoughall and spat on the grass. 'I
already told the coroner everything.'

She smiled warmly. 'You have answered his questions
sufficiently, thank you. However, new questions have
arisen and I was rather hoping you could help us once
more. Did you grow up in this house?' She nodded toward
his home.

'Why is that interesting to the coroner?'

'A mere formality.' She knew the answer. Sévère had
checked the registry.

'I was born here, as was my father.'

'How old are you?' This she also knew.

'Twenty-seven. No, twenty-eight. Is that important?'

'Oh, not so very much. You and Charlotte Hunt grew up together. Can you tell me anything about her?'

MacDoughall dropped his gaze, and grunted something Olivia didn't catch. 'Excuse me?' she said.

He lifted his head, looked at Hunt's house, and said, 'We didn't grow up together.'

'Are you telling me you know nothing of Charlotte?'

'She didn't speak.'

Olivia nodded slowly. 'I see. Well, Mr MacDoughall, here is your pruning knife. I thank you for lending it to me. It has been most helpful. I can see that you don't wish to answer my questions. You have seen, read, and understood the warrant. I will now take you into custody, and transfer you to our offices in London. You may pack a few things and inform your wife, but I must ask you—'

He held up both hands. The rake handle dropped to the ground. 'You cannot!'

'I very well can, Mr MacDoughall. And please be assured that I will. Unless, of course, you decide to answer my questions truthfully, here and now.'

He set his jaw, turned a shade of purple, then jerked down his chin once.

'Thank you. Did you grow up with Charlotte Hunt?'

'We were friends, if you mean that. I knew her well.'

'How would you describe her family?'

'The mother was distant and sickly. I rarely saw her, never talked to her much. The father, Rupert Hunt, I liked him. I never expected him to...' MacDoughall turned his face away. '...to do such a thing.'

'Did you ever notice that she was with child?'

'Mrs Hunt? No, she was old. Older than her husband, I believe.'

'I was referring to Charlotte.'

He sucked in air, his ribcage expanded. He let out a groan. 'I suspected it once or twice.'

'And then?'

'Nothing ever came of it, so I believed...I believed I was mistaken.'

'Hum.' Olivia pushed her hands into the pockets of her coat. She toed a clump of dirt aside and mashed it with her heel. 'The seven apple trees were yours?'

He looked up, pale. 'No. She...she knew how to graft. She and I learnt plant craft from my father and grandfather. She mostly watched. She had nothing else to do.'

'Did you ever see the Hunts burn blankets or rugs or other items one normally doesn't burn, or did you see them bury a small package or two?'

He shook his head violently. 'No. Never.'

'I am trying to understand how he did it. Rupert Hunt. How did he hide nine bodies, how did he hide all those bloody sheets? How could Charlotte have been with child seven times and no one saw it, and why did she never ask for help?'

Her eyes were sharply on him, analysing every twitch and every change of colour, every breath.

'She is a big woman. I imagine it was rather hard to see it, when she was heavy with child.'

'Did she have a nurse? When she was a child?'

Startled by the sudden change of topic, MacDoughall blinked stupidly. After a short moment, he recovered. 'Ah. No. It's not common here. Employing a nurse, that is.'

'Did she play with other children?'

'When she was young? Yes. She was quite normal. Except that she was mute.'

'Interesting,' Olivia said. 'She is in an asylum now. Her father told the staff that she's an idiot.'

MacDoughall jerked back as though he'd been punched in the face. 'No! Impossible. Why would he say that about his own daughter?'

'I don't know. He fathered her nine children.'

MacDoughall spat again. He shook his head, then nodded. 'That must be it.'

'Must be what?'

'He was done with her. He dumped her. Poor Charlotte.'

'Yes. Poor Charlotte. I will visit her today. Would you like me to say hello?'

For a moment, Olivia saw shock in the man's face.

'Better not upset her.'

'Very well. Have a nice day, Mr MacDoughall.'

When Olivia shut the garden gate, MacDoughall called after her, 'Don't tell Charlotte you talked to me.'


SHE FOUND an inn and ate a quick lunch, then took the South Eastern Railway to Tunbridge and up to Sevenoaks. She was certain the asylum staff would not be delighted when they learnt she was the assistant of Coroner Sévère, the man who had caused a fit of hysteria in one of their patients.

She thought about the book and the ink bottle and the curious statement Sister Grace had given, and she wondered if the asylum staff could be trusted at all.

---

THE MAID DELIVERED a telegram together with his four o'clock tea. Sévère took a sip of the hot and aromatic brew, and only a moment later, snorted it right back out. Through his nose. He coughed and sputtered, wiped his face with a hanky, and read the telegram once more:

COMMITTED MYSELF TO SEVENOAKS ASYLUM. *Back in 2 days. O.*

# THE SILENT VICTIM

*A* thin sickle of moon peeked through a gap in the clouds. Olivia watched the trees wave their twigs in the moonlight, and wondered whether she missed her old life.

What was there to miss? Nothing, really. For certain not the many men who'd had her. Perhaps the company of the other women? The laughter and silly stories they'd shared? Perhaps not. She found no regrets in her heart, no wish to return to Madame Rousseau's for even the shortest of visits.

Shivering with cold, she lay down in her bed and pulled the blanket up to her chin. She felt new, strange, other. She touched her lips, her breasts, and slid her fingers between her legs. For the first time in seven years, her body didn't have to serve anyone.

The memory of Sévère whispering "silk" against her thigh sent a ripple of heat through her.

'Get to work, woman,' she growled and kicked the

blanket aside. She pushed her feet into a pair of scratchy felt slippers, wrapped a robe around herself and turned the doorknob. Her slippers were as silent as a cat's paw on the hardwood floor.

As she pulled open the door, the soft creak of metal sounded as loud as an alarm bell to her. She stuck her head out into the dark corridor and pricked her ears. Nothing moved.

She tiptoed down the corridor and toward the north end of the house, past four doors, two on each side. The rooms of Sarah Bollard, Annie Swinfew, Emma Alexandra, and Rebecca Austin — they'd been committed to Sevenoaks Asylum for various forms of hysteria. Rumour had it that Sarah had sewn shut her abusive husband's coat sleeves and subsequently shat into them. He'd not been delighted.

The last door on Olivia's right was that of Charlotte Elizabeth Hunt, and opposite that was the communal sewing room. The staff had decided that deaf Charlotte wouldn't be disturbed by the other women chatting and doing their needlework.

Olivia peeked through the half-open door of the sewing room, and, seeing no one, moved on to the next door. The office was locked. She pulled two pins from her hair and picked the lock. A low, grating noise. The lock gave.

She stepped into the room and shut the door behind her. She'd seen an oil lamp on the desk and a box of matches next to it when she'd given herself into the good Sisters' care. Slowly, she stepped forward and probed with her fingers. When she found the lamp, she lit the wick, and carefully placed the matches back at where she'd picked them up. Then she opened drawer after drawer.

Patient files. There weren't that many and she quickly found Charlotte Hunt's. Committed in June by her father, Rupert Hunt, who'd stated that his daughter was addled in the brain and had always been so, and that, according to the family practitioner, there was no cure for her malady. No name was given for the practitioner.

A note by Dr Faulkner, Sevenoaks' physician, dated July 2, 1880, was next: "Miss Hunt takes delight in drawing flowers. Fresh air seems to have a positive effect on her nerves."

Below that was a note from August 15: "It appears as if Miss Hunt is merely deaf, and not of a weak mind. She has taken responsibility for the orchard and the rose garden, and seems to thrive."

And a note from October 1: "I believe that nothing is wrong with Miss Hunt other than her being unable to hear and speak. I have sent a letter to her father to enquire about relocating the patient."

Olivia wondered where Miss Hunt was to have been relocated, and if these plans had been changed. Had anyone talked to Charlotte about it?

She replaced the file and shut the drawer, turned off the lamp and left the room. Her gaze fell on the door of Charlotte's room.

One part of her argued that patience was her best friend in this case, the other part whispered *hurry!* Hunt's approaching trial was cutting her time short.

She turned the doorknob.

The moonlight zigzagged from windowsill to rug,

across the dark silhouette of a desk to her left. To her right stood a bed. Someone lay in it. She couldn't make out a face. Was Charlotte Hunt turned toward her, or away from her? Olivia tilted her head and listened. Soft, regular breathing.

She tiptoed to the desk and picked up one of the books that lay there. Moving it into the sliver of moonlight, she leafed through the pages. There were drawings of plants. A simple shape at the border of some of the pages drew her curiosity, and she lowered her face to the page, trying to crank open her pupils as far as possible. Could it be the pupa of an insect?

A cough issued from the bed. Olivia dove behind the desk. Her heart hammered. She hadn't placed the book back to where she'd taken it. It still lay open in the moonlight.

Miss Hunt moved. A little at first. As though she dreamt. A sigh, and the blanket was thrown aside.

Olivia felt sweat tickle her spine.

The scrape of something metallic. Another sigh. A trickle of liquid. Olivia bit her knee so as not to make a sound. Miss Hunt was using her chamber pot.

---

'GOOD MORNING, MRS HEWITT.'

Olivia rubbed her eyes and sat up. The sun had not yet risen. 'Good morning, Sister Agatha,' she said with a theatrical yawn.

'Rise, and thank our Lord for a new day, Mrs Hewitt. The others are already up and about. Prayer and singing will begin in a moment. Then you can take breakfast. Sister Grace will assign your work.'

'Thank you. I was hoping... Oh, please forgive my audaciousness, but I was hoping I could help in the gardens.'

Sister Agatha smiled mildly. 'You are new. You will soon learn our ways. I will let Sister Grace know you've enquired about the gardens. Wash and dress now. Mrs Bollard has water duty this week. She'll be here shortly.' With that, she left and shut the door.

Sarah Bollard entered before Olivia had time to push her feet into her slippers. Sarah was a quiet woman whose left hand was crippled, her crooked fingers curled to a fist. 'I'm sorry, it's ice cold,' she said, as she put the jug down.

'Thank you,' Olivia said. 'I'm Mary Hewitt. I arrived yesterday afternoon. I heard about the coat sleeves. Brilliant!'

Sarah Bollard dropped her head hastily, a shy smile and a flush of colour in her face.

'You can do needlework with your hand?' Olivia pointed her chin at Sarah's left hand.

'I manage. Why are you here?'

'I had a stillbirth, and my husband believes the baby died because I didn't want it.'

'Did you not want it?'

'No, I didn't. It was my husband's.'

Sarah's mouth formed an "oh" but she refrained from commenting.

'What's your work?' Olivia asked.

'Emma and I launder. Emma Alexandra...'

'Why is she here?'

'She took a lover. Her mother-in-law found out and told her husband.'

Olivia snorted. 'Unbelievable. I bet the husband has a hundred mistresses.'

Sarah clapped her hand to her mouth, and after the initial shock had passed, she giggled like a child. She stopped herself when a bell sounded.

'Prayer time! Hurry up now!' she said, and flitted from Olivia's room.

THEY SANG in a small chapel that had been erected behind the main house. The prayer, though, was performed lying flat on the icy stone floor.

'Humbly lie face down, so that the Holy Touch can seep into your uterus,' Sister Octavia had explained.

'My bladder will probably catch the chills,' Olivia muttered against the flagstones.

BREAKFAST WAS A SILENT BUSINESS. One doesn't talk while eating what the Lord hath provided, even if the Lord provided only a slop of burnt porridge. Olivia wondered if the Lord had ever bothered to read the instructions on porridge preparation, or how to work stove and pot.

She forced the food down her gullet, helped by tea so thin it tasted more like wash water than anything else. She avoided looking at Charlotte Hunt, who sat right next to her.

Sister Grace did indeed assign garden work to Olivia, and (Thank the Lord, Miss Hewitt! Thank the Lord!) she also assigned Miss Hunt to supervise Olivia during her initial days.

'Good gracious! I believe I thanked the Lord a hundred times today,' Olivia whispered to Charlotte. 'I hope he doesn't burn our lunch.'

Charlotte didn't react. Olivia poked her elbow into Charlotte's side. 'Didn't you hear me?'

Charlotte's eyebrows drew up. She shook her head, and placed her hands flat onto her ears.

'Oh, dear! Are you telling me you are deaf? No one told me. I'm *so* sorry! Oh, what am I saying? You can't understand a word anyway.'

Charlotte, looking mildly annoyed, touched her finger to Olivia's lips and then indicated her own eyes.

Olivia squinted stupidly. 'Excuse me?'

Charlotte shrugged, and turned away.

Olivia followed her into the tool shed and was handed a pruning knife. They picked their way to the orchard and she saw that most of the apple and pear trees had already been pruned, but not the cherry, plum, and peach trees.

She poked Charlotte again. 'It's almost mid-March; we need to finish pruning the apple trees.'

Charlotte made round eyes. Olivia babbled on, 'Pomaceous trees are to be pruned between January and March. Why are you looking at me like that? You are not *quite* deaf, are you?'

Again, Charlotte indicated her eyes, and then Olivia's mouth.

'Oh! Forgive my stupidity!' Then she said very slowly, 'You. Can. Read. Lips?'

Charlotte nodded, hoisted up her skirts, tucked them into her girdle, and scaled the ladder that leant against one of the trees. She began to cut away the twigs which grew on the undersides of the branches. Olivia did the same on the branches low enough to reach from the ground.

Aside from prayer every two hours, a dip in cold water before lunch, and sunbathing while being wrapped up in a wet wool blanket — all beneficial to the female nervous system — the day went on like this: Olivia was talkative and enthusiastic, annoying even to herself, all the while shadowing Charlotte. She hoped that her many questions about plant craft would prompt Charlotte to fetch her journals and better explain what she wished to say. Charlotte, however, seemed utterly comfortable in her silence. All Olivia could get from her was an occasional movement of her head in assent or disagreement, and a finger pointed at grafting knots, buds, or twigs. Olivia felt like ripping her hair out.

When night fell, she lay in her bed knowing that by tomorrow afternoon she would have to report to Sévère. And aware that she mustn't break the law to gather evidence, she felt the clench of predicament. Then she stopped herself.

Will I be breaking the law? she wondered.

She could hardly send a telegram to Sévère asking if, under certain circumstances, it was legal to burgle a room in order to secure evidence. Didn't policemen do this all the time?

Deciding the law was on her side and, hence, she wouldn't be breaking the contract she'd made with her employer, she flipped the blanket aside, pushed her feet once more into her felt slippers, and silently left her room.

Charlotte Hunt, however, was wide awake when Olivia entered.

# COCOON

*O*livia jerked awake. Her heart kicked her ribs, her mind stuttered. It took her a moment to realise that she was back in Sévère's house. Her *home*. What was it that had awoken her? Something she'd dreamt. Something important about the case. The asylum.

Yes! There it was again. The butterflies!

She jammed her feet into her slippers, drew closed the lapels of her night robe, and left her room. Hastily, she covered the short distance to Sévère's door and knocked.

'Sévère?'

No answer.

She knocked again. 'Gavriel, I need to talk to you. I know it's very late and I'm sorry, but… I think I was all wrong. I didn't come back empty-handed from Sevenoaks at all. I think I know who killed Charlotte's children. I just didn't see it until now.' She thumped her head against the door in frustration. 'Damn. Why was I so blind? Gavriel, are you awake?'

Still no answer.

She pressed her ear against the wood but heard nothing. He'd retreated to his private rooms at half past eleven, saying he was tired. Was he such a heavy sleeper?

She tried the door. It was unlocked. 'Gavriel?'

She took a few steps into his room. The meagre light from the corridor hinted at the furniture.

The bed was made.

And empty.

---

'GOOD MORNING. Did you have a restful night?' Olivia enquired, as she entered the dining room.

'Yes, thank you.' Sévère didn't look up from his newspaper. She noticed that the tension she'd sensed in him upon her return the previous day had vanished. Whatever woman he had had, she must have served him well.

Olivia sat and poured herself tea, picked a muffin, and began to eat. 'Can a verdict be overturned or amended if new evidence is found that was not available at the original inquest?'

He folded the paper and placed it aside. 'One cannot appeal against a coroner's ruling. Not even the coroner himself. One can, however, seek judicial review in the High Court. Why are you asking?'

'I have a hunch. Well, perhaps more than a hunch. Though I'm not sure if…'

'Put it to me, let's discuss it and see what comes of it.'

She placed her half-eaten muffin on the plate and drank a sip of tea. 'I did some thinking last night. And I stumbled over a queer thing. Charlotte's journals are filled with drawings of plants, how to graft, how to prune, how to... Well, everything related to plant craft. She's been given responsibility for the asylum gardens. She learnt the craft from MacDoughall the elder when she and MacDoughall where children. She loves it.' Olivia tapped her index finger against the table top. 'This is important here. She loves gardening. She loves plants.'

'Go on.'

'When I entered her room the second night, she was awake. I couldn't just run away, so I blurted out that she hadn't heard my knocks. And next to come to mind were apical buds. Mr Pouch had said something about apical buds being snipped off when an expert does the grafting, remember? I told Charlotte that I kept thinking about grafting techniques, and that I couldn't sleep because of the apical buds. I needed to know what was so important about them and if she could explain it to me. She showed me sections in her journals. Sections dedicated to grafting techniques and various trees. Apples, peaches...

'I kept asking stupid questions, pretending I didn't quite understand her mute explanations, so she would show me more. I hoped she would slowly open up and perhaps tell me something personal. Something about her children, or her father. She didn't, of course. But then...

'I didn't pay much attention to it when I saw it. Drawings of small insects on the page borders, illustrating the lifecycle of a moth: from egg to worm to pupa to adult insect. She had drawn them in all her journals, except the newest. I believe she began drawing in that one a year or two ago. Then there are four older journals, the oldest is from 1869. She's thirty-three now, so she used this journal when she was twenty-one. If I remember correctly, this journal begins not with an egg, but with a pupa. As though she'd noticed it too late, because it was her first.'

She groaned, and rubbed her brow. 'Damn I wish I could look at all of them right now to make sure I'm not mistaken!'

Sévère sat silently and waited.

'If I remember correctly...no, I'm quite certain that I do remember correctly.' She shut her eyes and slowly nodded.

'Yes. Seven life cycles through the years. Two had been corrected. She added a second egg, a second worm and pupa later. She used a different pencil, a sharper one. Nine, in total, became moths.'

She looked up at Sévère.

'And?' he said.

'The moths that hatched were small, dark things. Unpretty. Their frontal wings were darker, striped. The back wings were much lighter and plain. I believe they were all depictions of a codling moth.'

'A what?'

'A codling moth. An apple tree pest.'

Sévère blinked, said, 'Hum,' pushed himself up from his chair, and left the room.

---

OLIVIA FOUND him in his office, cloaked in cigar smoke.

'The Burns case. I can work on that instead. It's not as

complicated,' she said, and sat down heavily at the other side of his desk.

'I gave that case to Stripling.'

'Oh. Well… I don't know what to say. I got carried away, it appears.'

'It appears?'

She sighed and leant back, her gaze following the ribbon of cigar smoke curling up toward the ceiling. 'I didn't want her to be the murderer. I wanted him to have done it. It's stupid to feel this way, I know. It's just that…she seems so innocent. I cannot imagine her kneeling in her bedroom, putting a knife to her own child's throat.'

'Nine times,' he said softly. 'What does a murderer look like in your opinion?'

'I don't know.'

'Precisely.'

'Gavriel?'

'Hm?'

'Do you regret it?'

'Our partnership? No. Why would I?'

She looked at him now. 'Because I wasted your time.'

'Did you now?'

'I was fantasising instead of investigating.'

'Were you now?' A flash of amusement.

'Are you mocking me?'

'I wouldn't dare.' He stubbed out the cigar, folded his hands and said, 'Now. While I must admit your observational skills are excellent, I must also point out the weaknesses of your theory. If Charlotte Hunt saw her unborn children as pests, how does that fit to the careful arrangement of their remains in the flowerpots? Johnston's opinion is that these children had been cherished.'

'How does their violent death fit with them having been cherished?' Olivia retorted.

'Precisely. Who has ever said that the person who killed these infants is also the person who buried them in flowerpots or the person who drew moths into journals?'

Embarrassed, Olivia dropped her head. 'I'm not good at this, Sévère. It was a stupid idea to make me your assistant.'

'You've trained yourself to prejudge. A client steps into your room, and you gauge him and his likely actions based on what you see in his face. It's time you learnt to distinguish fact from opinion.'

She looked up, a dangerous flicker in her eyes.

'Very well, then. Hunt's trial is in ten days. We haven't identified the father of the children, nor have we got a word out of Charlotte Hunt, who's now our main suspect. She's also our main problem. Should your theory be correct, Miss Hunt has fooled a lot of people for a very long time. Perhaps she's also fooled the father of the victims, but we should not forget that he might be her accomplice... What is it?'

Olivia, sitting bolt upright and big-eyed in her chair, shook her head. 'Nothing. Go on, please.'

'Hunt is protecting his daughter. We can't expect him to cooperate. He doesn't want her sent to gaol or the colonies. She might even be hanged if there weren't the possibility that she's insane. He, as well, might be her accomplice. But whatever the case, he will not testify against his own daughter. Dammit! How do we get a most uncooperative, emotionally unstable, and deaf woman to give evidence against herself?'

'I will speak to her,' Olivia said with a hoarse voice.

'Excellent. Talk to MacDoughall first.'

'I will.'

'There's a farm—'

'Yes, I'll ask there, too. Anyone who might know about a man who entertained a relationship with Charlotte Hunt. I'll knock on many doors. Do I need a new warrant from you?'

'Only if you require the help of the local police,' he answered.

'Do they usually share gossip?'

'They might.'

'Well then, I'll need that warrant.' She looked at him expectantly.

'You are aware that these drawings in no way prove that Charlotte Hunt killed her children?'

She leant back in her seat and nodded.

'Let's go for a walk to invigorate our mental faculties.' He rose and opened the door for her, stopped himself, and shut it again. 'Olivia, I need to say one more thing.'

'If it's about the prostitute you visited last night, there's no need to talk about it. I couldn't care less about your choice of bedmate,' spilt from her mouth.

Puzzled, he squinted at her. 'That was not what I wished to say. But if you do feel a need to talk about other women, I believe I prefer the discussion to take place in the evening after we both have had a brandy or two.'

She blushed violently. 'I do not wish to discuss it. As I already said.'

'Very well then.' He looked at the hand that still held the doorknob. 'Olivia, this case is difficult. You'll have to get used to the idea that we might not be able to apprehend the murderer. You need to accept the possibility that an innocent man might be hanged.'

She nodded and said softly, 'I know. I will begin with digging around the apple trees on Hunt's premises. The codling moth, the newborns buried under apple tree saplings. She probably buried them right there.'

'Stripling and I will accompany you. He can do the digging.'

---

STRIPLING WASN'T lucky this time, either. It was raining buckets as he dug holes along the line of apple trees.

Mr and Mrs Sévère had walked away, both protected by their large umbrellas. He wondered what she was doing here. She couldn't possibly be planning to interrogate witnesses?

His gaze travelled up and down the line of apple trees. Must be thirty, forty yards, he thought. Was he supposed to dig all that up in one day?

---

'MAY I SPEAK TO YOUR HUSBAND?' Olivia asked Celia MacDoughall.

The woman wiped her hands on her apron. 'He's picking up manure at Miller's. The farm down yonder.' She jerked her head in a noncommittal direction.

'May I come in?'

'If you want to talk to my husband, you'd better go down to the Millers.'

'It can wait. It's raining cats and dogs, and my toes are freezing. You wouldn't have a nice fire and a hot tea for me?'

Reluctantly, Celia MacDoughall stepped back. Olivia shook the rain from her umbrella and coat, and thanked her for her hospitality.

'How are your children?'

'Fine, thank you.' Celia offered Olivia a towel and placed a teapot onto the table.

'Your boy's cold is gone, I assume?'

Celia threw a sharp glance at her. 'What's that man doing over there?' She tipped her chin toward the window that provided a glimpse of Hunt's orchard.

'Officer Stripling is excavating evidence.'

'But Mr Hunt confessed!'

Olivia nodded slowly and stared into her mug. 'Do you believe he did it? Killed nine newborns?'

Celia shrugged. 'I don't know. If he said he did it, he must have done it, mustn't he?'

'The coroner has his doubts.' Olivia made it sound as though she believed Sévère had no clue about anything.

Celia caught the bait. 'Have you ever met him?'

'Rupert Hunt?'

'Yes. He might look all friendly and kind. But... Anyway. I'm sure he did it.'

A wail sounded from the bedroom, and Celia left to pick up her infant. When she sat back down at the table, the soft sheen of a nursing mother in her eyes, Olivia said,

'I'm sure you are correct. It sickens me to think of it. Nine infants. Just like yours.'

The jab had instant effect. Celia looked up, horrified. 'I don't want to think about it, let alone talk about it. How can a man do such a thing? And dig them down in the middle of the night, and no one knows anything. Thank the Lord the Hunts are all gone!'

'I wish I had met Charlotte. Poor woman…' Olivia said softly.

Celia blew air through her lips. 'Pshaw!' And with a blush, she fell silent.

'She threw an ink bottle at the coroner,' Olivia provided.

No answer.

'And a book. It just missed his head. He briefly considered apprehending her.'

'He should have. That woman did quite a bit of front door work all over Redhill.'

'With your husband, too?'

'Not since after we got married. I made sure of it.'

———

SÉVÈRE'S new umbrella withstood the first gale for precisely half a second. Then a rib broke. He made it to Redhill's general practitioner with his left shoulder soaked.

'May I speak with Dr Thorpe?' he said when a maid answered his knocks.

'He's presently attending to a patient. You may sit in the hall. May I take your coat and umbrella?'

Sévère didn't have to wait long. A thickset man in his seventies wheezed through the hall and left. Then Dr Thorpe called, 'Next, please!' through the open door of his office.

Sévère introduced himself, and Thorpe answered, 'I was wondering when you'd pay me a visit. Nine concealed births — the practitioner must know something. He's probably romantically involved, if not an accomplice. Isn't that how detective stories go these days?' He held out a hand and shook Sévère's. His moustache twitched with a smile.

'I came here for the gossip,' Sévère replied.

'Ah! You wish to know who the father is. Well, it wasn't me. May I offer you a cup of tea? You look like you need it. Perhaps a towel, too?'

'Very kind of you, thank you.'

Dr Thorpe called for the maid, who delivered the requested objects swiftly.

Sévère, now significantly warmer, stretched his left leg. 'Rupert Hunt fathered his daughter's children.'

'Did he now?' Thorpe showed genuine surprise.

'You didn't read the papers?'

'I rarely do. It's a waste of time, if you ask me. These days, reporters don't report anything. They write what sells best. What's the use of reading that?'

'You prefer detective novels?'

Thorpe laughed, wiped his moustache, and said, 'Did you come to borrow a book from my library, or to question me?'

'I was hoping for hot tea, to be honest.'

'Ah! I see. Your tactic is to calmly lean back and let the

culprit talk himself into a corner. Well then. I am not the father of Charlotte Hunt's children, as I've already said. I'm greatly surprised Rupert Hunt is the one. I'd have thought a pig farmer had done the deed. I'm even more surprised the gossip of Hunt being so deeply involved in this tragedy didn't reach my ears. It usually does.'

Sévère raised an inviting eyebrow.

'Miller. Unbecoming wife, four unbecoming children. He had an eye on Charlotte. Everyone knows it. Even his wife.'

'Did anyone else have an eye on Charlotte Hunt?'

'Not that I know of.'

'Hum,' said Sévère, drank his tea and scratched his neck. His eyes scanned the office for several long moments, and, when he thought Dr Thorpe had fidgeted in his chair long enough, he said, 'Rupert Hunt stated that you've diagnosed his daughter with insanity.'

Thorpe looked aghast. 'Before making such a judgement I would have had to examine the patient in question.'

'You've never seen her?'

'No, not as her doctor. I've met her in passing several times. But as you know, she doesn't speak.'

'Mr MacDoughall stated that Mrs Hunt was sickly. Surely you must have seen her on occasion?'

'I did not. The Hunts weren't fond of learnt medical men. They preferred the services of Miss Dunham. She's the local witch. Although she prefers the term *wise woman*.'

Sévère pulled out his notebook. 'Her full name and address, please.'

'Aliya is her first name, I believe. Aliya Dunham. She lives in the Brook. I can arrange for a cab, if you wish.'

---

STRIPLING'S SPADE MET RESISTANCE. He cursed. Not another body! He dug around it and extracted a bundle of what looked like a cut-up and bunched-up rug to him. The hole was filling up with rain quickly. A thin strip of light-coloured clay bled into the dark muck. Stripling pulled the heavy package onto the lawn and peeled layer upon layer of the thick, dirty-brown fabric aside.

He spat on the grass. There was nothing but light-coloured clay inside the bundle.

Stripling wiped the rain off his brow and kept digging.

---

ALIYA DUNHAM HAD NOT BEEN at home. Sévère had poked around her hut and her chicken coop, and then taken the cab back into Redhill. At the Miller farm he ordered the driver to stop.

He enquired after Mr Miller, and a farmhand pointed him toward the pigsty.

Sévère tiptoed around puddles that stunk of urine, almost slid off the wooden boards that served as a walkway across a mud pit, and finally entered the stable. Two men with pitchforks looked up. Sévère was surprised to see MacDoughall.

'Coroner,' MacDoughall said, and stuck the fork into the manure.

'Mr MacDoughall, Mr Miller. I need to ask you a few questions regarding the murders of nine infants in your neighbourhood.'

MacDoughall looked at Miller. Miller gave a small nod.

They made for the main house, and entered. To his surprise, Sévère found Olivia chatting with Miller's wife. The latter threw her husband a cold glance.

'Good day to you, Mr Miller, it is a pleasure to finally meet you. Mr MacDoughall, how are you doing today? Hello, Gavriel, may I speak with you for a moment?'

Olivia saw the triple lines deepen on Sévère's brow. They stepped out into the corridor and she shut the door, put a finger to her lips, and pressed her ear to the wood.

'They know,' hissed Miller's wife.

'Be quiet!' Miller answered, and then they talked in voices so low that Sévère and Olivia couldn't understand what was being said.

Olivia pulled Sévère down by his collar and whispered into his ear, 'According to Celia MacDoughall, Charlotte Hunt warmed a lot of beds. Even MacDoughall's and Miller's. It appears that half of Redhill had the opportunity to father one of Charlotte's children. If this is true, I wonder why the Sevenoaks staff told you she's afraid of men.'

Sévère regarded Olivia with interest. A corner of his mouth twitched. Then he opened the door and stepped back into the room.

---

STRIPLING'S STOMACH roared with hunger. He'd had enough, he truly had. Hours of digging in the pissing rain. He would probably come down with a cold, or worse. And for what? Dirty sheets and a cut-up rug.

---

THE TWO CHESTNUTS' new shoes rang sharply against the cobblestones. Olivia shut her eyes, glad the evening entertainment at the Berks hadn't been as disastrous as she'd feared. Sévère hadn't seemed the least bothered by the fact that everyone believed him a little deranged for having married below his station. Lord knows what she's doing to tie him to her thus. Lord knows why he makes her work in his office. *Assistant*. Ha! A girl of unknown parentage, raised at an orphanage in Reading, they say. Her twin had been taken away soon after birth, they say.

'You are very beautiful tonight,' he said, without taking his eyes off whatever lay behind the brougham's window.

'You are to refrain from courting me. We agreed on this.'

'If I were courting you, I would use pretty words to get into your bed. I must disappoint you. I've merely stated a fact.' He looked at her now. 'Why did Charlotte bury her children in flowerpots and give them to her father? Could it have been revenge? Could he have known... No, I don't believe he knew. He'd never have allowed his housekeeper to touch them.'

'Why did you leave the dining room when I told you about my theory of the codling moth?'

'I needed to think. My apologies if I was too abrupt.'

'I know what it means now. I don't mind if you do it.'

'You believe I stormed out because I was disappointed in you.' It was a statement, not a question.

'The trial begins in two days. Did you speak with the High Court?'

'About what precisely? That Charlotte Hunt draws plants and their pests? That we found sheets and an old rug that might or might not have been soaked in blood before someone covered them with muck? That several men have accused Charlotte Hunt of promiscuity?'

She lowered her head. 'Is this the most depressing part of your occupation? Trying to make others see?'

'It's the most gratifying.'

Olivia balled her hand to a fist and rapped her knuckles on his knee. 'How do we get a confession from Charlotte?'

'Aren't you forgetting something?'

'I don't know. Am I?'

'You suppose that the jury will believe what you believe. Let me ask you this: if both Charlotte Hunt and Rupert Hunt admit to the killing of these nine infants, and each continues to insist the other is lying, to whom will the jury give more credit? To the old man who says very little? Or to the woman who can't say anything at all, and who is an inmate of an asylum?'

'Are you saying that Rupert Hunt has no chance whatsoever?'

'He has a good chance to get what he wants. We, however, will probably not get what we want: the arrest of the murderer. We might have to settle for much less.'

When the brougham came to a halt and the coachman

opened the door for them, Sévère said, 'It's not about catching the murderer anymore, Olivia. It's about not getting an innocent man hanged, no matter how much he wants it. This mess is my fault. I've been sloppy and complacent.'

# TRIALS & ERRORS

*S*he sat facing him in the smoking room. The customary cigar smouldered in the crystal ashtray. Her fingers balanced a glass of brandy on her armrest. He watched how the liquid left oily trails on the thin glass as she turned it in her hand, her gaze unfocused, her lips a hard line.

She opened her mouth, shut it, and inhaled.

He knew he had to wait until she'd sorted her thoughts into a narrative. Olivia theorised more freely when she had the time to chew on and spit out her thoughts bit by bit.

'Charlotte's first journal begins with a pupa, not an egg. It was her first pregnancy. She probably didn't know the signs and only realised it when the child inside had grown large enough. Odd, isn't it? That even before she saw it, it already felt like a pest to her.'

Sévère said nothing. He had the impulse to challenge

statements as soon as they were uttered. As a young man, this reflex had hindered him more than it had helped. Especially at court. It had taken him years to realise that in order to listen, one had to be silent. In order to understand, one had to allow the other to make himself understood. Or herself. He would deliver his counter-arguments once she'd emptied her glass.

'I can imagine she pretended to graft the apple tree saplings for him as a farewell present. While in fact, they were a revenge. Or perhaps they were a keepsake? She must have known that her mother was dying, and that her father would then send her away. But why did Hunt tell Dr Faulkner that his daughter was addled in the head?'

Olivia cast a glance at Sévère. 'Did he know that she had killed her own children? Or was it her promiscuity that made him say it? And how can parents be blind to their own child's pregnancies? Impossible! Damn, I wish I could talk to her mother.' Her gaze drifted out of focus. 'Her father put her into a Christian institution, although the family preferred the services of a wise woman. It sounds a bit pagan to me. Did you confiscate the journals?'

'I told you I sent Faulkner a telegram.'

'Oh, yes. I forgot.' She massaged her brow.

'I haven't received them yet. Which is odd. He wrote that he sent them out four days ago.'

'I'll take the train to Sevenoaks tomorrow, if you wish, and enquire at the post office. If they have no records of Faulkner's package, I'll pay Sister Grace a visit. I've always wanted to confiscate something.' She wiggled her eyebrows at him, and, all of a sudden, sat up straight. 'Fuller's Earth is meant for cleansing. It was all over the sheets and the rug. They were wrapped around it. But it's clear that no one attempted to wash them, launder them. It makes no sense with all the blood on them. But why take handfuls of it and wrap it into the sheets? Do you believe that...'

She drifted off again.

'Believe what?' Sévère said.

'That it was some kind of ritual. That she saw her children as things that needed cleansing.'

'Hm.'

'What?'

He eyed her glass. There was only a drop left.

'It is irrelevant, Olivia.'

She leant forward, eyes sharp and narrow. 'How can the motivation of the killer be irrelevant?'

'It is highly likely that we will never get a satisfying answer as to what Charlotte's motivations might have been, neither in private nor in court. Evidence to link Charlotte Hunt to the killings is weak at best. Besides, the trial concerns Rupert Hunt, not his daughter. It is him we need to worry about, not her.'

'But—'

He growled in response. 'Two days, Olivia! We have two days. What is more important to you: to be right and have the last word in the matter, or to save Hunt from the gallows?'

She turned her gaze away. After a moment of consideration, she nodded faintly. 'What is your plan?'

'I've given Hunt's attorney all relevant information and informed the assizes as to the new witnesses that need to be heard. Subpoenas have been issued. Dr Faulkner is still insisting that Miss Hunt is unable to give evidence. I wonder why he shields her. You said that he'd written in her file that nothing seems wrong with her mind. He even suggested having Miss Hunt removed from the asylum. I wonder why Mr Hunt never answered Faulkner's letter.'

Sévère's attention was distracted by his left knee. It had begun to tremble. Not visibly, but he could feel the vibrations down to the marrow of his bones. A prickling rushed up his leg and a stabbing pain followed. He told himself to take slow, measured breaths, and wondered when the pain would grow unbearable, when he would have to use his crutch, and employ a manservant to help him use the stairs. When he would have to signal defeat.

'Gavriel?'

Gruffly, he said, 'I'll send a warrant to the Redhill police to summon all men between twenty to forty-five years of age, should it become necessary to identify each and every one of Charlotte's lovers.'

'That must be three, four hundred men! Why the dickens would you do that?'

He felt an urge to lie down and guzzle all the alcohol he kept in the house. He unclenched his jaw and spoke, 'To force Charlotte Hunt to give her statement. She'll not wish to be paraded before all of Redhill. Bringing up the issue will also slow the trial. We might need more time.'

He slapped the armrest to announce the end of the

discussion. 'Very well. You will take the first train to Sevenoaks tomorrow morning. At present I need to think about two inquests I'll be holding tomorrow. Good night, Olivia.'

He didn't meet her gaze. Instead he busied himself with his brandy, tapping his fingertips against the glass as though solving a problem of great proportion.

From the corner of his vision, he saw her rise and approach.

She held out her hand. 'You are entirely hideous, with or without your limp.'

An involuntary laugh burst from his chest. It sounded more like a cough than anything else. 'You are a wicked creature. Very well, then. This is what you bargained for.' His hand grabbed hers, her wrist, her shoulder, and then he pulled himself up.

She steadied her stance as he leant heavily on her.

'You should eat less,' she suggested.

'Is your courage failing you already?'

'I merely made a humorous statement. Shall we walk to your bedroom, or do you first need the water closet?'

'My dear wife, I feel a tad too invalid tonight to do it in the lavatory. I suggest we make use of my soft bed instead.'

'Sévère, really! If you keep jesting like this, I will push you down the stairs.'

'Well then, perhaps another night. Shall we?'

THE CLERK at Redhill's mail office had neither record nor recollection of Dr Faulkner's package.

When Olivia banged the knocker against the asylum door, she didn't need to make an effort at looking official, effective, and cold.

'Mrs Hewitt!' Sister Grace's surprised look quickly turned to puzzlement.

'My name is Olivia Sévère. I'm the wife and assistant of Gavriel Sévère, Coroner of Eastern Middlesex.' She pulled out her warrant and held it under Sister Grace's nose. 'I came to confiscate Miss Hunt's journals and to ensure that you, Dr Faulkner, and Miss Hunt appear at court tomorrow morning at ten o'clock. Should I get the impression that any of you plans to disobey the High Court's orders, the Redhill police will apprehend you and transfer you to the Old Bailey to give evidence. May I come in?'

'I recommend we talk in our office.' Sister Grace stepped aside.

'Thank you, but I will first talk to Charlotte,' Olivia replied, strode past the nun and banged her fist against the door to Charlotte's room.

'She's in the orchard.'

Olivia entered the room. Without much ado, she picked up the journals and placed them into her briefcase, opened all drawers of the desk and searched the shelves. The ink bottle, pen and pencil were gone. One journal was missing. She took a step back, surveyed the room, and left.

'I assume she's drawing?'

'I couldn't say,' Sister Grace said. 'Aren't you ashamed you lied to us?'

'I can't say I am. If you wish to accompany me to the orchard, I must ask you to refrain from talking or signing to Charlotte until I give you leave to do so.'

Sister Grace grabbed Olivia's shoulder. 'What is this about?'

'Charlotte's father has confessed to nine murders he did not commit. It is Charlotte's statement that can save him from the gallows. Why, in your opinion, is she unwilling to give it?'

The nun's gaze flickered. 'Is she unwilling to give the statement, or is she unwilling to leave this sanctuary and place herself at the mercy of men?'

'Are you so eager to sign a man's death sentence?' She stepped around Sister Grace and found Charlotte in the garden, hunched over her journal. She was drawing the small, simple shape of a moth larva onto the border of the right-hand page.

———

THEY TOOK the brougham to the Old Bailey. Olivia bent forward and straightened Sévère's cravat, then pulled down the veil of her hat.

'If you do not have the nerve to attend Hunt's trial, go back home,' he said.

'You have a way of making me feel better instantly.'

'Whatever you allowed that man to do to you, it does not matter anymore.'

'I'm not worried for myself, you idiot! I'm worried your career will be ruined by the Chief Magistrate announcing to all of London that an official of the Crown is married to a whore.'

'As I've said already, it does not matter. You are Olivia Sévère. Miss Mary does not exist. Should you indeed bump into Chief Magistrate Frost today, please do so as my wife, and not as his strumpet.'

Her hands curled to fists, and she had to unclench one to stick her index finger into his face. 'If you didn't need your visage intact today, I would knock out your front teeth.'

His mouth did a satisfied twitch. 'There's the warrior. Keep her there and walk into court with your head held high. Do not be afraid of Frost or any of your former clients. Keep these fists balled, if you must. Ah! Here we are.' The brougham stopped and Sévère alighted. He held the door open for her, then excused himself and rushed ahead to consult with the defence attorney.

Olivia took the flight of stairs up to a lobby, then a second staircase. She kept her head low, her veil down. She could deal with Frost after the trial, if she had to. But now, she was feeling utterly out of balance.

As she slunk through the hectic lobby, she glanced up for a moment. A marble dome. It made her feel entirely insignificant. Where should she go? Straight ahead? The door to the left? She asked a policeman, and he led her to the gallery where the public was to be seated. When she told him that she was with the coroner, he harrumphed and pointed down toward the attorneys' desks. She spotted Sévère in conversation with a wigged, gowned man.

People were pouring into the courtroom. She pushed ahead. Sévère looked up, and waved her closer.

'May I introduce my wife and trusted assistant,' he said. 'Olivia, this is the attorney for the defence, Mr Bicker.

'It is my absolute pleasure, Mrs Sévère!' The man shook her hand. His glasses sat slightly askew. Olivia resisted the urge to straighten them for him. She lifted her veil.

He smiled broadly. 'Now I see why the Coroner has given up his long-cherished bachelorhood.'

She blushed, and dropped her gaze. As was expected of her. 'Gavriel, where do you want me?'

'The judge might wish to send away the womenfolk when we reach the grisly details. You'd better sit over there with me.' He indicated a row of chairs behind the newspapermen, waved at the usher, and dismissed her with a nod.

The usher led her to a seat where she would have a good overview of the whole spectacle.

She scanned the hall. The bustling of the audience on the stairs and up in the gallery. The clerks and barristers in their gowns and white, curly wigs. A sword was hanging on the dark wood panels just above where the judge's head would soon be, its tip pointing skyward. She wondered, briefly, if the weapon had ever been used. Where was the judge, anyway?

She stretched her neck, and felt a sudden chill. There

was the prisoner's dock. Rupert Hunt would soon be sitting there. And it had been her doing. Had she not broken into his office and taken his beekeeping book...

A stillness befell the room. An official stood and gave the order for the court to rise. Sévère chose the moment of commotion to join Olivia.

The judge was admitted, and with him three robed men.

'Why does he carry flowers?' Olivia whispered to Sévère.

'To cover the stink of Gaol Fever.'

'I don't smell anything.' She sniffed to make sure she hadn't missed something obvious.

'It's an outdated tradition.'

The men mounted the dais and seated themselves. The judge placed the posy of flowers onto his desk.

Rupert Hunt was brought into the prisoner's dock. His ear trumpet was placed in his hand, and when he had put it into his ear, the charge was read to him. Upon the question how he pleaded, he lifted his head high and said with a voice as clear and strong as a young man's, 'Guilty!'

The world did not tip off its axis, no one cried foul. The clockwork of justice kept ticking on as though one man's fate did not matter.

The jury was sworn in, and then a barrister rose and began his opening speech for the prosecution. Olivia paid little attention. Her eyes were stuck to Rupert Hunt, more haggard and whey-faced than she remembered him.

Bicker stood and said that, yes, the prisoner pleaded guilty, but that the defence would show during the course of the trial that Rupert Hunt was lying to protect the real killer. A *boo* sounded from the audience. The judge rapped his gavel against his desk.

The first witness was called in: Mrs Hopegood, Hunt's housekeeper.

She stood in the box, hand still firmly pressed to the Bible, and gave her statement in a small voice. The defence attorney rose and asked only one question: If Rupert Hunt had been surprised by the discovery of a skull in his flowerpot. Yes, of course. He'd been utterly shocked.

Then he sat, and Mrs Hopegood was released.

Next, Dr Baxter was called into the stand, followed by Dr Johnston. Before the latter could dive into the details, the judge bade all women and children in the audience to leave the courtroom.

Once the shuffling and rearranging had quieted down, Johnston continued, followed by Inspector Walken and Coroner Sévère. Then, the trial was adjourned until after lunch.

SÉVÈRE APPEARED calm as Olivia watched him and the defence attorney talk in hushed voices. But she recognised the furrows on his brow and the whiteness of the knuckles of his left hand that grabbed the cane.

Finally, he walked up to her. 'We are missing Aliya Dunham. Where the blazes is she?'

Olivia shrugged.

'I left a note at her house that she should report to my

office. She didn't. I sent two telegrams which she didn't answer. She received a subpoena. No answer. Dammit.' He was about to check his watch when the judge entered, and the trial was reopened. 'Send a telegram to Redhill police. I need them to arrest Mrs Dunham and convey her to court by tomorrow morning, at the latest,' he whispered, and she slunk from the hall.

Olivia didn't get far.

'Now, what's this? A dove!'

She scrambled back from the man who'd caught her by her wrist. She recognised him immediately and bit her tongue. The taste of blood made her gag.

'Excuse me, sir, but you are confusing me with someone else.' Her voice sounded unnaturally high.

Chief Magistrate Frost's grip around Olivia's arm tightened. He raised an eyebrow and hissed, 'Am I, now? Why did you disappear? I see you dressed like a *lady*. For whom? Who is the man?'

From the corner of her vision, she saw someone in uniform. A policeman. 'Sir? Sir! Help me, please, this man is accosting me!'

Frost didn't move an inch. 'PC Lester, arrest this woman for loitering,' he said to the hastily approaching constable.

'What? Are you jesting?' She tugged at her arm, but Frost didn't let go.

'Mr Frost, sir, you wish me to take this woman into custody?'

'Indeed. She is a common whore, and was just now offering her services to me.'

That was when Olivia decided to make a ruckus.

It took five seconds for the door of the courtroom to burst open, a further two seconds for Sévère to step through and wrench Mr Frost's hand off his wife.

'Explain yourself, man!' he said to the Chief Magistrate.

'As I already said to Constable Lester here: I found this woman loitering in the lobby. She even offered her questionable services to me.'

'Are you mad?' Olivia squeaked.

Sévère raised his voice. 'Are you calling my wife a prostitute?'

'What is this circus?' The usher elbowed himself through the onlookers, followed by the judge himself.

'Coroner Sévère, Chief Magistrate Frost, you will be removed from court should you—'

'May I?' Olivia interrupted.

'And who are you, Miss?'

'I am Olivia Sévère, wife of Coroner Sévère. I had just left the courtroom and was on my way to dispatch a message to Redhill police station to apprehend a witness who apparently ignored a court order, when this *creature* brutally grabbed my arm and called me a whore.' For effect, she spat at Frost's lapel.

'Is this true?' the judge thundered.

Frost, now pale, looked down at the saliva dribbling down his waistcoat, then at Olivia, Sévère, and back at the judge.

'It happened as my wife said. I asked her to send a telegram in my name,' Sévère said calmly. 'This was merely minutes ago. Then I heard my wife scream, exited the courtroom, and saw the Chief Magistrate assaulting her.'

The judge's eyes narrowed on Frost's face.

Frost bowed his head. 'This is... I am most...' He cleared his throat. 'I am lost for words, my lord. It appears I have confused this woman for another I knew from the House of Detention. My sincerest apologies.'

'I demand reparation,' Sévère growled. 'He has treated my wife in the most foul fashion.'

'An apology is in order, I should think,' the judge said to Frost.

'Thank you, my lord, but I don't want an apology from a man who believes he can treat a woman like a slab of pork at the market — be she a prostitute or not. With your permission, I will take my leave now, and let you continue your trial. My apologies for the disturbance.'

She gifted Sévère a small smile and left, but not without noticing the expression of incredulity on Frost's face.

The last thing she heard was a grunt of protest from Frost when the judge ordered both men to his chamber as soon as the trial was closed for the day.

---

OLIVIA RETURNED FROM THE TELEGRAPH, quietly entered the courtroom and sat down next to Sévère. She put her mouth to his ear, and said, 'Thank you.'

He gave a curt nod.

Mrs MacDoughall was telling the court that she'd been a neighbour of Rupert Hunt for the past nine years, since the day she and her husband married. They had two children, and no, her husband did of course not entertain other relations, but yes, he'd done so before they'd begun their courtship. No, he hadn't courted Miss Hunt; she had courted him. No, she didn't have any knowledge of Miss Hunt having been with child. Ever.

Next, her husband was called onto the witness stand, and swore upon the Bible that he would say the truth and nothing but the truth.

The prosecutor stood and asked, 'Mr MacDoughall, you and Charlotte Hunt grew up together?'

'We were neighbours, yes.'

'You were childhood friends?'

'Yes, we were.'

'When did Charlotte's interest in you change into something more than friendship?'

'I cannot say precisely.'

'What do you mean, you cannot say precisely? Does a man not know when a woman shows romantic interest in him?'

Laughter in the audience. The judge threw an angry glance up at the gallery.

'I couldn't tell when *precisely* her interest in me grew, but she signalled it when I entered my fifteenth year.'

'Of what nature was your relationship thereafter?'

'That of occasional lovers.'

'How occasional?'

'We had...relations, on and off. She wouldn't let me see her for months, and then she was all over me again. I broke it up when I met Celia. My wife.'

'Can you describe Miss Hunt's relationship to the prisoner?'

'It was a good relationship.' He caught himself, and added, 'A good father-daughter relationship.'

'They were close?'

'Yes.'

'He was a loving father?'

'Yes.'

'Would you say that the relationship between Mr Hunt and his daughter was in any way queer?'

'No.'

'Mr MacDoughall, you have heard the prisoner plead guilty to having fathered nine children and to having brutally murdered them moments after their were born. The children of his own daughter. Would you say that this is in no way queer?'

MacDoughall seemed alarmed and confused.

'Was my question unclear to you, Mr MacDoughall?'

MacDoughall inhaled and said, 'As I said, the relationship between Mr Hunt and Charlotte was in no way queer. Not from what I observed.'

'Do you agree that an intimate relationship between Mr Hunt and his daughter might have been possible, from what you observed?'

'I have not observed anything like that.'

'But it is possible?'

The attorney of the defence stood and reminded his colleague to cease his attempts at putting words into the mouth of the witness.

Olivia's gaze slid to the men of the jury. Two scribbled away in their notebooks. She looked back at the defence attorney. It was his turn to interrogate the witness.

Bicker nodded to himself, and scratched his whiskers. 'Mr MacDoughall, according to the very limited statement of the prisoner, the prisoner had relations with his own daughter, in the course of which he fathered nine children. You were close to the daughter of the accused. Did you ever see her with child?'

'I might have suspected it once or twice.'

'How could you not be certain? A woman's body is either with child or it is not. Toward the end of the pregnancy, there cannot be any doubt about this, can there? You have two children with your wife. Shouldn't you know the symptoms?'

MacDoughall blushed. 'Yes.'

The attorney waited, then said, 'Would you please answer my question.'

'I have never seen Charlotte with child.'

'Thank you.' Bicker sat, and MacDoughall was released.

A ripple of excitement went through the courtroom when Rupert Hunt was called into the witness stand. The prosecution asked only one question. Had he done it. Yes, he'd done it.

Bicker rose again, and walked up to Hunt.

'Mr Hunt, I sincerely doubt you did it.'

Hunt adjusted his ear trumpet.

'While my dear colleague over there might be satisfied with a mere "I did it," the jury and I will need a little more convincing. You see, justice will be done only when there is sufficient evidence. The slightest doubt and...*fooof!*'

Bicker waved his hand as though to swat at a fly. He straightened his lapel, let his gaze sweep over jury and audience, and said, 'How precisely did you murder your own children?'

Hunt's ear trumpet sank to the desk upon which the Bible lay. He mumbled something and shook his head.

'Excuse me?' Bicker said loudly.

'It happened precisely as Dr Johnston described it.'

Everyone in the hall could see Bicker grind his teeth.

'Thank you, Mr Hunt. You are released for the moment. I now call Charlotte Elisabeth Hunt into the witness stand!'

Hunt stood abruptly and grasped Bicker's arm. 'No! You mustn't!'

The judge demanded order in the courtroom, to little avail.

Hunt, protesting until spittle wet his chin, was removed to the prisoner's dock. When Charlotte was led in, the room hushed. She held her head low, and seemed to walk on feathers. Hunt called out to her, but she did not lift her gaze, did not look at anyone.

'Miss Hunt, we understand that you are deaf, but that you can read lips. Is this correct?'

She nodded once.

The prosecutor stood. 'My lord, the movement of the witness' head does in no way indicate that she understands Mr Bicker's questions.'

'What do you suggest, Mr Wimsey?' the judge asked.

'A question that requires more than a simple yes or no. Would Mr Bicker please ask the witness how many men are in the jury.'

The judge nodded at Bicker and Bicker said, 'Miss Hunt, it appears as if my dear colleague would like you to tell him how many jurymen you can see.'

Charlotte looked confused, pointed at her own eyes, then at the prosecutor and made a wiggling movement with her fingers in front of her face.

'You wish to know whether he can't see the jury properly?'

She nodded and smiled. Her beautiful face transformed into something ethereal. Men held their breaths. Some hastily arranged their wigs and robes.

Charlotte held up her hands, spread ten fingers, curled them, and spread them again. Twenty men in the jury.

The charm was broken. Nervous giggles erupted here and there.

'Thank you Miss Hunt. To ensure that you understand why you are here, I will give you a short summary. The skeletons of nine newborns have been found in seven flowerpots. These flowerpots belonged to your father, Rupert Hunt. He has confessed that he fathered these children and murdered them as soon as they were born.'

Bicker paused.

Charlotte swallowed, and methodically shook her head.

'The prisoner, Rupert Hunt, also has stated that these children were yours. I will now ask you simple questions to each of these statements, that you might answer with a nod or a shake of your head. Do you understand?'

Charlotte nodded once. A stray curl slid off her shoulder.

'Did your father murder these nine children?'

Rupert Hunt's cry 'Don't, Charlotte!' cut through the tense silence.

The judge rapped his gavel.

Hunt stood, and waved his arms. 'Charlotte, look at me! Do not speak ill of her!'

The usher hurried toward Hunt, the judge hollered 'Quiet!' and Charlotte looked calmly upon her father. She touched her hand to her heart, then stretched it out toward him.

Hunt howled, was wrestled down and led from the room.

The judge, now red-faced, brusquely swiped the posy of flowers from his desk, and pounded his gavel once more for good measure.

'This was most enlightening,' Bicker said, when the room had calmed down. 'Now, Miss Hunt, where were we? Ah! Is Rupert Hunt guilty of the murder of your nine children?'

The prosecutor rose, and Bicker flapped his hand at him. 'I apologise for my lack of proper wording.' He turned once more to Charlotte, who was still shaking her head violently to answer the previous question. Bicker asked her, consecutively, if her father had killed one, or several, or all of her children.

And she kept shaking her head.

'Thank you, Miss Hunt. Would you, by any chance, know who did it?'

She glanced down, and shook her head.

'Miss Hunt. Miss Hunt!' Bicker tapped his fingers onto her desk to catch her attention.

She looked up.

'It is now your word against your father's. I doubt it sufficient to change the verdict—'

'He influences the witness!' called the prosecutor.

'I merely explain the process to her.'

The judge signalled to Bicker to go on.

'Can you confirm that these were your children?'

Olivia sat up straight, barely able to contain her curiosity.

Charlotte nodded. Her eyes were glistening.

Bicker swallowed his next question, considered for a moment and said, 'Do you know who killed them?'

Charlotte shook her head, clearly confused.

'Can you speculate as to... No, forget what I said.' He was about to continue, but stopped when Charlotte began to sign.

Her stomach, seven fingers held up. Her arms formed a cradle, nine fingers held up. Her hand to her cheek, her head tilted to one side, her eyes closed.

'You slept—'

She cut him off with a slashing gesture. Her stomach, the cradle, her head to one side and her eyes shut.

'They were born dead?'

*Yes!* she nodded. And again, *yes!*

Bicker silently caressed his lapel. He harrumphed, and asked if she was absolutely certain. Yes, she was absolutely certain.

'Thank you, Miss Hunt. Your witness.'

The prosecutor stood. 'Miss Hunt, you might be unaware that Dr Johnston from Guy's hospital has examined the remains of your children, and found that all suffered a violent death.'

He watched her pale, then added, 'Their throats had been slashed.'

Charlotte's face lost all colour, her hands grasped at the desk, her shoulders slumped, and she dropped out of the witness stand.

The trial was adjourned until the following day.

Sévère looked at Olivia, one eyebrow drawn up. 'Now, that was interesting.'

---

'WHAT HAPPENED in the judge's chamber?' she asked when he climbed into the waiting brougham.

He shut the door, and, ignoring her question, said, 'As I am now deeply involved in this matter, I need you to tell me precisely all that has occurred between you and Chief Magistrate Frost.'

'I doubt you want to hear this.'

'It is more a need than a want.'

She inhaled and began, 'He has two penchants: sodomy, and underage girls. I am quite certain that I was one of the very few experienced women he uses. Usually, he pays for maidens, often very young ones.'

'How young?'

'Nine, ten years old, if he can get them.'

'Who delivers them?'

'I heard from two other women, prostitutes like...' *Like me,* she'd almost said. Sévère's eyes flickered dangerously. 'They told me a madam arranges for underage girls for men like Frost.'

'For men like him, or for him?'

'Both, of course. What are you planning to do?'

'A very delicate matter. One needs to handle it expertly...' he mused.

'Handle it expertly?' Her voice had grown cold.

'Accusing him openly without proof would be madness, don't you think? I am not certain I should confront him at all.'

'That certainly is one way of handling it expertly.'

'Whatever I do, it will risk your past being made public. You won't be able to go anywhere without experiencing the repercussions. No...' He tapped his index and middle fingers against his lower lip. 'What we might need are the services of a newspaperman.'

He scrutinised her for a long moment, nodded, and said, 'Yes, I think this might work. We will take our time to carefully collect evidence against Frost. The man ought to rot in gaol for years. I will speak to an acquaintance, a scribbler of horribly sensational gibberish. He might be just the man to unearth grisly secrets. All we need from him is a nudge to start an avalanche.'

Satisfied, Sévère leant back and crossed his legs. 'Now, tell me what you think of Charlotte's queer behaviour today. '

'To me, it did not look like she was putting on a show. She truly fainted when she heard about the violent deaths of her children. But this makes no sense...' Olivia brushed her hair behind her ears.

'Hum...' said Sévère. 'When I visited her at the asylum, I believed that Sister Grace conveyed to Miss Hunt what I'd asked her to say. That her father had confessed to having killed her children and that her statement was needed. But in fact, I didn't hear her say it. All I heard was a great commotion. I wonder why the asylum staff repeatedly shielded Charlotte from the truth.'

'Isn't that what one does with the insane?'

'But she is not insane! That was what Faulkner wrote in his file. You said so.'

'I know,' she answered. 'But please explain to me why she's still an inmate in a lunatic asylum.'

---

'MISS HUNT, I do hope you have recovered, yes?' the prosecutor asked.

Charlotte nodded. She clasped a handkerchief in her right hand, and ran the nail of her left index finger up and down the Bible.

'I must remind you that you are still under oath.'

A nod.

'Now. Would you please tell us who the father of your nine children is, Miss Hunt?'

A slow turning of her head, then a curt shake.

'You must answer my questions — all of them — truthfully. If you refuse to do so, you will be held in custody until you give a full statement.'

A nod.

'Excellent. Did Rupert Hunt father your children?'

A violent shake of her head.

'Who was it, then?'

She scanned the courtroom for a few long moments, then shrugged.

'He is not in the room?'

She shook her head.

'I will now call out names, and you will indicate with a nod or a shake of your head whether or not you have had relations with that man.'

Disapproving grunts and murmurs issued from the audience. Bicker stood. 'What does this have to do with the issue at hand?'

'I wish to outline the character of the witness.'

'Get to the point, Mr Wimsey,' the judge said to the prosecutor.

'I will, my lord.' He turned back to Charlotte and said loudly, 'Alexander MacDoughall.'

A nod.

'Peter Miller.'

A nod.

'Rupert Hunt.'

*No,* she signalled. *No.*

Mr Wimsey read more than twenty names off his list and every now and then, Charlotte nodded. With each nod, the audience grew more restless. What kind of woman had so many lovers? Only a whore, surely?

'You stated that all your children were stillborn. Can you explain?'

She looked around her desk as though searching for something to express her thoughts, then she stood and stepped out of the witness stand.

The judge was about to protest, but Wimsey asked for a moment's patience.

Charlotte put both hands to her stomach, grunted as if in pain, knelt and lay down on the floor. People stood up to see better, effectively blocking each other's view.

Charlotte swung her hands down along her body. Then she closed her eyes, her chest heaved. Immediately, she jumped up, held up a finger, stepped around the spot on the floor she had just occupied, and picked up an imaginary bundle. She rocked it in her arm and carried it away. Then she lay down again and shut her eyes.

Prosecution, defence, jury, and judge stared down at the scene. Charlotte opened her eyes, trying to find understanding in the faces around her, then she stood, brushed off her skirt, and returned to the witness stand.

'Were you trying to convey that someone took away your child after birth?'

A nod.

'Who?'

A shake of her head and a shrug.

'Miss Hunt, do I need to remind you that you can be apprehended for refusing to give evidence?'

*I slept,* she signalled again and shrugged.

Wimsey grunted and told her she was now the witness of the defence.

'Miss Hunt, do you recognise these?' Bicker held up several journals.

A nod.

'Are these yours?'

A nod.

'Did anyone but you draw in these journals?'

She squinted, and cocked her head. Bicker repeated his question and she shook her head.

'So it was only you filling the pages?'

A nod.

'Very well. It appears as though you are a hobby

gardener. You were given responsibility for the gardens at Sevenoaks Asylum. Is that correct?'

A nod and a smile. Bicker inhaled a wobbly breath.

'Are you proficient in plant craft?'

A nod.

'Well then,' he continued, and strode behind his desk. He picked up an apple tree sapling.

'Miss Hunt, did you graft this apple tree?'

Her hands came out to cup the naked, dry roots of the small tree. Her mouth formed an "oh", and she looked up at Bicker as if to say, 'Why did you kill it?'

'Did you graft this tree, Miss Hunt?' he asked softly.

A nod.

'Did you give it to your father along with six others?'

A nod.

'Did you bury the remains of your infants in the pots that you then gave your father?'

A slump of her shoulders.

'Miss Hunt?'

A nod.

'Did your father know that your children were buried in these pots?'

A shake of her head.

'Why did you bury your children in flowerpots, and give them to your father?'

She frowned and looked at her hands. With trembling fingers she pointed at the prisoner's dock and waved her hand to the right. Then she pointed at herself and waved her hand to the left. Then she indicated the ground, pretended to take something from there with both her hands, hold it in her arms, and to her bosom. She waved to her left again and shook her head. Then she waved to her right and nodded.

It took a long discussion between the judge, Mr Bicker and Mr Wimsey until finally the explanation to Charlotte's gesturing — which grew more and more hectic with every repetition she was asked to perform — was found to be thus: She knew that after the death of her mother, her father felt unable to attend to the house, the premises, and his daughter. She knew he would go to London, and that she would be sent to a place for women. She didn't want to leave her children behind, but she couldn't take them with her, either. So she made her father a farewell present: seven apple tree saplings she'd grafted for him. She didn't tell him what was hidden in the pots.

The courtroom had fallen utterly still. Bicker let his eyes roam the jury. Then he said softly, 'Miss Hunt, I need to ask you again. Did your father kill your children?'

*No.*

'If you were asleep, how could you possibly know whether or not he did it?'

She set her jaw, squared her shoulders, and tapped her fingers against her brow and her heart. Then she gave a single nod. *Because I know.*

THE PROSECUTION CALLED Dr Faulkner into the witness stand, and questioned him as to the state of Miss Hunt's mind. Surely the jury couldn't trust the statements of a woman who was an inmate of an asylum and who has had more lovers than any decent person should have?

Faulkner confirmed that Miss Hunt's mind is of perfect health. He had no doubts as to her trustworthiness. Her father did commit her, but Faulkner soon realised that nothing was wrong with her. Nothing but her being deaf and mute, that is. Why keep her, then? Because she had nowhere else to go.

Unsatisfied, the prosecutor nodded to Bicker, and seated himself.

Bicker massaged his temples, grunted, and said that he had no questions for the witness. Faulkner was released, and the trial adjourned until after lunch.

---

'Mrs Dunham, you resisted a direct court order. Would you care to explain yourself to the jury?' Bicker asked.

'I was unaware of such an order,' the small woman answered. She appeared to have sprung directly from the forest, with her green shawl, her fine-boned features, the freckles dusting her nose, and her fire-red hair.

'How is this possible? You received the order five days ago.'

'My chickens received it, but not I.'

Someone giggled. The judge struck his gavel against the desk.

She rearranged her shawl and said, 'I had retreated into a safe and nourishing space to allow my spirit to journey through subtle realms.'

'Excuse me?'

'My dear sir, you might be unaware of your own history, but I am not. I celebrated spring equinox and, while doing so, I was not at home to receive any letters from officials of the Crown, or otherwise. I resided in the forest for five days, and ate only what the Great Mother provided.'

The prosecutor opened his mouth, shut it, and shrugged at the judge. The latter signalled to him to get on with it.

'Very well, Mrs Dunham, would you—'

'Miss Dunham,' she corrected him.

'Ah, yes. *Miss* Dunham. My apologies. Would you tell the jury of your connection to Miss Charlotte Hunt, and to the prisoner, Mr Rupert Hunt?'

'I was occasionally summoned by the family when they needed the expertise of a healer.'

'I see. How would you describe Miss Hunt's health?'

'Sturdy.'

'And the health of her mind?'

'I would think she has a perfectly clear head.'

The prosecutor huffed. 'Have you ever attended a birth?'

'Yes, I have.'

'As a midwife?'

'Yes.'

'Did you ever work as a midwife for Charlotte Hunt? Or did you attend one of her births?'

'No.'

'No?'

She shrugged and answered, 'No. Mrs Hunt was proficient enough in these matters.'

Olivia grabbed Sévère's wrist.

'Were you aware that Charlotte Hunt had been with child?'

'I was.'

'How often, in your opinion, had Miss Hunt been with child?'

She narrowed her eyes at him. 'I cannot say precisely, but I dare guess three to five times.'

'Did you ever ask yourself why she was never seen with any of these children?'

'I did not.'

'And why, I wonder, would you not be surprised that all of Charlotte Hunt's children were dead?'

'Because the woman is cursed.'

The judge groaned.

'Please elaborate,' Wimsey said, half-amused.

'Just look at her. Every man is drawn to her. And she can't carry even one healthy child. She's cursed.'

'What do you mean by "she can't carry even one healthy child?"'

'They were all stillborns. I don't know why Mr Hunt said he killed them. It makes no sense to me.'

'How do you know they were stillborn? You said you didn't attend the births of Miss Hunt's children."

'Mrs Hunt told me. She was the one who helped her daughter.'

'Mrs Hunt helped her daughter give birth?'

'That is what I just said, didn't I?'

'Did you ever see the children?'

'No. They were buried within the hour.'

'Do you know where they were buried?'

'In the orchard.'

'How do you know?'

'Mrs Hunt told me.'

'Thank you, Miss Dunham. Your witness, Mr Wimsey.'

Sévère extracted his wrist from Olivia's grasp, and slunk from the room as Wimsey stood. Puzzled, Olivia followed Sévère with her gaze.

Wimsey cleared his throat. 'Miss Dunham, could you tell the jury if Mrs Hunt was the only person who tended to Miss Hunt during childbirth?'

'This is what she said, yes.'

'Was Mrs Hunt the only person who had access to the newborns?'

'I believe so.'

'Do you know if Mr Hunt had access to Charlotte Hunt while she gave birth?'

'What are you thinking, dear man! This is women's business.'

'I did not enquire as to my own thoughts, Miss Dunham. I was asking if you knew whether Mr Hunt was present in Miss Hunt's birth chamber.'

'He couldn't have been in the room. I'm absolutely certain of this.'

'What makes you so certain?'

'Mr Wimsey, I don't know about your preferences, but I would think that a man has no business peeking at a woman's private parts when—'

A *bonk* issued from the dais. 'We've heard enough, thank you, Miss Dunham,' the judge said. 'Does the prosecution have further questions for the witness?'

Wimsey shook his head.

'Well, then. All witnesses have been heard,' the judge

announced. 'The council will be given time to prepare their closing speeches. The trial is adjourned until tomorrow morning, ten o'clock.'

Olivia left the courtroom to find Sévère. The lobby gradually emptied, but there was no sign of him. She took a cab home. He wasn't in his office, either.

———

SÉVÈRE REAPPEARED IN THE MORNING. He took his seat next to Olivia, excitement shining in his expression.

'Where have you been?'

'Shh!'

'My lord, before the closing speeches can be given, I need to inform the court of a recent development. As of eight thirty this morning, Mr Hunt has pleaded not guilty.'

The judge nudged his spectacles down the bridge of his nose, and looked sharply at Mr Bicker.

'And did he care to explain this?'

'Yes. In fact, he is now willing to give a full statement.'

Hunt was called into the witness stand. Olivia lent forward, as did everyone else in the room. Except for Sévère, who smirked contentedly.

'Mr Hunt, you pleaded not guilty, is this correct?'

Hunt grabbed his ear trumpet a little harder. 'Yes, it is,' he said.

'Please explain to the jury why you gave false evidence, and why you have changed your mind and now wish to come forward with the truth.'

'When I said that I had fathered and killed the children of my daughter, I did so to protect her. And I also…'

Here, he was drowned out by the audience, who booed and clapped and laughed, but couldn't agree to a uniform response to this new development. The judge demanded silence, and Hunt went on, 'I also did not wish to speak ill of my dead wife. One doesn't speak ill of the dead.'

'Just to clarify, Mr Hunt: you lied to the coroner, the police, the coroner's jury, the High Court, and to this jury?'

'Yes, I did.'

'I do not see what could possibly justify this behaviour.'

Is that what a good defence attorney would say? Olivia wondered, and chewed on the inside of her cheeks. She threw a quick glimpse at Sévère. He seemed entirely comfortable, and not the least bit surprised.

'All blame and all consequences are mine to bear.' Hunt bowed his head to the jury. 'When Mrs Hopegood, my housekeeper, showed the skull to me, I knew at once that the seven pots must hold all nine of Charlotte's dead children. At first, I had no explanation of why she had done this. I thought she might have intended this as some kind of spite. I haven't been a good father to her. I let my wife poison my daughter's thoughts, and I allowed my daughter too much freedom. I knew she'd been with child. When it happened the first time, I was outraged, of course, and then…'

He sighed, and shook his head. 'And then I decided it was women's business. I suspected no ill deed when my wife told me the first child was stillborn. And the second and third. I found it strange when the fourth, the fifth were stillborn, too. But my wife insisted that it was so, that Charlotte's children were all too weak to live.'

Hunt looked at every single jury member and said hoarsely, 'And what man expects his wife to be a cold-blooded murderess? Can you imagine how it feels to watch the evidence laid out, to listen to the witnesses and have my suspicions confirmed? That my own wife had put a knife to the throats of our own grandchildren? I find it hard to accept. I will never understand why she did it.'

He dropped his gaze and wiped his eyes. 'I swore to myself to never speak of Charlotte's children. She was living in an asylum far enough from Redhill, that I believed the gossip couldn't reach Sevenoaks. When I saw the skull Mrs Hopegood had dug up, when I knew the police and the coroner would be alarmed, I feared that...'

He braced himself, calmed his breath, and continued, 'I feared my suspicions would be confirmed. I couldn't bear it. Charlotte believed what her mother had told her: that her children were born dead. And I couldn't take that from her. She didn't deserve that. I feared that my daughter would truly go mad if she learnt that her own mother might have... Had murdered them. Her babies. That is why I lied. And I believed, and still believe, that I deserve to be hanged for my failure. I didn't protect her. And...'

His shoulders were trembling. He inhaled a deep gulp and said, 'I believed it better to simply disappear. To confess to a crime I didn't commit, to go to gaol, be hanged. Charlotte would have never known. She's deaf, she can't read. The nuns wouldn't have told her what happened to me. I thought she wouldn't mind. But then... Suddenly, all is out in the open and she's on the witness stand and puts her hand to her heart and offers it to me.'

Hunt wept openly. Bicker handed him a handkerchief. The ear trumpet dropped to the desk, and the prisoner buried his face in the embroidered silk.

Bicker stroked his lapel, nodded once and turned to the jury. 'I have no further questions.'

The prosecutor rose, opened his mouth, but nothing came out. He cleared his throat and finally said, 'What makes you think the jury will believe this new version?'

Hunt blinked, put his ear trumpet back into his ear and Wimsey repeated the question.

'Because it's true,' Hunt said.

Hunt was returned to the prisoner's dock, and the judge asked if the prosecution needed more time to prepare the closing speech.

Wimsey waved a hand in dismissal and said, 'The statement of the prisoner has no bearing on the evidence.' Then he laid out every grisly detail of how the infants must have found their end, he illustrated the incredibility of Charlotte Hunt: an asylum inmate with a knack for fornication. And the similar lack of credibility of Hunt himself: a man who seems to have no qualms about stating under oath first one thing and then another, a man with neither alibi nor, obviously, honour. The queerness of Miss Dunham: a woman who lives in the woods, looks like a fairy, and excuses her failure to turn up at court with *having celebrated spring equinox*. Ridiculous!

Bicker smiled at Wimsey as they traded places. He reminded the jury that the only solid evidence for

Mr Hunt having committed the crime was his own confession, and that this one piece of evidence was now void. He laid out how Charlotte Hunt's children found their grisly end at the hands of her mother, and that, according to Mrs Dunham's and Miss Hunt's statements, Rupert Hunt had had no hand in the murders.

He fell silent and let his gaze sweep across the courtroom. Then he smiled and nodded and said, 'Even if Miss Hunt, Miss Dunham and Mr Hunt had said nothing at all, the evidence does not link Mr Hunt to the murders. The Crown has failed in its first duty: to establish the guilt of the prisoner, Rupert Hunt, beyond all reasonable doubt.'

Bicker took his seat and the judge asked the jury to retire and begin their deliberations.

'Jesus!' Olivia groaned into her hands. 'Is it always as nerve-racking as this?'

Sévère mildly smiled to himself.

'Why the dickens are you looking like the cat that stole the cream bucket?'

'Because I *am* the cat that stole the cream bucket.' He winked at her, stood, brushed lint off the rim of his hat, and said, 'Please excuse me. I have to arrange for one more thing before the verdict is read.'

And with that he was gone. Olivia felt like the fifth wheel on this circus waggon.

Four and a half hours later, the jury returned, took their seats, and the judge addressed them, 'Men of the jury, have you agreed upon your verdict?'

'We have.'

'Do you find the prisoner, Rupert Hunt, guilty or not guilty of the murder of nine infants?'

'We find him not guilty.'

---

'A MOST SATISFYING end to our first case,' Sévère announced, as he filled two glasses with brandy. He handed one to Olivia, who sat curled up on her armchair, wrapped up in a woollen blanket, her hair wet from bathing.

She took the drink from his hand and gave him a quizzical frown. 'That's a queer way of describing the outcome of a case with no outcome whatsoever. The only thing we have accomplished is the death of seven apple trees. Oh, and we made Hunt's premises impossible to sell. No one wants to live in the house of a mad killer. Yet, you are entirely satisfied, which makes me worried about your sanity. And why the dickens did you disappear right in the middle of Dunham's witness statement?'

'I thought she was about to be released from the witness stand.'

'Ah. Well. She was. But where were you?'

'I went to the witness room. I needed to see Charlotte's face when Aliya Dunham was brought in.'

Olivia sat up.

'Absolutely as expected.' He wiggled his back snug against the cushions, and grinned. 'Miss Hunt was surprised to see Miss Dunham. A moment later, they sat together and happily conversed. One woman told the other that she was with child once more. Miss Dunham's face fell, and she made the sign of the devil. Miss Hunt began to weep. And now it gets interesting: Dr Faulkner—'

'Why wasn't he questioned by Bicker?' Olivia interrupted.

'Because Faulkner had said everything that needed saying. If Bicker had asked any more questions, Faulkner might have let slip that he had withheld the truth from Charlotte and that he had refused to hand over her journals. Anyway. The interesting bit is… Dammit, Olivia, you spoiled the climax of my story!'

'My sincerest apologies. Please go on. I will chew my fingernails, if this makes you feel better.'

'Please do. The interesting bit is this: when Charlotte began to weep, Dr Faulkner rushed to her side. They are lovers.'

'Goodness gracious, Sévère! A man comforts a woman, and you think of intercourse.'

'Faulkner held her and kissed her wet cheeks. Then, when he noticed that everyone was looking at them rather perplexed, he explained that all was in order, for he and Charlotte are to be married in a fortnight.'

'What? Didn't you say he has children?'

'He's a widower.'

'Oh.'

'Indeed. And he's the father of Charlotte's unborn child. For once, her child has a future. Miss Dunham joined the weeping, then. Faulkner didn't kiss *her*, of course. So!' Sévère, clearly drunk on the unusual developments of the day, as well as the excellent brandy, had just warmed up his tongue.

321

And so he continued while Olivia watched with fascination the unfolding of a man she knew as controlled and shuttered. 'Most puzzle pieces have been laid out, and the story of the nine bodies unfolds thus: Miss Hunt could always take her pick from a long list of suitors. Apparently, men liked not only her beautiful face, but also that she spoke rather little. Her mother was the lunatic in the family. She believed that all men were inherently evil. Perhaps that is why she rarely left the house, or perhaps it was because her mind had slowly poisoned her body. Perhaps both. Charlotte never went to school. For obvious reasons. So it was only her mother who educated her, and, to a limited extent, also her father. But he was a male of the species and thus not trustworthy, according to the mother.'

Sévère stopped and gazed into his glass as though to find the proper words. A little less enthusiastic, he continued, 'Each of Charlotte's children was a thing that could not be. When Charlotte's pregnancies began to show, she didn't dare leave the house. Charlotte gave birth attended only by her mother, who took away her child at once, and told her that it was stillborn.'

'Why did Hunt commit her to an asylum? And what about his daughter's supposed fear of men?'

'What else could Rupert Hunt have done? Considering his daughter's age and reputation, no man in Redhill would have offered for her in marriage. And she was hardly in a position to provide for herself. Hunt had also hoped to shut her away from men. So he chose an asylum led by nuns. He didn't share his wife's views, but he believed it better for his daughter. Why Sister Grace believed Charlotte Hunt had suffered at the hands of a man, I don't know. Perhaps she simply didn't want to believe that Miss Hunt had a taste for men. I still have to ask her about Miss Hunt's outbreak of hysteria. My guess is that, first, I asked her about her dead children, effectively reminding her of something she wished to forget, and then she learnt from Sister Grace that her father had been incarcerated. Naturally, she was upset. As to Faulkner's letter about Charlotte Hunt's relocation: Faulkner never sent it. He'd already fallen in love with her. And, he said, he wanted her to have a child of her own. One that wasn't buried under an apple tree.'

Sévère's nervous energy had entirely evaporated. He was about to refill his glass, but then thought better of it. He inhaled and said hoarsely, 'I asked Faulkner about the codling moth. He said that I should have looked more closely at the worm she'd drawn in her new journal. It was the larva of a swallowtail... May I ask you something, Olivia?'

She looked up. The fire illuminated her pale skin; her hair seemed to emit small sparks.

'You mentioned that you have plans for your life once you've collected enough funds. Tell me: what will you do and where will you go?'

She turned her gaze back to the hearth. 'You would laugh if I told you.'

'I promise I won't.'

For several long moments she said nothing. Sévère stretched his left leg closer to the warmth, gradually coming to the conclusion that she'd never answer.

Until she suddenly said, 'The sea.'

She cleared her throat and sat up straighter, as if to prepare herself for an attack. 'My parents and I lived near Hamstead on the Isle of Wight before we moved to London. I will purchase my grandfather's house by the sea. In the past fifteen months, I've been sending small amounts of money to the landlord to ensure he does not sell to anyone else. In a little less than three years' time, the property will be fully paid for, and I'll go back and re-open my grandfather's apiary.'

'This is...unexpected.'

'Did you believe I would open a brothel?'

'No, most certainly not. I believed you'd wish to do something with that brain of yours.'

'One needs a brain for beekeeping.'

'But one doesn't nurture one's intellect with it,' he replied.

'There are other things that need nurturing.'

Sévère opened his mouth, and shut it. He gazed into his glass and said softly, 'I don't think this will suit you. But I do understand your motivation.'

'You don't understand one bit.'

'Perhaps you underestimate me.'

'The topic is closed.'

He lit a cigar and balanced it on the rim of the crystal ashtray, inhaled the rich scent and spoke with a trace of mockery in his voice, 'You always close a topic when you fear my irrefutable counterarguments.'

She rose and faced him. 'As per mutual consent, our marriage exists on paper only. You, however, repeatedly cross the boundaries we agreed upon. You are my employer, and nothing more. Your money only gets you so far. Good night, Coroner.'

He watched her silent retreat, the soft closing of the door, listened to her her fading footfalls.

The fire crackled and rain tapped against the windowpanes.

Sévère placed his long legs on the footstool, picked up the cigar and puffed it until he felt lightheadedness settle in on him.

---

END

---

**Continue reading for a preview of the next book in the series**

# SPIDER SILK

## KEEPER OF PLEAS BOOK 2

ose bunched up a handful of dirty-brown hair that she'd snipped off the neighbour dog's wiggly backside. She added four matches she'd taken from Olivia's room, and wrapped everything in a sheet of paper she'd found beneath Mr Sévère's desk. She wasn't supposed to enter his office. But then, she wasn't supposed to do a lot of things she did.

As she worked, a warm evening breeze sneaked through the window and lifted wisps of her hair. The tip of her tongue poked out of her mouth, curling up, snake-like. She caught herself, tucked her tongue between her teeth to hold it still, and gazed out the window. Standing on tiptoe, she surveyed the courtyard.

Higgins was grooming the horses. The sun had slipped behind the houses.

Everything was in place.

She struck a match and put it to the crumpled paper, then held her breath and let the burning missile fly. She watched its trajectory, a grin dimpling her cheeks as it landed in the courtyard with a dramatic *poof*.

The chestnuts jumped.

'One. Two... Three.'

'Aaaaaalf!' Higgins bellowed from below.

Alf being the kitchen boy. He sported two very large ears, of which the left was more lopsided than the right. This condition alone had earned him Rose's distaste when first they'd met.

He would get those ears pulled in a moment. She hated Alf, he was... Well, silly, clumsy, and naive was how one could best describe him. He was two years her senior and a brat. The feeling of dislike was mutual.

Alf often took a beating for things he hadn't done. What a dumb boy! No one suspected her, of course. Not ever. Girls don't build stink bombs, they don't climb out of the attic's top window, and traipse about the roof. And a girl would *never* throw a dead cat down the chimney.

Ever.

Rose loved being a girl.

She waved whiffs of the stink bomb's aroma out the window, then shut it, and tiptoed down the dark stairwell to the third floor, to the second floor, and — after making sure the servants weren't around — she slipped into Olivia's room.

'Where have you been?' Olivia asked, squinting at Rose through the looking glass.

The girl grinned, her gaze traveling up and down Olivia's form. 'You look horrible!'

'As I should.'

'Are you catching thieves and murderers?' Rose asked, eyebrows perching high on her brow.

Olivia patted her mutton chops, and spoke with a dark and dramatic voice, 'That, my dear First Mate, is my destiny: to save mankind, to stop evil from spreading. Damn, this itches.'

Rose giggled, and Olivia shooed her away, 'Off with you to the kitchen, landlubber! Cook hates it when you let your dinner go cold.'

A toothy grin, two fingers to her temple. 'Aye, Captain!' And Rose dashed from the room.

———

'HE'S NOT COMING,' Olivia whispered and looked up at Sévère, who said nothing in reply. 'At least I know now what a rhinoceros is going through.' She crossed her eyes toward the putty on her nose that was in the way wherever she looked. She decided on the spot to never mock anyone with old potatoes for noses. It was a miracle they could walk straight, considering their obstructed vision. Tentatively, she pressed her fingers to the fake enlargement, then yanked her hand away as the putty began to wobble.

Sévère threw an irritated glance at her, and hissed, 'Stop it already! It's coming off.'

She stuck out her tongue, then directed her attention toward the house across the street. Windows spilt murky light onto the pavement and a lone, stubborn whore.

'I wonder why business is so slow to…to—' Olivia held in the sneeze, else she might shoot her fake nose off her face. Perhaps even the prickly mutton chops. Damn that vile shoe polish she'd put on her eyebrows! And damn this entire investigation!

She curled her fists so as not to claw at her disguise and throw it into the nearby piss puddle. She coughed once, then said gruffly, 'What do we do now?'

'Patience,' Sévère whispered, and leant against a lamp post, right hand in a trouser pocket, the left lightly tapping the knob of his cane against his hip.

Olivia's gaze touched upon his face that was partially hidden by his cap, partially lit by the cigarette that smouldered at the corner of his moustached mouth.

She huffed. If investigating a crime meant to wait *months* for something — anything — to happen, hoping that it could be used in court, then she wasn't made for this. She lacked Sévère's calm patience, and doubted she'd ever attain it. She'd reached the point of "shoot first, ask later."

'This isn't working,' she grumbled softly, and then louder, 'Well then, my dear chap,' as she elbowed Sévère, and motioned toward a woman across the street. 'Shall we be on our way, or are you *still* lusting after that foxy girl?'

'I wonder if she might like to see the both of us,' he said casually, a dark glimmer in his eyes. He scanned the brothel's windows once more, its entrance, the street. The redhead smiled at them and lifted her skirts to show her ankles.

Olivia whistled and set off across the street, ignoring Sévère's muffled protest.

She stopped as a group of youngsters came running, and stepped aside to avoid collision. Without success.

A boy bumped into her, and his hands probed her trouser pockets as swift as fleas. She pulled up her knee but missed his testicles. Her right arm swung. Her fist made contact with his cheekbone.

A moment later, she was on the ground, stomped by a herd of furious young men.

———

'GODDAMMIT, Olivia! Would you please allow them to pick your pocket next time? There wasn't much to steal anyway!' Sévère's finger brushed the tip of her bleeding nose, then plucked off the putty that hung from her nostrils. 'This might hurt.' He pulled at the left mutton chop.

'Ouch,' Olivia said.

'One more.' And off came the other mutton chop. He extracted a handkerchief from his pocket, and dabbed at her nose and the cut on her upper lip. He was worried about her right eye. It was swollen shut.

'Can you move your jaw?' he asked.

She tried to open her mouth, and winced.

'What about your ribs? Might anything be broken?'

Olivia laughed. Or grunted. He wasn't quite sure which.

Sévère stood. 'Cabbie!' he called to a nearby hansom. 'To Sillwood Street!'

'Let Johnston sleep. I'm all right,' she spoke through clenched teeth.

'I will not discuss this.'

'I won't, either!'

'Excellent.' He helped her up and into the waiting cab.

Once the horse had fallen into a fast trot, he said, 'We need to revise our tactics. For three months we've been tailing this...subject.' He was so furious at Olivia, he'd almost let slip the name of the man they were working so hard to apprehend. The cabbie might be able to hear their conversation over the rattling of wheels.

Sévère ground his teeth. 'The handful of witnesses we have managed to talk to are unwilling to give statements. Honestly, considering their position and the position of the subject in question, I would be reluctant, too.'

From the corner of his vision, he saw her sitting up straighter.

'Go on,' she said, her voice dangerously soft.

'What I mean to say is...' He balled his hands to fists. 'Damnation! This is not what I envisioned to happen!'

'If you give up now, I will do it alone.' She sank against the backrest. 'I don't have to abide by rules set for men like you.'

'Dammit, Olivia! Have you ever seen me give up? No. I said we have to revise our tactics. There's nothing wrong with that. Ah, here we are.'

'I don't need a doctor. I'm all right, really, Sévère.'

He squeezed his eyes shut and exhaled. 'Humour me. Just this once.' As he tapped his cane to the hansom's roof, he heard Olivia mutter something that sounded much like *overbearing weasel brain*.


A SLEEPY SERVANT opened the door for them and beckoned them in. Sévère apologised profusely to her, and to

Johnston who came descending the stairs in robe and tattered slippers

'My goodness,' Johnston muttered, eyeing Olivia. 'What the deuce happened? Why are you in men's clothing?' And then to Sévère, 'And when did *you* grow a moustache?'

'We were tailing a suspect.' Sévère ripped off his moustache and tucked it into his waistcoat pocket.

'We?'

'Oh, it's fun,' Olivia said, and flapped a dismissive hand at Johnston. He seemed not to hear her remark.

Johnston led them to the drawing room and held a candle to Olivia's face. 'My bag and the leeches.' He snapped his fingers at the waiting servant, who rushed out of the room and returned a moment later with the requested items.

'You may retire.' Johnston waited until the servant had shut the door, then dropped his voice and said to Olivia, 'How did you come about your injuries?' He flicked a sideways glance at Sévère that wasn't any too trusting.

'You don't believe...I would...' Sévère stammered.

Ignoring Sévère, Johnston gazed gently but enquiringly at Olivia.

'I had a disagreement with a band of pickpockets,' she supplied, and shrugged.

Johnston nodded as though such occurrences weren't unusual in the least, and beaten up wives of coroners paid him visits at least twice a week.

He rubbed the bridge of his nose, nodding once. 'My apologies, Sévère. The husband is always the first suspect. To me, and to you.' Johnston went to turn up the gas light at the wall, then lit an oil lamp and moved it closer to his patient.

Sévère mumbled agreement, and watched the surgeon run tender fingertips over Olivia's face. When she flinched, Sévère grabbed her hand.

'You can let go of me, Sévère. I won't run away, I promise,' she said.

He dropped her hand.

'I feel no bones shifting, my dear,' Johnston said softly. 'But I would like to see the swelling around your eye lessen. Two leeches should do. It won't hurt.'

Olivia smiled up at him. 'Don't worry. I've had worse.'

Johnston froze. 'You've had worse? When was that?'

'When I was a child. There was that boy in the neighbourhood...'

Johnston's gaze was sharp, but Olivia's expression was so innocent that one could not but believe her.

Sévère observed the interaction, and found himself quite surprised that his friend was fooled by his wife.

Johnston placed the leeches onto Olivia's swollen eye, disinfected the cut on her upper lip, and then excused himself to find a cup of tea for her.

'I know how we can apprehend him,' Sévère said in a low voice.

'You do?'

He nodded. 'We've been doing it all wrong. He's always a step ahead of us, and we've allowed it. We've chased him. This time we'll set a trap.'

Olivia's healthy eye narrowed.

Sévère continued, 'Unfortunately, for this to succeed,

we have to enter into rather…shady areas of legality. We'll need a young girl as bait.'

'No! *That* we won't do.'

'Why ever not? Call a prostitute into the witness stand instead? The jury won't believe a word she says. But a young girl that hasn't been ruined…' Slowly, he nodded. 'Why didn't I think of this earlier?'

'If you do this, I will divorce you. What do you believe will happen to the girl after you and the court are through with her? Even if Frost never touches her, she'll be ruined. Her name and her face will be public property. *The girl who was almost raped.* I have a better idea for you, Coroner.'

Sévère straightened his shoulders. Whenever his wife called him *Coroner*, he knew to prepare for battle.

'Why not simply change your lovely legal system so that the voice of a woman is given as much credit as the voice of a man?'

'That would be like trying to convince people God does not exist,' Johnston's voice sounded from the door. 'You cannot fight belief with logic. And I can't believe what I just heard. Should I apologise for overhearing your heated discussion on how to lure a young girl into prostitution?'

Groaning, Sévère rubbed his brow. Olivia touched his hand, and said, 'Allow me.'

He nodded.

'Dr Johnston,' she began, and sat up straight. 'We've been trying for months now to obtain evidence against…a man with considerable political power. We know he is paying seductresses to gain access to underage girls. And we know he has been doing this for years.'

Johnston sat down in a chair opposite Olivia. He completely ignored Sévère.

'How do you know?'

'I know because...' She flicked her gaze to Sévère who shook his head minutely. 'We just know. And we can't tell you all the details. I hope you understand.'

'No, I certainly do *not* understand. What I *do* understand is that an injured woman is my guest, and so far she's been telling me only half-truths. Or half lies. I am not quite sure which. I do understand that her husband is the Coroner of Eastern Middlesex — a position of political power, although not considerable. And both have been arguing about forcing a young girl into prostitution.'

'It's not what you think—'

'How, then, is it, Mrs Sévère? Your husband is about to lose my friendship, and I do wonder if I have enough evidence to report him to the authorities.'

'Johnston, listen to me,' Sévère interjected.

Johnston stuck his index finger in Sévère's face. 'I am not talking to you, lad. I am talking to the lady. So, Mrs Sévère, I'm listening.'

Olivia lifted a hand to rub her brow, but remembered the injury. She sucked in a breath, held Johnston's gaze, and told him about her abduction at the age of nine, the various boarding houses and brothels she'd called home, that her marriage to Sévère was a mutual business agreement, and that her past was to be kept secret, so that she could work as his assistant without damaging his reputation. And she told him about Chief Magistrate Frost's appetites.

Johnston stood, placed the saucer he was still holding onto a nearby table, and left the room without a word.

Sévère stared at Olivia, about to speak, when Johnston returned with three glasses and a bottle. He poured whiskey, and handed a glass to Olivia, and another to Sévère.

With a grunt, Johnston tipped his drink into his mouth. His Adam's apple bounced, and he smacked his lips. 'Well, then. May I assume your knowledge of Chief Magistrate's illegal and, I must say, extraordinarily disgusting activities stems from personal experience?'

Olivia dipped her chin.

Johnston harrumphed, refilled his glass, and hurried the contents down his throat.

'By the Queen's mammary glands,' he muttered. 'A criminal Chief Magistrate... Ahem. I agree with your wife, Sévère. Do not use an innocent as bait. Do you have a trustworthy midwife at your disposal?'

Sévère shook his head no.

'In that case, you will need a surgeon or physician whom you can trust. And I don't mean to stitch up your wife every time she's injured. Well...that, too. But what you need is a medical man who is discreet and ever at your disposal. One who is qualified to testify at court that a girl's maidenhead is no longer intact, and that physical evidence clearly shows she's been taken against her will.'

Sévère coughed. 'Are you volunteering?'

'Of course I am. Why else would I venture such a forthright speech?'

'I think the swelling is going down,' Olivia said. A fat leech let go of her brow and dropped to her lap with a soft *plop*.

End of preview

***Spider Silk***
is available at all major retailers

# ON THE USE OF BRITISH ENGLISH
## IN THIS BOOK

I have avoided overuse of Victorian-era spellings and punctuation, because British readers might believe the prose to be littered with Americanisms.

While the Victorians used, for example, *leaned* and *leant*, and *spilled* and *spilt*, I had to decide for one of the two versions. And so I picked the one with a Victorian flavour (*leant* and *spilt*). Other words didn't fare as well. The Victorian *Mr.* is now the dot-less and more British *Mr*, and all the *Judges* and *Jurymen* have been de-capitalised to modern *judges* and *jurymen*.

However, the Victorian *Coroner of Eastern Middlesex* is his original self, because he's much hotter than the *Coroner of East Middlesex*.

So there. Now you know.

# ACKNOWLEDGEMENTS

*M*agnus, my lovely husband, for reading all the awful first versions.

My brave test readers Robyn Montgomery and Irina Kraft, and my awesome editors Sabrina Flynn, Nancy DeMarco, Rita Singer, and my prof reader, Tom Welch.

Carlina de la Cova for joyful discussions of neonate skeletonisation and 19th century postmortems, and for checking all my dissection scenes for correctness.

Eliška Frank for neonatal C2s and C3s.

Luke Kuhns for scanning 1880s Coroner case files from the London Metropolitan Archives for me. Sadly and unexpectedly, we did not find Jack the Ripper's toe nail clippings among the files.

Pete Andrews for entrusting me with his granddad's beautiful beekeeping books.

Any errors in court procedures, medical procedures, history of Victorian London, etc., are mine and can be attributed to artistic freedom or failure to detect them.

James Vincent McMorrow and Kerry Muzzey for inspiring music.

74755432R00191

Made in the USA
Columbia, SC
05 August 2017